Who hasn't thought Pride and Prejudice could use more dragons?

Praise for Maria Grace

"Grace has quickly become one of my favorite authors of Austen-inspired fiction. Her love of Austen's characters and the Regency era shine through in all of her novels." ***Diary of an Eccentric***

"Maria Grace is stunning and emotional, and readers will be blown away by the uniqueness of her plot and characterization" ***Savvy Wit and Verse***

"Maria Grace has once again brought to her readers a delightful, entertaining and sweetly romantic story while using Austen's characters as a launching point for the tale." ***Calico Critic***

I believe that this is what Maria Grace does best, blend old and new together to create a story that has the framework of Austen and her characters, but contains enough new and exciting content to keep me turning the pages. ... Grace's style is not to be missed.. ***From the desk of Kimberly Denny-Ryder***

PEMBERLEY
MR DARCY'S DRAGON

Maria Grace

White Soup Press

Published by: White Soup Press

Pemberley: Mr. Darcy's Dragon
Copyright © 2016 Maria Grace

For information, address
author.MariaGrace@gmail.com

ISBN-10: 0-9980937-1-8
ISBN-13: 978-0-9980937-1-0 (White Soup Press)

Author's Website: RandomBitsofFaascination.com
Email address: Author.MariaGrace@gmail.com

Dedication

For my husband and sons.
You have always believed in me.

1
Chapter

A great many people only hear what is comfortable and convenient for them to hear. Far oftener than might be expected, that is a very good thing indeed.

Twilight was Elizabeth's second favorite time of day, just slightly less appealing than dawn and nearly as interesting. She settled into her customary spot in the parlor, the little faded chair near the window. Long shadows danced across the worn rose-patterned carpet. Waning sunlight warmed the cozy room to soporific levels, leaving the children yawning even as they protested, they were not tired.

Mrs. Bennet sat back into the sun-bleached sofa cushions and grumbled under her breath. "Children ought to mind the first time they are told a thing. Sister Gardiner is far too lenient with them."

Neither Jane nor Kitty gave any sign of having heard. No doubt Mama did not intend to be heard, so Elizabeth chose to ignore her.

Sometimes preternatural hearing was more bane than blessing.

Papa and Uncle Gardiner exchanged raised eyebrows over the card table. The long-suffering expression in Papa's eyes suggested he would like to have words with her, but was unlikely to expend the effort.

Daniel Gardiner bounded up to Elizabeth, hands clasped before him, an unruly shock of blond hair falling over his eyes. "Please Lizzy, Mama says we must go to bed. Will you tell us a story?"

Samuel scurried up beside him, blinking up at Elizabeth, "Pwease, Lizzy, pwease."

The child was far too adorable for his own good. Elizabeth scooped him into her arms. "If your Mama agrees, then of course, I will tell you a story."

Joshua and Anna rushed to their mother and tugged at her skirts. "Mama, pray let us have a story."

Aunt Gardiner took their hands and smiled at Elizabeth. "Are you certain you want to? I do not expect they will allow you to stop at only one."

"I should be delighted. There is hardly anything I enjoy more than telling stories—"

"With dragons?" Daniel grabbed her hand and squeezed.

"Yes, dwagons!" Samuel bounced in her arms.

Mama huffed and muttered something under her breath, something that it was best Elizabeth pretend not to hear.

"What other kind of story is worth telling?" Elizabeth chuckled and ushered the children upstairs.

With Aunt Gardiner's assistance, the children settled into the nursery and dressed for bed. The room
was awkwardly tucked into a gable, all odd angles and
shadows. Had it been drafty and dusty, it would have
been a frightening, unfriendly place. But with bright
yellow moiré paper on the walls and crisp green curtains at the window, it was snug, comfortable and
playful. Exactly what a nursery should be.

"Climb into bed. I shall return in a moment." Elizabeth looked directly at Joshua, the middle of the three
boys, who was most adept at avoiding bedtime.

He hung his head and pouted as his mother placed
a firm hand between his shoulders and propelled him
to the little bed beside his brothers.

Elizabeth hurried to her room, collected her birdcage and returned.

"Is that her?" Anna asked, pointing at the cage. Her
sweet face peeked up above the little coverlet.

"Yes, it is. If you promise to be very quiet and not
startle her, I will uncover the cage and you may watch
her whilst I tell your story. Perhaps if you are all very
good, she might sing for you afterwards."

"We will be very, very quiet, we promise." Anna
glanced at her brothers with a pleading look. With her
wide, dark eyes and silky hair, Anna reminded everyone
of Jane, but her personality was far more like Elizabeth's.

"Boys, do you agree?" Aunt Gardiner folded her
arms and cast a stern look at her sons.

"Yes mama," they murmured, eyes fixed on the
birdcage.

Elizabeth nodded and unbuttoned the quilted cover
surrounding the cage. The candlelight glinted off iridescent blue and green feathers. Tiny wings buzzed

and the creature hovered above the perch.

"You remember April from the last time you were here. April, these are my cousins, the Gardiner children." Elizabeth gestured at the children.

April looked up at Elizabeth with something resembling annoyance.

Anna pressed up on her elbows. "She is so beautiful. I have never seen anything so beautiful in my life!"

April flew closer to the side nearest Anna and poked her dainty, pointed beak between the bars.

"Oh, she likes me! Lizzy, she likes me!"

"Indeed she does, but don't startle her. Here, I will set her cage on the table nearest you if you promise to be very still."

"I will, I will!" Anna tucked back under the coverlet and held herself very stiff.

Elizabeth sat on the little bed beside her. "So you wish to hear a story about dragons? Then I will tell you one, but I do not think you will believe it."

"But we will, surely we will." Daniel flipped to his belly and propped up on his elbows.

"You think so now, but very few can believe the tale I will tell. It is not one for the faint of heart."

"We're not!" Joshua cried in hushed tones.

"That may be, but still, I expect you will be surprised to learn that England is full …" Her eyes grew wide as she pressed a finger to her lips. "… of dragons." She leaned close and whispered the word.

"Where are they, Lizzy? I have never seen one." Anna's expressive eyes darted from April to Lizzy and back again.

"Everywhere, they are all around."

"Why can't we see them." Daniel huffed.

"Children, if you do not allow your cousin to tell

you the story, then I shall put out the candle, and we shall leave." Aunt Gardiner tapped her foot, and the children ducked a little farther under the covers.

"You see them all the time, but you do not recognize them for what they are. Dragons are very good at hiding in plain sight. They speak spells of great persuasive power, convincing you that they are anything but a dragon, but most people cannot hear them directly. They think the dragon speech is their own thought, and they go about never questioning those ideas."

"Is there a dwagon in the rwoom now?" Samuel cast about the nursery, breathing hard.

"If there was, it could not be a large one, could it? The room is quite small. Any dragon here with us would be so small there would be nothing to fear from it."

"There are small dragons?" Joshua's brow furrowed as he worked over the idea. He was such a perceptive, thoughtful, mischievous child.

"Small ones, medium size ones and very large ones indeed. One of the largest is the monster Saint Columba encountered in the river Ness in Scotland."

"River dragons? That monster drowned a man! If there are dragons here, aren't you afraid they will eat you?" Daniel's words tumbled out almost all at once.

"I am glad you have asked, for that is exactly the story I wish to tell. Now lay back on your pillows, and I will tell you why I am not afraid of dragons." Elizabeth waited until the children complied.

April zipped around her cage twice and settled on her perch, looking at Elizabeth as if to listen to the tale herself.

"Long ago, back in the age of Saint Columba, dragons ravaged our land. For hundreds of years, man and beast were at war; man against man, dragon against dragon, dragon against man. Chaos reigned. In the year nine hundred, it seemed as though the dragons would wipe out the race of man in the British Isles."

"Was it like the war in France?" Joshua whispered from behind his blanket.

"As bad as Napoleon is, this was far worse. But Uther Pendragon rose to the throne. He was unlike any man born before him, for he was able to hear the dragons."

"The dragons' roar was silent before Uther?" Daniel asked.

"No, it was loud and terrifying, like thunder in a storm. Everyone heard that. But what Uther perceived was different. He heard them speak. Some spoke in very high, shrill notes that sounded like the whine of a hummingbird's wings."

"Like April?" Anna whispered.

Elizabeth's eyebrows rose as she glanced at Aunt Gardiner. "Yes, just like that. And others spoke in a voice so deep it felt like the deep rumble of thunder. Uther could detect those voices, not just the fearsome noises. He suddenly understood what the dragons had been saying all along."

"What did they say?" Samuel pulled the blanket up to his chin and chewed on the edge.

"The dragons were weary of war and they wanted peace as much as men did. So, the wise king Uther invited them to meet with him in a large, deep cave. His advisors warned him not to go into the cavern, for he would never come out again. The dragons would devour him, leaving the race of man without a king, and the war would surely be lost."

"Did the dragons eat him?" Daniel asked.

"Of course not," Joshua hissed, "Lizzy would not be telling the story if they had."

Aunt cleared her throat and tipped her head toward the older boys.

"Uther treated them with respect and the dragons welcomed him as a foreign king. At the end of a fortnight, Uther emerged from the cave carrying a red shield emblazoned with a gold dragon. A mighty falcon with feathers that shimmered like polished steel rode on his shoulder, a gift from the dragon king. Some say a peace treaty was written on that shield, but none could tell for certain, for no one could read the dragon language then."

"Dragons can write?" Daniel gasped.

"Some of them, just as some men can write, and read as well."

"Is that why so many men have falcons, like Papa? To be like king Uther?" Joshua rested his chin on his fists and stared at her.

"Indeed it is. And the reason ladies keep pretty birds, like April, since ladies do not keep falcons."

"I think April is far prettier and sweeter than a falcon. I should very much like to have one like her someday." Anna yawned and stretched.

"Perhaps you shall, dear. But now it is time to sleep." Elizabeth rose.

"Will you not tell us another?" Daniel sat up, but his mother waved him back down.

"It is late. I will tell you another tomorrow. But, since you have listened so very well, April will sing for you. Lie back on your beds, and I will let her out so she can."

The children obeyed and Elizabeth opened the cage. April zipped out and flew two circuits around the room, hovering over each child and inspecting them as she went. She flew to the middle of the room and hovered low over the beds. Her sweet trill filled the room.

The children yawned. One by one their breathing slowed into the soft, regular pattern of slumber.

April warbled a few more notes and landed on Elizabeth's shoulder.

Aunt Gardiner smiled, pressed her finger to her lips and slipped out. Elizabeth picked up the cage and followed.

"Will you return to the parlor?" Aunt Gardiner asked.

"After I put the cage away." Elizabeth turned down the corridor toward her room and slipped inside.

"You called me a bird! How dare you call me a bird!" April shrieked in her ear.

"You need not shout. I can hear you quite well." Elizabeth held her hand over her ear.

"Why did you call me a bird?" April launched off her shoulder and darted around the room. The candle-light glinted green off her feather-scales.

"You were the one telling them you were a hummingbird, not I."

"What else should I have them believe? That I am a cat?"

Elizabeth pressed her lips hard. April did not like to be laughed at. "Certainly not! You do not look enough like one for even your persuasive powers to convince them of it."

"It is one thing for me to tell them I am a bird, but quite another for you." April hovered near Elizabeth's face.

"The children are too young. We cannot know if they hear you."

"They all do. Coming from two parents who hear, what would you expect?"

Elizabeth's jaw dropped. "Aunt Gardiner does not hear you."

"Yes, she does. Not as well as her mate, but she does, and so do the children. You must tell their father as soon as you can. They all need to be trained."

Elizabeth held her hand up for April to perch on. "There is plenty of time. It is not as though Uncle Gardiner is a landed Dragon Keeper, only a Dragon Mate."

"I do not understand why you humans are so insistent upon making distinctions among us based on size. A Dragon Mate may not have a huge landed dragon to commune with, but they are Dragon Friends nonetheless. We of smaller ilk are just as important and just as proud. And we are far more convenient, not being tied to a plot of ground or puddle of water." April flipped her wings to her back and thrust her dainty beak-like nose in the air.

Elizabeth stroked her throat with her index finger. April leaned into her. "There, there now, you do not need to get your feathery little scales in a flutter. You need not be jealous of Longbourn. He is a cranky old thing. Grumpy, and not nearly as pretty as you."

"Nor as good company."

"You are the best of company, my little friend."

"Of course I am. Who would not rather spend their time with a fairy dragon than a dirty, smelly old wyvern?" April presented the other side of her neck for a scratch.

"I would not let Longbourn hear you say that. He does have quite the temper."

April squeaked in that special annoying tone she saved for anything related to the resident estate dragon.

"You will wake the children."

"Then you could begin training them."

"They will be as cranky as Longbourn, and I will leave them to you." Elizabeth smoothed the soft scales between April's wings.

The fairy dragon really did resemble a hummingbird, though she was much prettier and far more nimble.

"Oh, very well. I do not like cranky anythings; not dragons, not people, not anything." April's head drooped.

"I must return downstairs. Do you wish to come? I know you do not like being alone when we have company about."

"Does your uncle have his horrid cockatrice with him?"

Elizabeth chuckled. April had never met a cockatrice she approved of. "Rustle? Of course he came. But he prefers to keep company with Longbourn in the cavern. He does not favor so much female company."

"Your mother insulted him when she called him a mangy looking falcon." April cheeped a little laugh.

"I do not blame him for being insulted. So do you wish to come or not?"

"I do indeed. I have some very important news to share with the official Dragon Keeper of Longbourn."

"What else have you not told me?"

"It is my news, and I will share it myself." April launched off her finger and lit on Elizabeth's shoulder.

No point in trying to out-stubborn a dragon, even a very small one. "Very well, I shall leave the door open though, in case you tire of mere human companionship and wish to return to your sanctuary." Elizabeth propped the bedroom door open with a little iron dragon doorstop.

April nipped her earlobe. Fairy dragons did not like to be teased.

Voices wafted up the stairs. Mama complaining— again—about the lack of eligible young men in the neighborhood to marry her daughters. And—lest any of them forget—the cruel injustice that they had no sons, and the estate would go to some horrid cousin at Mr. Bennet's demise.

"She is right, that is a problem." April tapped Elizabeth's ear with her beak.

"I know, but what is to be done? The law is the law and we must abide by it."

"But what if he cannot hear us? That would violate a far older and more important law. An estate with a dragon must have a Keeper who can hear."

"We do not know that he cannot. Do not work yourself into a flutter. Papa has invited him to Longbourn. I am sure we shall meet him soon. Then we will know for certain and can decide how to proceed."

Papa and Longbourn had already decided, quite some time ago. Neither Mama nor April need know that yet.

"So he has given up on any further mating? I do not blame him, she is rather horrid. He should have found a woman with some sense—or who could at least hear."

Elizabeth stopped and glared at April. "You are speaking of my mother, you know."

"What of it? My own was nearly as stupid as a hummingbird and got herself eaten by a cat, not even a tatzelwurm, but an ordinary cat." A shudder coursed the length of April's tiny body.

"While your kind may not be attached to your

brood mothers, humankind is. I would have you re-frain from insulting mine." Elizabeth gently soothed ruffled feather-scales into place.

April snorted and looked away.

Elizabeth continued into the parlor.

"I suppose you filled the children's heads with more of your dragon fantasies." Mama rolled her eyes and stabbed her needle into the bodice she embroidered.

Why was she so opposed to all things draconic? So determined in her opposition that neither Rustle nor April could persuade her into a fondness for them.

"The children love her stories so much. There is no harm in them." Aunt Gardiner did not look up from her own sewing, but her jaw tensed just a mite.

"She does not like your mother, either." April nipped Elizabeth's ear. Again.

That was not April's most endearing habit.

"So my children are fond of dragons, are they?" Uncle Gardiner chuckled and played a card from his hand.

Papa grumbled under his breath and studied his cards.

April launched from Elizabeth's shoulder and hovered in front of Uncle's face. "Of course they do, you nit. They hear us as clearly as you do. You had best do something soon about it or they will be thinking all of us are as cross and crass as that mangy Rustle-creature you keep."

Uncle began to choke and dropped his cards. Papa's eyes bulged. He stared from April to Elizabeth. Aunt's jaw dropped as her sewing sank to her lap.

So, April was correct, Aunt could hear, too.

"I … I just remembered there is a … a business matter I need to discuss with you, Gardiner. Let us to my study. Lizzy, join us. I will need you to write for me."

"I do not understand why you do not hire a proper secretary. It is not right that Lizzy should be so involved in your business." Mama huffed, her feathers as ruffled as April's.

Papa laid down his cards and rose.

That was always a sore point between them. Mama could have at least offered to help him, but no, that was a hireling's work in her eyes. If only she could understand how he resented the disease that gnarled his hands and pained his joints, taking away his ability to do so many things. Even holding cards was difficult for him now. Mama really should know better than to continue pressing that issue.

Perhaps April had a point about Mama.

Uncle followed him out.

April flitted back to Elizabeth. "Well, come along. Do not give that old biddy consequence by even responding."

Elizabeth curtsied to her mother and departed. Tomorrow she would probably enjoy an ear full of complaints about allowing that 'annoying little bird' out of her cage. No wonder Rustle kept to the caverns when visiting.

Papa closed the study door behind her.

Densely packed with books and papers, the room was cluttered and dusty. But the tomes, some ancient, were part and parcel of Papa's business. She picked her way past the stacks on the floor and around the desk.

Uncle pulled three chairs into a cluster near the fire and brought a graceful carved perch into the center. Carved of mahogany, the heirloom had been in the family for over a century. Papa said it was carved by the first Bennet to host a companion dragon. That companion, a cockatrice according to family lore, had a fascination with the human chair. He insisted on having one of his own. So, his Dragon Mate carved a perch to match the back of a set of dining room chairs that had long since left the family.

"Will you join us?" Uncle gestured toward the perch.

"His manners are much more pleasing." She lit on the perch and presented her throat for a scratch.

Uncle took the hint and scratched that particularly itchy spot just behind her left ear. April trilled.

"You will put us all to sleep if you do that, and then you will not be able to share your news." Elizabeth yawned, a little more deeply than necessary to make her point.

April flittered her wings, the fairy dragon equivalent of a huff and foot stomp.

"Ah yes, Elizabeth is right. It seems you have some rather significant observations regarding my children?" Uncle sat back, eyes fixed on April.

"Your children and your mate. All of them can hear. Your mate is a bit hard of hearing, but she heard me quite clearly in the parlor, about the children."

Uncle laced his hands together and bounced them off his chin. "You are certain? Entirely certain? All of them?"

"With two parents who hear, it could hardly be otherwise." April cocked her head one way then the other.

"But Rustle—"

"—is a cloddish old cockatrice with all the perceptive powers of a lump of clay. I doubt he willingly gives your children notice at all." April tossed her head.

"He does not prefer their company, but I would have expected him to be more tolerant if they could hear," Uncle said.

"He does not tolerate anyone with equanimity, not even his own kind." Papa winked.

"He likes Longbourn well enough." Elizabeth chuckled.

April grumbled low in her throat. From a bigger dragon it would have been a frightening growl, but from her, it was laughable.

"Do you think she is right, Lizzy?" Papa tapped his fist to his chin.

"Fairy dragons are most perceptive to such things. I told them the legend of Uther tonight. Something about the way they listened and watched April—I think she is right."

A smile lit Uncle's face and his eyes grew very bright. He threw his head back, sniffling.

"Congratulations—all of your children! That is something to celebrate." Papa shuffled toward the crystal decanter.

Elizabeth met him there, poured the three glasses he indicated, and passed them around.

"We must drink to the occasion!" Papa raised his glass.

They lifted their glasses and sipped the fiery brandy.

April perched on Elizabeth's hand and stuck her nose into the glass.

"Be careful, only a sip or two or you will be flying into the windows again." Elizabeth giggled.

"I know how to handle my brandy, thank you." April flipped her wing and splashed a few drops on Elizabeth's cheek.

"I shall begin their training immediately." Uncle balanced his glass on his knee.

"That is not the only news I have to share." April

returned to her perch.

"You have more? I can hardly imagine what else you could tell with us." Papa leaned back in his wingback, a funny little half smile lifting his lips. As much as he preferred the estate wyvern's company, he did have a soft spot for April—she hatched on his study hearth, after all. She could say things to him he would tolerate from no one else.

"More good news, I am proud to say. I have made a very important discovery in the orchards, on the sunrise side of the estate. But you must act quickly, very quickly I would say." April hopped from one foot to the other. "I have found a clutch of eggs, fairy dragon eggs!"

Papa and Uncle sat up very straight.

"Are you certain they are fairy dragon eggs?" Papa set his glass aside and leaned in very close.

"Would you mistake one of your own children for a puppy? Of course I know my own kind's eggs!"

"And the brood mother?" Papa asked.

"I have not seen her in at least a fortnight. She is a wild dragon and has forgotten her clutch for more interesting things. Foolish little twitterpate." April cheeped shrill disapproval.

"Her twitterpation may very well be our good fortune." Elizabeth chewed her knuckle.

"It would be much better for them to hatch in our presence. Even if they choose not to stay, they will have imprinted upon men, and that is always a benefit. It has been some time since we have had a hatching on the estate." Papa stoked his chin. "I think you should take Mary as well. It would be good for her to find a Dragon Mate of her own."

"She has been jealous of me for quite some time.

Who could blame her?" April thrust her head up high.

"Would you like to keep company with another fairy dragon? I should worry you would become jealous." Elizabeth stroked April's proffered throat.

"If it is your sister's companion, I will tolerate another. But only one." April laughed a peculiar high pitched trill. "I would suggest you speak to Rustle though, he will have a more difficult adjustment in store."

Uncle gasped. "You would recommend my family as Dragon Mates?"

"If your wife is to learn to hear more clearly, she needs a companion. I hardly imagine Rustle deigns to speak to her regularly. Your children would benefit from being properly taught by a companion of their own. After all, look what I have done for Elizabeth."

Papa and Uncle snickered.

A sharp rap—Hill's knock—sounded at the door and it swung open. Her wizened face peeked in. "Sir, a courier just come, with one of those letters you said you always want brung immediately."

Papa met her at the door. She handed him a thick letter tied with blue tape and fixed with a large blob of blue sealing wax, an embossed wyvern embedded deep in the wax.

He shut the door and trundled back to his seat.

"Are you expecting news from the Order?" Uncle braced his elbows against the chair, ready to spring to action.

"No, I am not." He fumbled with the seal and handed it to Elizabeth. "Open this."

"Are you sure, Papa? This looks quite important."

"All the more reason. If it is, you will be involved in some way, no?"

She snickered. "I cannot argue."

"Besides, with Collins coming to visit soon, and the chance that he is dragon-deaf, we must face the possibility that you will marry him and take up the role of Dragon Keeper. Even if he does hear, Longbourn may still insist that you marry him. You know how much he hates change. If you are already acquainted with the Order's business when Collins arrives he will be less likely to try and keep you from it later if he does hear, and if he does not, the Order's business will be yours to manage." Papa rubbed his eyes with knobby thumb and forefinger.

"I am not ready for her to marry!" April squawked, flapping her wings.

"I am inclined to agree." Uncle's lips folded into a deep frown. "Surely this cannot be her only option."

"In this, I am afraid, Longbourn's opinion outweighs yours." Papa's brows creased. "Go on and read the letter for us, Lizzy."

Elizabeth cracked the seal and unfolded the letter, swallowing back a bitter tang. It was not as if she and Papa had not been discussing it. There were certain decisions dragons were entitled to make for their Keepers. Longbourn had schooled her in her duty to the estate and dragonkind since she was ten years old, but it had always seemed like something far off.

Perhaps Collins inherited the family legacy and could hear dragons. Perhaps he was a decent sensible man who would understand …

Papa coughed. "Lizzy, the letter?"

"Yes, sir." She smoothed the letter over her lap. "It is from the office of the head of the Order, the Earl of Matlock, addressed to the Most Honorable Historian of the Order. He writes: A serious crime has been committed, one that threatens the Pendragon treaty and the peace between man and dragon. A firedrake egg has been stolen and hatching is imminent." She gasped and pressed her hand to her chest.

April launched off the perch and hovered at Elizabeth's shoulder.

"What egg?" Papa joined April in peering over her shoulder.

Elizabeth traced down the spidery handwriting with her fingertips. "The egg of the Lambton Wyrm!"

"The last Lambton Wyrm passed five years ago, at the same time as the master of that estate." Uncle leaned forward, elbows on knees.

"Five years is the right time for the egg to incubate." Papa shambled to his shelf and retrieved a thin book bearing the same wyvern image as the letter's seal.

One of the dragon genealogies. He had such records for every major-dragon in England: every ancestor, every descendant and their Keepers.

He flipped through it as he returned to his seat. "Yes, yes, here is the date. December 1806, the egg was laid. This is very bad indeed."

April darted around the room. "Bad? Bad you say? It is far worse than bad. It is tragic and dangerous and awful indeed."

"If a dragon with the power of a firedrake hatches without human presence—" Elizabeth shuddered.

"It will not imprint, leaving us with a wild dragon, seeking to fill its belly with the most convenient prey." Papa paced the length of the room, a heavy, labored process. "In time, its presence will be discovered and parties will rise up to kill it. I well know the histories, Lizzy."

Uncle stood and leaned against the back of his chair.

"We could find ourselves returned to the days of dragon war. What has been done to recover the egg?"

Pray let it not be so!

Elizabeth held her breath and scanned the letter. "Here, here, there is hope! The egg has been traced to a … a militia regiment from Derbyshire. Several cockatrices, in Norfolk near Caistor where they last encamped, believe they smelt it on some of the soldiers. You have been contacted because the militia is coming to Meryton soon! The Order is sending the keeper of the Lambton Wyrm here as well. You are to assist him in any way possible in the recovery of the egg."

Papa turned to Uncle. "You will stay on to help me manage this affair, will you not?"

He winced as he spoke. How much did it cost him to ask for assistance once again? This did not bode well for his temper.

"I will need to take a brief trip back to London to arrange business with my clerk, but he is a good man. He can manage for the duration."

"Whilst you are there, you ought to visit the secretary of the Order for additional news. Lord Matlock seems certain that we will be host to a major-dragon hatching." Papa raked his thinning hair back. "The first in over a hundred years."

April settled back on the perch. "I do not see why you should make such a to-do. I was hatched here a decade ago and another clutch is due to hatch soon. Just because it is a firedrake does not make it so different."

"But dearling, you cannot burn us to crispins when you are irritated. You just nip at ears." Elizabeth ducked and covered her ears.

"Do not make light of the seriousness of the situation. It is all the more important now that you find those fairy dragon eggs. If they hatch wild, they could interfere with the other hatching—dear little dimwits are likely to think they are protecting an egg from us." Papa turned to April, deep creases furrowed in his brow. "Can you find the clutch again or shall we send Rustle with you?"

"Your time would be better spent setting him to smell for the Lambton egg. I know exactly how to find my kind."

"I will be to London tomorrow at first light. I will return in a day, two at the most. Should the fairy dragons hatch whilst I am gone—"

"We shall assist your wife, do not worry." Papa removed his glasses and pinched the bridge of his nose. "Did Matlock say when the keeper of the Lambton Wyrm would arrive?"

"Not precisely, just in the next few days. He is supposed to identify himself to you when he arrives." Elizabeth pointed to the information in the letter and handed it to him.

"I expect all of us shall be involved, before all is said and done. This business takes precedence even over Mr. Collins. We must pray it is resolved successfully or I shudder to think of the consequences."

Fitzwilliam Darcy's horse stood in a nondescript little meadow along a nondescript little path, near a house Darcy had neither heard of nor cared about until now. Until it had become central to everything.

He shaded his eyes and looked up into the bright

morning sky. Walker circled high above, silhouetted against the thin clouds.

"Your fondness for that bird is entirely baffling." Charles Bingley pulled his horse alongside Darcy's. His boyish smile and energy might have been contagious had other concerns not been so pressing. "You care so little for people or society, but for that bird you would move heaven and earth itself."

"Do not sell yourself short, my friend. You come in a close second."

Bingley laughed, but it was true. Bingley was a very good friend, but not as good as Walker.

Walker had been with Darcy since Darcy's birth. He had comforted Darcy through the loss of both his parents and firedrake Pemberley; kept him company through the lonely days at school. What more faithful friend could there be? Of course Darcy would do anything for him.

"See there, over that hill, I believe that is Netherfield Park." Bingley pointed into the rising sun. "A beautiful prospect, I should say."

The dark shadow of a house rose out of the horizon. It would suit Bingley's purpose well enough. But it suited Darcy's needs far more.

"The house is handsome at a distance." Darcy stared into the woods.

The local landscape showed all the signs of karst terrain. No doubt there were several caverns nearby. Some might be large enough—

"But you will scold me that I should not accept anything sight unseen. I assure you I will not. I have an appointment with Mr. Morris, the solicitor for the property, at half past ten. He has consented to tour the house and grounds with me. In the meantime though,

I should like very much to peruse the woods a bit and see the grounds I may be hunting for myself."

Good, he had taken Walker's suggestion easily—perhaps a little too easily. It was uncanny how well Bingley took dragon direction. Then again, perhaps not. He was awfully apt to follow the opinions of anyone who presented them strongly enough.

"Far be it from me to suspend any pleasure of yours. Lead on." Darcy gestured for Bingley to ride on.

With any luck, Bingley would happen upon the dragon caverns without realizing what he discovered. And if not, Walker was there to convince him there was nothing of interest to be seen.

The bridle path led into the deeper woods, just right for hunting. The game trails suggested a substantial herd of deer roamed the wood. Enough to feed a wyvern.

So the local dragon-estate had connections to the Duke of Bedford. No other way to have got a herd here. Was the Dragon Keeper simply frugal, preferring his dragon to feed off wild deer instead of his own flocks or did the dragon prefer wild game to mutton?

Something tiny, blue and fast zipped past Darcy's face. He started. His horse shied and bolted.

"Mary! Look out!"

A flash of white caught his eye and rushed toward a red cloaked figure standing with her back to him and pulled her away just in time.

He reined in his horse and returned to survey the damage.

"You are a better horseman than that! Pay attention and control your worthless beast!" Walker dove through the trees and landed on a branch several arms' length above him.

Two young women panted beside the trail. The one in white peered up, past him and into the trees toward Walker.

"Trespasser!" The blue blur buzzed past him and between the young women, disappearing somewhere behind them.

"Pray excuse me. My horse was startled. It is not at all like him." Darcy bowed from his shoulders.

It would not do to blame the iridescent blur for all the mischief. Did the women even realize what it was?

"Indeed, nor is it like you, Darcy." Bingley rode up to them. "Pray forgive us for startling you. I have come to see Netherfield Park. Do you know it?"

"Indeed we do, sir, the grounds border my father's estate, which you are currently traversing." The woman in white's eyebrow rose and she cocked her head in a most impertinent fashion.

Walker squawked and flapped his wings. "Do not stare, Darcy. Females of your kind take on all manner of ideas when you do. Follow me, and I shall lead you back to the Netherfield's grounds."

"Your ... falcon, sir?" Her eyes narrowed just a bit and she slipped her arm over the red cloaked woman's shoulders.

Darcy nodded.

"I should caution you, my uncle's falcon is apt to hunt free on our estate. He does not always take well to others in his territory." She adjusted the market bag on her shoulder.

Something about the way she said 'falcon' and stared at Walker made the skin on the back of his neck prickle. If she was a daughter of the estate, then it was entirely possible she knew Walker was no falcon.

"I will keep that in mind. I would not wish to see

any conflict between our … birds." Darcy glanced up at Walker.

"Yes, she does hear, and I am not a bird," Walker squawked.

"If you follow the path to the left, it will take you back to Netherfield." She pointed to the fork in the path.

"Then we will be on our way. I hope to properly make your acquaintance soon." Bingley touched his hat and headed off.

"Get on with you." Walker launched from the branch and made a low pass over his head.

Darcy hesitated one more moment, then turned to follow Bingley. Walker was right. He had business more important than investigating a woman who heard dragons. Distractions of any kind—and time—were the enemy now.

"So we have met my new neighbors." Bingley clucked his tongue. "Unofficially of course, but still. They were both very pretty young ladies, unmarried too."

"Always the first two things you notice about a woman. Really, Bingley, you are as marriage minded as any of the mamas of the *ton*."

"I am tired of all the raised eyebrows and recommendations that I marry. They come from all sides now, men, women, sometimes I swear even the horse would tell me so."

"I would not," Walker screeched.

"You see, even your bird agrees." Bingley threw his hand up toward Walker.

"I am not sure he agrees, Bingley. Besides, when have you begun taking advice from everyone and their horses?"

Bingley stopped his horse and turned to look at Darcy. "I am lonely. My sister is an adequate house-keeper, but I want more than that to come home to. Her tongue and temper are sharp. I want a friend and a comfort, not a litany of complaints and dissatisfactions."

"It sounds like you want a good hound, not a wife."

"Just because you are content to be by yourself, does not mean that all men are. I intend to make the acquaintance of our neighbors and every young woman in the neighborhood. I aim to find a wife. What better place to do it than close to home?"

"So you have decided to take Netherfield sight un-seen, after all?"

Bingley grumbled and urged his horse into a fast walk.

Though the decision might be rash, and not even in Bingley's best interest, it could prove helpful. What better excuse for Darcy to stay nearby than to offer Bingley help in leasing his first estate? He might also accompany Bingley in meeting with the local estate's owner, attracting as little attention as possible to his own presence. Exactly what he needed most right now.

Elizabeth held her breath as the two men disap-peared into the forest. The clop of their horses' hooves faded into the noises of the woods. At least one of them was a Dragon Mate, perhaps even a Keeper, it was difficult to tell. Papa would need to know.

"Well, that one was a crosspatch." April darted out from the silk flowers of Mary's bonnet. "But what can you expect from someone who keeps a ratty old cockatrice as a companion?"

"Do be fair. That was hardly a ratty cockatrice, but a very fine specimen of the species." Elizabeth held her hand up for April to perch. "What is more, you were being most incautious, flitting about here and there. You look like a tasty snack to one who does not know you. You may not like to be told what to do, but if you are not more careful I will keep you indoors where you are far safer."

Elizabeth and Mary covered their ears. April was in such a temper she might well draw blood.

"Do you think the fair-haired one really will take Netherfield?" Mary untied her bonnet and inspected it.

Her hands still trembled, poor dear. She lacked the constitution for such excitement.

Elizabeth took the bonnet. "Oh, really? Another hat picked to pieces? Must you?" She waved it at April.

"I have told you a hundred times—no more than that, I am sure. If you would simply leave me a place to perch—"

"On a hat?" Mary asked.

"Where else? I am certainly not going to ride in your reticule."

"Enough, enough. We are not here to argue fashion or even to gather gossip about the new neighbors. Though I think it behooves us to discern if both of them can hear, that can wait. We have a clutch to find—assuming it has neither been eaten by a visiting cockatrice, hawk nor weasel, nor hatched on its own." Elizabeth tweaked the disheveled ribbons and passed it to Mary. "I will repair it for you when we get back."

"Come along then." April hovered in front of Elizabeth, then darted ahead.

They wove deeper into the woods until thick

branches obscured the sunshine and dropped the temperature. Cool loamy smells with a hint of several varieties of dragon musk filled her nostrils. Papa found the scent unpleasant, but it comforted her soul like nothing else.

The path faded into a narrow, ragged trail that only the deer would use. Was that—yes—a broad, clawed footprint nearly obscured by the swipe of a tail. Longbourn had been here recently, too.

April lit on a tree trunk. "Here." She gestured upward with her wing.

The branches began ten feet up. The little nest was at least twenty feet high.

"You do realize we do not have wings," Elizabeth muttered.

"You never asked how high it was."

April was such a twitterpate.

"What are we to do? I know you are willing to climb trees, but this is too much even for you." Mary peered up at the nest.

Elizabeth looked about. Nothing to stand upon. The brood mother had made a good choice of nesting sites. That boded well for the intelligence of the hatchlings. Only winged creatures, a weasel ... or a tatzelwurm could reach that.

She pulled the market bag off her shoulder and opened it.

"Why are you holding a bundle of dried cod in the air?"

Not merely dried cod, dried cod with a touch of salt, and a sprinkle of white wine.

"Do put those away! They stink!" April sniffed and sneezed.

Elizabeth waved the fish though the breeze. "There

is a tatzelwurm that lives in these woods. He is excessively fond of dried cod and a scratch behind the ears."

"A wild dragon? Why would you call one to us?" Mary gasped and covered her mouth with her hands.

"Not wild. He has no Dragon Mate, but he imprinted. Papa says he hatched in the Longbourn barn. Our great-grandfather assisted the hatching."

"But why does he not live with us then?"

"Our great-grandmother detested cats. They kept terriers to deal with the rats."

"But could not the tatzelwurm convince her that he was anything but a cat?" Mary glanced at April.

"I might be able to, for I have such a sweet voice." April preened her wing. "But most have to content themselves with lesser persuasions."

A nearby shrub rustled. Elizabeth crouched and peered into it. Two large, emerald eyes peered back. She pulled a piece of cod from the bundle and tossed it toward the bush.

Raspy rumbles, quite like purring, erupted from the leaves. Two large, thumbed paws and a furry head emerged and inched toward the fish, snatched it and pulled back into the branches.

"Good day, Rumblkins." Elizabeth extended another fish, but did not toss it. "I am pleased to see you still enjoy my offering."

"It would not hurt for you to bring them to me more often." His deep voice was raspy and rough as he spoke through a full mouth.

"You could come to the house more often."

"Not since your housekeeper threw a shoe at me." He swallowed a huge gulp and emerged from the bush in all his glory.

His face and tufted ears were decidedly feline.

Striped tabby fur with white tips on his toes and ears covered his whole front half. Magnificent large paws, with extra toes giving the impression of thumbs, sported razor sharp claws. Behind his shoulders though, the fur faded into deep brown scales that covered the length of his long, thick, snake-like body.

"It was not our housekeeper, but my grandmother's. The current housekeeper, Mrs. Hill, has quite the soft spot for cats and will put out a pan of milk if she sees one. Rub yourself around her ankles and purr and you shall have fish any day you like."

"Like this, you mean?" He circled her ankles, rubbing his cheeks over her feet and rumbling.

She offered another fish. "Exactly."

He ate more slowly this time.

"Perhaps you would be willing to assist us with a task of vital importance. I have an entire bundle of cod to offer for your help."

He looked up, a fishtail hanging from one side of his mouth. "What do you want?"

"Above us is an abandoned fairy dragon nest with eggs near hatching. It is too high for me to reach. We want to bring the eggs back to the house so they can imprint when they hatch."

Rumblkins licked his broad paw and washed his face. "I like eggs. Almost as tasty as fish."

April swooped over his head, chittering. "You will do no such thing. I did not bring any of you here for a meal!"

Rumblkins reared up and swiped at her, not trying very hard to hit her.

"You are a horrid, flea-bitten bundle of fur."

"And you are a senseless bit of flying fluff." He batted at her again, clipping the edge of her tail.

April spun and wove drunkenly, colliding with Elizabeth. She caught hold of the edge of Elizabeth's spencer and clung hard.

"Do you really want your woods populated with wild bits of senseless winged fluff?" Elizabeth asked as she righted April on to her shoulder.

"I could just eat the eggs."

"But then you would not have an entire bundle of cod."

Rumblkins chirruped in that funny way cats did and curled his serpentine tail around his forepaws. "You have a good point. If I bring the eggs to you, will you keep them away from the woods after they hatch? That would be far less effort than catching them and eating them."

April squawked and plunged her face under the collar of Elizabeth's spencer.

"We cannot force them, but they will be made very welcome and encouraged to stay. Some of them might even become companions to my Aunt and Uncle's family and move to London."

Rumblkins' eyes widened and his mouth gaped in a feline rendition of a smile. "And you will give me the fish?"

Elizabeth patted the market bag. "You can smell them, I am sure. They are yours when we have the eggs, safely. There will be no fish if the eggs are damaged."

His long, forked tongue flicked out and licked his lips. "I like fish very much."

Elizabeth opened the bag and showed him the contents.

He drew a deep breath, eyes half closed, and rumbled. "I will bring the eggs."

His front half walked to the tree and his back half

slithered to keep up, an odd, awkward looking movement on the best of days. He pulled up with his claws until his tail wrapped around the trunk, then quickly disappeared into the branches. If there was something a tatzelwurm could do well, it was climb.

Elizabeth held her breath. This was risky. He could decide to eat the eggs easily enough and April might never forgive either of them for it. As much as he loved fish, he might just do that for the sport of it. Dragons, tatzelwurms in particular, were not entirely predictable, nor reliable.

But there were few options. She could not climb herself. Cockatrices loved eggs, so appealing to Rustle for assistance would have been certain disaster.

She squeezed her eyes shut. Hopefully the stranger's cockatrice had not—

Mary leaned into her ear and whispered. "He comes, and I think I see an egg."

Rumblkins' descent was far slower than his ascent, but when he made it to Elizabeth's feet, he placed a tiny, mottled blue egg at her feet.

She picked it up and replaced it with a small piece of fish. "Thank you. How many more are in the nest?"

He held up one paw. "One for each paw. Must I get all of them?"

"Only if you wish not to have wild fairy dragons disturbing your peace."

He bared his teeth and growled as he made his way back up the tree.

Elizabeth rewarded him for the second egg and produced the promised bundle of cod for the third. Rumblkins pounced on it with savage glee.

As much as she loved dragons, it was difficult to watch them eat.

Mary collected the eggs into her padded reticule and tucked them inside her spencer. "The shells are quite warm. I do not think it will be long before they hatch."

"Thank you for your help. Remember, you are welcome at the house anytime you wish." Elizabeth curtsied.

Rumblkins lifted his head and shook it, sending bits of dried fish flying. "I shall keep to my woods if you have a flock of senseless flits about, thank you."

April squawked, but remained hidden in Elizabeth's spencer.

"You could be bothered to bring me some of these more often, you know." He crunched on a fish head.

"I shall consider it. Perhaps you might catch a few of the rats that are plaguing the hens." Elizabeth tucked the empty bag over her shoulder.

"Perhaps you should get a cat."

"I am sure he would like fish as well as you, and be far easier to deal with."

Rumblkins grumbled and growled. "If the housekeeper throws anything at me, I swear to you I shall bite her."

"You will find her very amiable." Elizabeth leaned down and scratched behind his ears. "Bring her dead rats and she shall give you a pillow by the fire and all the fish you can stuff your fanged, furry face with."

He leaned into her hand so hard, he nearly fell over, eyes rolling back in his head.

"I will let her know where you like to be scratched. Good day." Elizabeth curtsied once more, and they turned back for home.

"Do you think it was a good idea to invite him to the house?" Mary asked.

"A house cannot have too many dragons. Mrs. Hill

is a gentle soul who is easily persuaded. Between that and her love for cats, I think they could make each other very happy—and take care of the rat problem in the poultry eaves."

Mary laughed and pressed her hand over the reticule in her spencer.

"You are not carrying chicken eggs." April flew between Mary and Elizabeth. "You do not need to be so dainty."

"Though it pains me, I must agree with her," Elizabeth said. "The eggs are more leathery than brittle. Unless you fall atop them, there is little chance you can damage them."

"I know you meant to comfort me, but knowing that, I now have one more thing to worry about."

Elizabeth put her hand on Mary's shoulder and stopped her. "What is troubling you?"

"Nothing at all. Why do you think—"

"Mary, please. You do not have to play that game with me. I am not Mama and will not scold you for your concerns."

Mary's eyes brightened, and she dragged her hand down her face. "How do you do it?"

"Do what?

"The dragons. Every single one I have seen you deal with, they all like you. You know where each of them lives. You know the right things to say and do to make them happy. You always seem to know just what they want and need. What is your secret?"

"You hear them just as well as I do. There is no secret."

"I could never have convinced Rumblkins to help us. I would not even have thought to try." Mary glanced down toward the eggs. "I know Papa has in mind for me to be Dragon Mate to one of these little ones, but I have no idea how I will do it. Why would a hatchling like me in the first place, not when you, Aunt Gardiner and even the children are about? Who would not prefer their company? Rustle is so grumpy to me. Longbourn hardly speaks to me at all. I may be able to hear them, but what matters that if none of them care to speak to me?"

Elizabeth gestured at a fallen log and sat down. She slipped her arm over Mary's shoulder. "There is no secret, truly. Dragons are very much like people. The only difference is that they do not hide their thoughts or feelings as we do. We are taught to be polite and reserved, but they have no such impediments. If they think it or feel it, they will say it. Their wants are simple and they will let you know them if you ask."

"You should have heard what Longbourn said to me the last time I went to groom his scales. He did nothing but complain and criticize. How do you tolerate it when they can be so … difficult?"

"I prefer to regard them not so much as critical, but honest." Elizabeth tipped her head back and peered through the branches into the sky. "All told, I try to appreciate it for the gift it is."

"You are speaking in riddles."

"How many times have you wondered what someone was truly thinking? You know that they do not mean what they say, but you do not know what they honestly think. Does that not bother you?"

"Of course it does." Mary dusted a leaf off her skirt.

"With the dragons, you always know what they are thinking. I find it refreshing and far safer than dealing with our own kind. If you treat a dragon as you wish to be treated, without false civility and ceremony, but with honesty and respect, you will find them very agreeable creatures."

"You make it sound so simple."

"I suppose that having a touch of impertinence makes it all a bit easier. But, I am certain you are quite up to the task." Elizabeth rose and pulled Mary to her feet. "Come, we should bring the eggs to Papa. He is probably pacing the floor waiting for us even now."

2
Chapter

Papa was indeed waiting most impatiently, with a hatching box stuffed with straw already sitting near the fire in his study. Close by, a basket overflowed with flannels and old towels. A treacle and blood sausage— a meal most easily digested by dragon chicks—hung by the fireplace, ready to feed to the hungry hatchlings, and a kettle stood ready on the hob. In honor of the occasion, many of the customary stacks and piles had disappeared, leaving the walkways clear and the tables piled high.

Three tomes lay open on the desk, revealing hatching lore dating back hundreds of years. Papa always refreshed his memory before a hatching. His encyclopedic knowledge on the matter had earned him great respect among the Order. He was often invited to attend important hatchings. He had been present at more than any living member of the Order and had brought Elizabeth to several.

He carefully studied each egg, holding them up to a candle, then to his ear. Faint cheeps could be heard from them. A very good sign indeed.

A few days, a se'nnight at most for the hatching. The eggs must not be left alone, not even for an hour. Their social plans must be curtailed until the hatchlings were past their need for hourly feedings.

Thankfully that only lasted a few days. With any luck at all, it would be Mary and Aunt Gardiner cast with managing that task. The last thing Elizabeth needed was another fairy dragon turning to her for companionship. April's demands quite filled her days.

Two days later, soft post-dawn sunlight streamed into the morning room as the family gathered for breakfast. The chamber was tidy and snug, with crisp white curtains and pale blue-green walls. The round table and plain chairs took up most of the space, with a neat sideboard pushed tight along the wall opposite the window. No matter how few people were in the room, it always felt rather full of company.

Aunt and Uncle remained upstairs, breakfasting with the children where the little ones might chatter and giggle as much as they wished without earning raised brows and dark scowls from Mama. No doubt Uncle would be enlivening their meal with a few dragon tales as well.

Ham, scones and porridge graced the table, with tea and a pot of coffee on the sideboard. Papa's usual mug of willow bark tea steeped beside his plate. It was his large mug—his pain must be particularly bad this morning.

With him hiding behind his newspaper, Jane and Mary quietly sewing, and Kitty and Lydia poring over the latest edition of *La Belle Assemble*, the tableau epitomized domestic familial bliss.

At least for a moment.

Mama swept into the morning room, a vague look of triumph in her eyes. "My dear Mr. Bennet!"

Elizabeth swallowed a gulp of too-hot tea and nearly dropped her tea cup.

Jane reached across her place and helped her set it on the table. Kitty leaned over Lydia's shoulder and whispered something. They both giggled.

Papa winced. That introduction always preceded a flurry of social plans, none of which would accommodate needy baby dragons.

"Have you heard that Netherfield Park is let at last? Mrs. Long has just been here, and she told me all about it."

"Is it not early for her to be paying a call?" Papa's eyebrow rose archly over his mug.

Mama waved his question away. "Mrs. Long came to me yesterday, and she says that Netherfield is taken by a young man of large fortune, from the north of England, by the name of Bingley. A single man of large fortune; four or five thousand a year. What a fine thing for our girls!"

"How so? How can it affect them?" Papa snapped his newspaper back into its creases and set it aside. His eyes sparkled—he enjoyed this little game. Perhaps a bit too much.

"How can you be so tiresome!" Mama snorted and took her place beside him. "You must know that I am thinking of his marrying one of them. It is a truth universally acknowledged that a single man in possession of a good fortune must be in want of a wife. Our girls are so very agreeable. It is very likely that he may fall in love with one of them. Therefore you must visit him as soon as he comes."

The light faded from Papa's eyes, and his shoulders stiffened.

Jane cast an alarmed look at Elizabeth. She detested conflict. Little got Papa's back up faster than being told he must do something—unless of course it was a dragon who told him so.

"A visit, you say?"

Jane squeezed her eyes shut and bit her lip.

"My dear, you must indeed go and see Mr. Bingley. Consider your daughters. Only think what an establishment it would be for one of them. Sir William and Lady Lucas are determined to go, merely on that account, for in general, you know they visit no newcomers—"

"Enough, enough, my dear Mrs. Bennet. You can cease your endless entreaties." Papa leaned back, tension flowing away.

What was he about?

Mama threw her hands in the air. "You take delight in vexing me. You have no compassion on my poor nerves."

Papa sipped his willow bark tea, looking far more smug than he ought. "You mistake me, my dear. I have a high respect for your nerves. They are my old friends. I have heard you mention them with consideration these twenty years at least."

"You do not know what I suffer!" Mama dabbed her eyes with her napkin.

"Nor have I any idea what I shall endure as I have actually paid the call just hours ago. The family was not there to visitors, so I left my card and one of yours as well, Mrs. Bennet. We cannot escape the acquaintance now."

Mama clapped and squealed. "Well, how pleased I am! I was sure you loved our girls too well to neglect such an acquaintance. Such a good joke, too, that you should have gone this morning, and never said a word about it till now. And so early!"

Mary glanced at Elizabeth, who shrugged.

"I believe we crossed paths with Mr. Bingley whilst Lizzy and I were walking the day before yesterday." Mary kept her eyes on the tablecloth.

"And you told me nothing of this? What happened?" Mama leaned toward her.

"A horse, out of control, almost ran over us on the path near Oakham Mount. Another man returned to check on us. He said he was here to see Netherfield Park, and that he hoped he would be able to properly make our acquaintance soon. I must conclude he was Mr. Bingley."

Lydia leaned across the table. "Oh, oh! Was he handsome?"

"What of the other man with him? The one who could not handle his horse?" Kitty nearly knocked over her teacup with her elbow. "It is even better if there are two gentlemen."

"Do not keep us waiting child, we must know." Mama waved her hand at Mary.

Mary's eyes bulged. Her conversation never attracted this much attention.

"I do not think he was a poor horseman. I think something startled his horse." Elizabeth glanced at Papa.

"Oh, not that foolish little bird of yours, Lizzy. You must keep it to its cage or better yet, turn it out of the house, and let it fly free. What will our new neighbors think of such a creature following you about? Really, that is too peculiar."

"Mrs. Bennet," Papa spoke through gritted teeth.

Mama's mouth opened and closed several times, but she knew well enough not to cross Papa when he used that tone.

They all did.

Mama leaned back, shoulders sagging. "Well, we must make the most of our acquaintance with him—"

Mrs. Hill trundled into the room with cards on a small silver platter. "A Mr. Bingley and Mr. Darcy to see the family." She curtsied.

Mama sprang to her feet and pounced on the cards. "Look how elegant. The printing, the paper, so re-fined!"

"Perhaps we should greet the men themselves rather than stand about admiring their cards." Papa offered her his arm and ushered her out of the morning room.

Jane followed, and the rest in turn.

Hill had installed their guests in the parlor where they stood near the fireplace waiting. Both men were finely dressed, but not dandies, conservative and polished. The parlor, with its faded fabrics and worn woods, looked a little shabby beside them.

They spoke in hushed tones that even Elizabeth's sharp hearing could not discern.

"Mr. Bingley and Mr. Darcy I presume?" Papa bowed from his shoulders.

"Mr. Bennet! I cannot tell you how sorry I am that the housekeeper did not direct you inside. We would have been most happy to have received you this morning. We had to come immediately and return your call. Allow me to present my friend, Mr. Darcy of

Derbyshire."

Darcy bowed a mite stiffly. "Pleased to make your acquaintance, Mr. Bennet."

When he straightened, a glint of gold caught her eyes. His pocket watch flashed in a sunbeam. An embossed wyvern, the sign of the Blue Order, emblazoned the cover. A signet ring with the same figure encircled the small finger of his right hand.

A Dragon Keeper from Derbyshire. He must be the Keeper of the Lambton Wyrm, Keeper of the missing egg!

Papa's eyes flashed to the pocket watch and back to Darcy's face. He glanced toward Bingley's watch. No such decoration. He probably could not hear dragons at all.

What a strange companion for Mr. Darcy to travel with, given his errand.

"May I present my wife, Mrs. Bennet, and my daughters?" Papa gestured toward them. "Miss Jane Bennet, Elizabeth, Mary, Kitty and Lydia."

They curtsied in turn.

Bingley bowed again. He was a handsome man, to be sure, and his temper seemed open and agreeable, just what one would wish for in a single man of good fortune. "Delighted to make your acquaintance, indeed."

Beside him, Darcy made a small bow but said nothing.

Mama sniffed in his direction. No doubt they would be treated to a long discourse on the man's rudeness later.

"Please sit down, be comfortable. I shall call for some tea." Mama rang the bell for Hill.

Bingley sat down on the settee. Mama waved Jane

and Lydia to his side as she took the chair nearest.

Of course Mama would direct her favorites to him. They were free to marry for normal considerations—affection, money, connections—but Elizabeth had no such privilege. As the eldest Dragon Hearer, she had a responsibility to the estate and to Longbourn.

Elizabeth swallowed hard. Jealousy was not attractive. All gifts came with a price. And hearing dragons was worth it.

Papa lifted an eyebrow at Mr. Darcy and twitched his head toward the door.

Elizabeth sidled between them and the rest of the company. Best make their escape as easy as possible. "So, Mr. Bingley, how to do you find Meryton?"

Bennet slipped out of the parlor, signaling Darcy to follow. Bingley appeared entirely happy, engaged with a room full of lively Miss Bennets, so he would hardly notice Darcy's absence. Best that way all told. If pressed, Darcy could easily claim he wanted to discuss land management with Mr. Bennet. While a bit of a stretch, it was hardly a lie.

"We shall not be disturbed here." Bennet shut the study door behind them.

His shoulders were bowed and his back stooped. He shuffled more heavily than his age alone would have implied. No doubt his feet were as gnarled as his hands. Could he even make it out to see the estate dragon? It could not be often if he did. Who tended the dragon for him?

The study was small, but serviceable. Shelves filled with books—books of dragon lore, dragon histories, genealogies, and titles he could not make out—lined the wall behind the imposing desk and an adjacent wall. Exactly what he would expect from the repository of the Blue Order's wisdom. Windows and a generous fireplace took up the remaining walls. Four comfortable chairs clustered near the fireplace, a unique dragon perch between them.

The space was not tidy, but the wooden box stuffed with straw near the hanging sausage could hardly be random clutter. He edged toward the hearth until he could peer into the box.

"Fairy dragon eggs." Bennet hastened across the room to stand protectively near the hatching box.

"Are you certain? I understand tatzelwurm eggs look very similar." Darcy crouched and peered at the eggs, but did not touch them.

"They do, but tatzelwurms do not put their clutches twenty feet off the ground, do they? Nor do they make the sounds you will hear if you listen very closely." Bennet hunkered down beside him and leaned close to the eggs.

Darcy did likewise, closing his eyes. Tiny trills came from the eggs, so faint it would be easy to dismiss entirely. His head fell back in a deep yawn.

"Have you any doubts now?" Bennet crossed his arms and chuckled.

"None at all." He rose and backed away from the eggs, shaking his head. There was a reason he did not prefer the company of fairy dragons. But still, to be able to attend an actual hatching, not merely read about it ...

Bennet opened the window. A sharp, welcome breeze blew through. "That's just the thing. Been hard to keep awake, standing watch over them."

Darcy joined him near the window, gulping in the bracing air.

"I received instructions from the Order concerning the Keeper of the Lambton Wyrm." Bennet wandered toward his desk and pulled a thick missive from the drawer. Fragments of blue sealing wax clung to the paper.

"My uncle is nothing if not efficient." Darcy clasped his hands behind his back and approached the desk.

It would have been far better had Matlock not interfered. Far better.

"Your uncle is the Earl of Matlock?"

"And I am the Keeper of the Lambton Wyrm, though the previous estate dragon far preferred to be known as Pemberley."

Bennet sat in a large wingback chair and gestured for Darcy to do the same.

"The Lambton Wyrm is a convenient fable, but hardly more true to fact than most dragon legends. Pemberley is a firedrake, not a wyrm."

"So you are Keeper to a royal dragon." Bennet tapped his fingertips before his chest. "That explains your bearing."

"I do not know whether to be flattered or insulted."

Bennet merely lifted an eyebrow.

Insulted it was.

Was Bennet rude, thick or irreverent? Few men addressed him with so much familiarity, especially once they knew his affiliation with Matlock and a firedrake.

"It bothers you? Most who deal with dragons have rather thick skins, as it were." Bennet folded his arms over his chest.

That accusation.

Again.

"You think I am no Dragon Keeper."

"Have you a dragon in your keeping?"

"Do not play games with me, sir. If you have something to say, come out with it directly." Darcy's hands knotted into fists.

This was not the first time he had fought this issue. Uncle Matlock and his cadre had quite worn it out. But discussing it again with this self-important nobody was beyond the pale.

"I find it difficult to respect a man careless enough to have a dragon egg—an estate dragon's egg and a firedrake no less—stolen from his own home. You must agree, it does not speak well of you, from any angle. And now, according to the head of the Order, I am to assist you in its recovery? Even if we do manage to find it—and for the sake of England and dragonkind, I pray we do—why should I see the egg back into your possession?"

A brutal, sharp cut, direct to the gut. But it was quick and clean. There was something to be said for that.

Not a great deal, but something.

"What you are carefully not saying, sir, is that you question my abilities as a Dragon Keeper and wonder if you should suggest to the new Pemberley, once hatched, that a new Dragon Keeper might be in order."

"At least you have spent time in the company of dragonkind, enough to know some of their ways. That is some reassurance." Bennet leaned back and his eyes narrowed.

Did he relish the thought of suggesting Pemberley make a meal of the last male of the Darcy line?

Probably.

"The egg will be recovered, make no mistake in that.

A wild firedrake—I cannot even conceive. It would send us back to the Dark Ages. It cannot be. But to send such a powerful creature back into the keeping of a man so careless, so—"

"Stop right there. You have no grounds to cast aspersions on my character."

"I have every place to do so. Do you know the last time an egg was removed from its inherited territory?"

"As I recall, it was in 1705."

Good, that startled the old man.

Darcy drew a deep steadying breath. It was time to put Bennet in his place. "How many eggs—major-dragon eggs are laid in a century—two perhaps? Never more than three—and that only happened once, in the century after the Pendragon treaty was forged. Of those seventeen major-dragon eggs since the treaty, how many have been removed from their keep? How many, sir? How many!!"

Bennet stammered.

He really ought to have made a better study of his dragon history.

"Six, sir, there have been six. One in three eggs has been tampered with. Even the Longbourn keep has once been meddled with. In 1379, your ancestor was a drunk and gambled away the egg in a game of cards. When he regained his sense—"

Bennet's face lost all color. "I know the story well enough, thank you."

"Then do not be so quick to cast judgement."

"What happened over four centuries ago is hardly my responsibility. It is not as though I could effect change to the past. But here and now, I can and I will. I must have satisfaction that dragonet Pemberley will have proper care."

"You are in no place to make demands upon me. You have been charged by the Order to assist me in the recovery, not to sit in judgement over me."

Uncle Matlock was already doing a sufficient job of that.

"An inquest should be held," Bennet snarled.

"Take that up with the Earl."

"As I recall, he is most conveniently your Uncle. Should you be found incompetent, his authority would be severely jeopardized. To keep his own position, he must protect yours."

How little Bennet understood. Matlock had younger sons whom he would be happy to set up as Dragon Keeper and master of Pemberley in Darcy's place.

Darcy slammed his fist on the arm of the chair. "How dare you!"

"Quite easily. It is precisely what you would do in my positon, with far less tact, I might add. It is what any Keeper loyal to dragonkind would do."

A screeching blur dove through the window. Prickles coursed down Darcy's spine. It landed on the perch, the force nearly toppling it.

Bennet reacted, but pulled back as Darcy grabbed it steady. At least Bennet had sense enough not to approach an unfamiliar cockatrice.

Walker flapped his wings as much for effect as to regain his balance. While he liked to make a grand entrance, usually he was far more regal about it.

Even in a rare moment of clumsiness, he was a spectacular specimen of his kind. Razor sharp beak and talons glinted in the sunlight with a vague metallic sheen. His head and shoulders resembled the falcon most people perceived him to be. Powerful wings extended as wide as Darcy's arm span. Feathers and scales gleamed—perfectly oiled and preened. But his eyes and forked tongue were as reptilian as his body and tail.

Walker sidled across the perch to look Bennet square in the eye.

"The unmitigated presumption of you! You question Darcy as a Keeper? Look at me." Walker stretched his wings and lifted his head. "Can you find fault with me? Would an inadequate Keeper have a companion such as me?"

Vanity was a cockatrice trait, but Walker took it to new heights.

"A companion dragon, even one such as yourself, is not the same as a major-dragon. Even you must agree."

Interesting how Bennet's tone turned far more respectful, even conciliatory, as he addressed the dragon.

Walker flipped his wings to his back and leaned so close to Bennet that his beak nearly touched his nose. "Then perhaps we should reflect on what kind of Keeper you are. Consider Longbourn—"

"He is quite well—"

"Longbourn is fat, lazy and sarcastic. He regularly fails to attend the Dragon conclave and all but refuses to perform his duties as presiding dragon of this parish. When he does deign to act, he is careless, forgetful and late. Over two years late in performing his last required census of the local wild and unattached dragons, as I recall."

Bennet's jaw dropped.

How satisfying.

Darcy rose and extended a hand toward Walker. "Perhaps an introduction is in order. Walker, may I present Dragon Keeper Bennet, of Longbourn."

Bennet bristled but held his tongue, clearly feeling the intended insult. A companion dragon should be presented to a Keeper, not the other way around.

Perhaps Darcy had spent too long among dragon-kind. The use of such insults really ought to be below him.

Walker squawked an acknowledgement. "So, Bennet, how do you explain Longbourn's dereliction of duties?"

"Those are his business. I do not manage his more than he does mine."

"And you think yourself worthy of taking another Keeper to task when you are hardly worthy of the title yourself?"

A tiny blue streak zipped through the window, chittering and scolding so fast Darcy could barely make out her words. After flying two dizzying circuits around the room, she wove between Darcy, Bennet and Walker and nipped Darcy's ear. He yelped and shooed her off, clutching his ear.

The blue fairy dragon hovered in front of his face. The color reminded him of something.

"What kind of Keeper do you think you are? You nearly permitted that dusty, feather-worn bird to eat me!"

Walker flapped his wings and snapped at her. Had he truly wished to, the little scold would have been a quick snack. The glint in his eye suggested he was amused, though, not annoyed.

The fairy dragon darted behind Bennet. "You see, you see!" she shrieked.

The door burst open and the woman in white on the path — Miss Elizabeth—stormed in.

No wonder the fairy dragon seemed familiar.

"April!" She sprinted toward her father, glowering at Walker all the way.

"No matter what she says, I do not eat other companions." He resettled his wings and lifted his head slightly.

Vain creature. He was seeking her notice, so he could snub her when she offered it. The trick was unattractive, but it would probably help drive his point about Bennet's inadequacies home.

"You are a gentleman's companion, so I should give you credit for that much civility." She coaxed the little fairy dragon on to her shoulder. "But still, I think you quite the bully for scaring her so."

Walker started. He was not accustomed to reprimand. "I should think you would have taught her some sense by now."

Miss Elizabeth's lip rose in a half smile—a positively draconic expression. "I shall consider that a compliment, if you believe me capable of teaching a dragon, even a very small one, anything. May I present my companion, April."

Darcy snorted. Every bit a senseless tuft of fluff as her companion.

Some help he would have out of this family.

Walker half spread his wings and dipped in his version of a bow. Not to the tiny blue fluff, but to Miss Elizabeth.

What?

He had little regard for men in general, but even less for women. Nearly tore the feathers out of Caroline Bingley's headdress the last time he saw her. What was he doing, showing such considerations to the forgettable daughter of a self-important keeper of an insignificant wyvern?

She curtsied to Walker and reached for him. Foolish girl would learn one did not touch a cockatrice uninvited. Probably never dealt with one before. She would be lucky if he did not draw blood. Would serve her right for her impertinence.

Capricious creature, he stretched his neck, reaching for her fingers. She found a spot of molting feathers and scratched. Ungrateful wretch, he all but cooed as she did.

What was Walker playing at?

"There is a place in the garden on the sunset side of the house, in the center of the roses. It is set aside for dustbathing. The bushes are thick and thorny enough to offer you privacy. The dust will soothe that molting itch for you." She stroked his cheek feathers with the back of her finger.

How did she know Walker was too vain to dust bathe where he could be seen?

Walker cheeped happily, offering another spot to scratch.

"I should thank you not to interfere with my companion or distract him from our task at hand." Darcy cut between her and Walker.

"Indeed, sir, I think your companion entirely able to speak for himself. He does not seem distraught." She blinked up at him with affected innocence.

Darcy growled under his breath. "Keep your senseless little flit away from him—from us—or I shall—"

"Shall what? Fall off your horse?"

"Elizabeth!" Bennet stomped and glowered. "That is quite enough. You, both of you, are excused."

She cast a look his way more toxic than basilisk venom and twice as plentiful. With a toss of her head, she stalked out.

Walker shrieked his displeasure. Full-on shivers coursed down Darcy's spine. Pray no one else in the house heard that or panic might ensue.

Walker launched from the perch, knocking it to the floor, and sped out the window.

Darcy pointed one hand toward the window and the other toward the door. "If this is the help I am to expect out of Longbourn, then I am better off proceeding without it."

"Arrogant fool. Have you any idea of the terrain here, the lay of the land? Are you aware of where something like a dragon egg might be hidden here? The number of small caves and caverns here is staggering. The task is far beyond you, and your Uncle knows it. You will realize it soon enough."

"Good day to you, sir. I will show myself out." Darcy spun on his heel and strode out before Bennet could reply. Or maybe he just chose to ignore Darcy. That was equally possible, though not nearly as satisfying.

The absolute gall of that nameless upstart! For all that Bennet might be an officer in the Order, the Bennets had only been Dragon Keepers for four hundred years. How could he presume to lecture a Darcy?

Dragon Keeper D'Arcy descended directly from the Pendragon line. His family had been hearing and keeping dragons for nigh on seven hundred years.

Bennet had no right to take such an attitude!

But then his family had never permitted an egg to be so wholly compromised as to be taken from its ancestral home.

Darcy had.

Five days later, Elizabeth and Jane walked through Mama's cutting garden, armed with baskets and shears. The vases in the dining room and entrance hall needed filling.

The midmorning sun inched toward its apex. The last of the morning freshness burned off into the day's heat—just enough to be noticeably warmer, but without with the oppression of the summer sun. A largely perfect day.

"I am surprised April is not with us. She loves the flowers so." Elizabeth clipped a large marigold blossom and tucked it in the basket.

"I am not sure she trusts the new cat Mrs. Hill has taken in." Jane pointed at Rumblkins, who carried a large rat toward the kitchen door.

He dropped it on the step and rose up to drum his forepaws on the door. Mrs. Hill opened the door with a happy gasp.

"You dear, dear creature." She crouched and scratched Rumblkins' throat until he purred loud enough to be heard across the yard. He rubbed against her ankles and wove around her feet.

"I have a treat for you. Wait just a moment." She disappeared inside, returning with a saucer of cream and a dried cod. "Just as I promised you! And you shall have another for every rat you bring me."

Dear Hill was exactly as Elizabeth had assured him she would be. She pressed her lips hard. It would be difficult not to gloat to the furry tatzelwurm later.

Rumblkins lapped the cream and started on the fish. Hill sat beside him, stroking his fur.

"I have never seen her so taken with a cat before," Jane said.

"I think she has never seen such a mouser before. But it is a good thing, I think. With fewer rats in the poultry, there are more eggs for us."

"And less salt cod." Jane giggled. "I know how you detest the stuff."

Elizabeth bit her knuckle. "I may have suggested it would not be inappropriate to make up a basket near the kitchen hearth for him."

He was a fine little dragon. There was no point in not seeking mutual benefit.

"I know Mama does not prefer cats, but she hates mice even more."

"And his purr is very persuasive."

Not that Rumblkins had much need to use it on Hill. Mama might be another story though.

"Indeed it is." Jane stared at Rumblkins, her brow knit.

Elizabeth studied Jane.

Was it possible she was beginning to hear? Some came into their hearing later in their lives—like Aunt Gardiner.

"Do you ever wonder—I think sometimes he is speaking in all those rumbles and purrs." Elizabeth bit her lip. That was more than she ought to say.

Jane chuckled. "You do say the oddest things, Lizzy. What an imagination you have. That sounds like a story you would tell our little cousins."

Elizabeth laughed along. It was the best way to conceal her disappointment. Dragons were the one thing she did not share with Jane. Sometimes it was easy enough to ignore, but at times like now, the cavernous gap between them ached like the death of a friend.

Hill rose. "So, shall you bring me another rat, or do you wish to come and sleep by the fire?"

Rumblkins batted the door and she opened it for him. He trotted inside, but paused and looked over his shoulder at Elizabeth.

"You are right. I like her very well indeed." He ended with a very convincing meow.

Cheeky little fellow.

Mrs. Hill shut the door behind him, mindful of his proud long tail.

"Are you not worried about April? That cat is such an adept mouser—"

"I am entirely certain of him. Just as certain as you are that Mr. Bingley is as handsome as he is charming." Elizabeth forced a smile.

Any more talk of the wonderful Mr. Bingley might well drive her to distraction, but it was by far the most expedient way to change the subject.

"He is, is he not? And his friend is very well-favored, too."

"That is Mama's opinion, and I believe it is strongly influenced by the ten thousand a year he is said to have."

"How can you say such a thing?"

"Very easily—"

"Lizzy! Lizzy!" Mary ran toward them.

"Stop and catch your breath or you shall make yourself ill." Jane caught her elbow.

Mary braced her hands on her knees, panting hard. "Papa says you are wanted immediately, Lizzy. I am to bring you myself."

"Of course." She handed Jane her basket and shears. "Should I send Kitty to assist you?"

"No, no. I am happy to walk by myself for a bit."

…and daydream of Mr. Bingley by the look on her face. Was it wrong to be jealous of Jane's freedom? Best not think of it now.

Elizabeth took Mary's arm and hurried for the house. "Is it time?"

"April says it is. Aunt Gardiner is already with Papa."

"And the children?"

"Lydia has taken them to play with the young Lucases."

"A convenient excuse to gossip with Maria about the Netherfield party?"

"Of course. I think he means to invent an errand for Mama, Kitty and Jane as well. He was seeking Mama when I left."

It would be best that way. The last thing they needed was the worry of keeping Mama at bay.

Mary paused and squeezed her hand. "Are you sure this is a good idea? What if—"

Elizabeth tugged her hand and urged her to continue. "Do not dwell on that. I am sure it will be fine. You have been talking to the eggs when you sit with them?"

"Until Mama suggested I needed a goodly dose of poppy tea if I was going to talk to myself so much."

Elizabeth snickered. If Mama knew what was actually going on, she would be the one needing great quantities of poppy tea.

They slipped into Papa's study. He had somehow managed to clear away the clutter. Probably stashed it under the desk, but still it was a good thing if there were to be four people and even more dragons within.

The windows were shut against any marauding dragons who might snack on the hatchlings. The curtains were half drawn, dimming the light for their sensitive eyes. The room smelt of clean straw and simmering soup.

Papa sat on a stool near the hearth adding slivers of blood and treacle pudding to a pan of simmering broth on the hob. The dragon chicks would eat well when they arrived.

How had he cut them when he could barely hold a knife? The things he could manage to do when dragon-inspired!

Aunt sat nearby. Rustle perched on the back of her chair. Odd that he did not use the perch. He generally did not prefer to be so close to her.

Rumblkins leaned against her legs, purring. She scratched his ears, anxious anticipation in her eyes. April perched on the hatching box, hopping from one foot to the other.

"Go sit with Aunt Gardiner, Mary. We have not long to wait." Papa said, beckoning Elizabeth to him. "Bring me those flannels."

She picked up a stack of three soft cloths from the desk.

"The hatchlings must have our scent as soon as they hatch. Rub each cloth along your throat and hands. Do not forget Rustle and Rumblkins, too. We will dry the hatchlings with them, to give them our scent."

Rumblkins enjoyed the attentions, even rolling over to present his belly for a rub.

Rustle did not.

He was a very different creature to Mr. Darcy's companion. Though hardly the ratty, unkempt bird April claimed him to be, he had none of the regal bearing of Walker. Almost like a gentleman wearing his best suit standing beside Beau Brummel. Clean and well kept, but somehow lacking in those fine details that set Brummel apart. Walker was definitely the Brummel of cockatrices.

"When will these flutterbobs get on with it?" Rustle peered over Aunt Gardiner's shoulder. "It is not a propitious start that they should already keep us waiting."

His words were slow and clear, very near to Aunt Gardiner's ear.

She half-closed her eyes and concentrated as he spoke.

"I think, yes—babies of all kinds are that way. Do you recall how little Joshua kept us waiting with the midwife declaring it should be today every day for a fortnight?"

"Indeed I do. That was very good, very good." Rustle touched her cheek with his wing. Apparently the discovery she was indeed able to hear had changed his attitude toward her. He would never credit April for the intelligence, though.

"Tell me again Papa, what do we do when they hatch?" Mary worried one of the flannels between her fingers.

Papa pointed at a ladle near the pan. Elizabeth ladled out three silver thimbles of broth, now richly colored from the blood pudding.

"It is best to allow the hatchlings to break free on their own. But if they cannot tear through the inner membrane, I have a small knife to cut through it. When their wings are free, you may pull the rest of the shell away, very gently. Then dry it with the flannel, talking very softly to it all the while. Tell it how welcome it is and offer it the broth. If it drinks, then offer it meat. Assure them there is plenty and invite it to stay. Offer it a name. If it wishes to leave, then take it to the window and allow it freedom to choose."

Elizabeth laid her hand on Mary's back and leaned close. "It will be fine. I promise."

April hunkered down in the straw between the eggs and threw her head back. She trilled a high sweet note. Soft cheeps came from the eggs. The one nearest Mary wobbled and rocked.

A tiny, sharp nose poked through the mottled drab-blue shell. April warbled encouragement. It was a good sign that it had managed to pierce the membrane on its own. The leathery shell tore halfway down and a wet little head poked through. Shiny jet-bead eyes darted back and forth.

Elizabeth nudged Mary. "She's looking for a familiar voice. Talk to her."

"Ah, what a sweet little thing you are." Mary whispered leaning close.

The tiny head twisted toward Mary, eyes fixed on her. She cheeped something that sounded like a question.

"Yes, it is me. I have been talking to you for the last few days."

She pulled one wing free and shook it, sending droplets of egg slime flying.

Mary reached for the flannel.

Elizabeth stayed her hand. "Wait until both wings are free."

April hopped to the half-free hatchling and pecked at the shell, scolding.

Impatient little thing.

Another wing broke free and the hatchling tried to flap herself away from the shell.

"Now, Mary," Papa said.

April side-stepped Mary's hand as she peeled away

the rest of the shell from the hatchlings' feet. The scraggly, wet fairy dragon wobbled onto Mary's waiting hand.

"There you go, dear. Give me a moment to get you tidied up. You will feel much better for it." She scrubbed it gently with the flannel.

Tiny feathers fluffed and dried. The soggy hatchling turned into a purple-pink heather-colored ball of fluff.

Fairy dragon chicks were nothing if not adorable.

The other egg began to quiver. Aunt Gardiner tended it as Mary offered the fluffy chick broth from the silver thimble.

She drank it down greedily.

Mary stroked her back with the tip of her finger. "Slow down, little one, there is plenty. I have meat for you if you like."

She warbled far more loudly than her size should have allowed. Papa produced a spoonful of blood and treacle pudding slivers on a china saucer.

If only Mama knew what her mother's tea set was being used for!

April flitted between the saucer and the hatching box as another head tore through its shell.

Mary offered slivers as fast as the chick could gobble them. "Slow down, you need not gorge. There is as much as you want."

The chick paused and stared at Mary, blinking, head cocked.

"I should like to call you Heather, if I may."

The tiny head bobbed up and down. "You may."

Her voice was so high and thin it was difficult to hear. That would change in time, but for now, it might make it challenging for Aunt to hear the chicks. Would that cause the other chick to look to Mary or her or to leave them altogether? Two chicks could easily over-whelm Mary—

"Hungry!" Heather demanded.

Mary obeyed.

Rustle and Rumblkins crowded close. Heather squeaked and backed away into Mary's arm.

Mary held the wet flannel up for Heather to smell. "They are friends, part of the Keep. Do not be afraid."

Rumblkins inched forward and sniffed Heather. He licked her soundly, though she shuddered. His raspy tongue fluffed her feathers so prettily, she gave him a bit of a cuddle before returning to Mary's hand.

Heather was a sweet little thing. April would have pecked him soundly on the nose.

Mary held Heather up to Rustle, who preened the feather-scales of her wings. She trilled.

He sneezed and shook his head. "So much fluff."

Heather cheeped a question at Mary.

"You are perfect, little one, simply perfect."

Aunt Gardiner applied a clean flannel to another newly hatched fairy dragon, revealing striking red-or-ange plumage.

"Oh, I have never seen one like him!" Elizabeth whispered.

He guzzled broth and snarfled down blood pud-ding, feet secured tightly around Aunt's finger. His voice was loud and demanding, far easier to hear than Heather's.

Brilliant!

In short order, he accepted the name Phoenix and fell asleep in Aunt's palm.

Rustle prodded him and Phoenix roused enough to land a sharp peck on the cockatrice's beak.

Rustle jumped back in a flutter of wings. "He will

do, indeed he will."

Aunt offered Rustle a generous lump of blood and treacle pudding for the compliment.

One egg remained, forlorn between the abandoned shells. Rumblkins batted at it. The egg toppled over, but did not move further. April landed beside it and pecked at it in an odd syncopated rhythm. She rolled it over with her feet and pecked again.

"Mine?" Rumblkins batted at it again.

April snorted and flitted to Elizabeth's shoulder.

"Not here, take it away from Heather and Phoenix." Papa's voice was grave and sad.

Rumblkins picked up the egg and trotted toward the door. Papa let him out.

Elizabeth rubbed the ache in her chest. Rumblkins was the only one who could look fondly upon an un-hatched egg.

"Perhaps you might allow me to examine the hatch-lings now?" Papa slipped in beside Mary.

She held up the sleeping Heather.

He picked up the fairy dragon and examined her carefully, muttering under his breath. "Yes, yes, very good. Well-formed wings, all her toes. A lovely speci-men." He returned the chick to Mary.

Aunt Gardiner offered Phoenix for Papa's inspec-tion. "Not many male fairy dragons are hatched, you know. Perhaps only one in four, I believe. You have a very rare little gentleman there, Maddie. Lovely, lovely color. That dark patch will become an eye ridge, a bit of a crest on his forehead when he is grown. You may find yourself very popular in London once your new companion becomes known."

Rustle hopped toward Papa. "I shall warn the cock-atrix who come to call that he and his visitors are not to be meddled with."

Rustle enjoyed a fair number of female callers, but that might change now. Aunt would probably not want the children exposed to such on-goings.

"So you find him acceptable, do you now?" Papa returned Phoenix to Aunt and directed Elizabeth to cut another slice of blood pudding for Rustle. "I am pleased to hear it."

"What do we do now, Papa?" Mary asked, stoking her check against Heather's fluff.

"I have prepared a 'sick room' in the attic for you and your aunt. You must go upstairs with the hatchlings and remain there until they no longer require constant feeding and attention. Usually for fairy dragons, that is three to five days. I am afraid that means you shall miss the assembly, Mary."

"I have no cause to repine, Papa." She sighed happily.

Oh the look in Mary's eyes! Somehow she looked like a new woman. Elizabeth blinked against her blurry vision. The little companion dragon might be exactly the thing to give Mary the confidence to come into her own.

"When they return, I shall tell them you both have taken a sudden fever and the apothecary said you must be separated from the rest of the family. Since Lizzy has already been exposed, she is the only one to tend you. Fanny does not like nursing, so I doubt there will be much fuss made over it."

Elizabeth snickered. And if there was, the resident dragons would be called upon to persuade Mama to see things their way.

"Keep the chicks warm and fed. Talk to them, and keep them close to you. They are apt to form very strong bonds with you—one of the fairy dragons' more endearing qualities."

April cheeped and flew toward his ear, but he covered it before she could nip. "That, by the way, is not an endearing trait."

April scolded, then alighted on Elizabeth's shoulder.

"Now, upstairs with you, and settle in. It will be a long few days for us all."

3
Chapter

Papa was right on all counts.

Mama was not at all unhappy to be excused from nursing. She did not ask how the apothecary had come so quickly nor did she bemoan Mary's expected absence from the upcoming assembly. All told, it was odd how little Mama asked. No doubt, Rustle and April, and maybe even Rumblkins had something to do with that.

He was also correct that the newly hatched chicks would be a tremendous amount of work for them all. April had required a great deal of attention in her hatchling days too, but those memories had faded over time. They came flooding back with each trip up and down the stairs with victuals and other supplies for all the sick room residents.

It was a shame that Mary would have to stay at home from the assembly, but then again, perhaps not. She was rarely asked to dance, so maybe staying at home would better suit her.

For Elizabeth's tastes, though, enjoying some company and a few lively dances would be just the tonic for too much time in the 'sick room.'

"Lizzy, please, help me with my hair." Jane peeked into the hall and beckoned Elizabeth in.

Evening sun shone directly in the windows, warming the room almost too much. The golden light suited Jane well though. She glowed in the sunbeams.

"I have never known you to be so anxious for a ball." Elizabeth took the brush and smoothed Jane's tawny tresses.

"Mr. Bingley will be there. At least he said he would be. He said he was fond of dancing."

"And of course, according to Mama, to be fond of dancing is a certain step toward falling in love. No doubt you entertain very lively hopes of Mr. Bingley's heart now." Elizabeth twined Jane's hair into an elegant twist and secured it with pins.

Where were those ribbons that would look so well with Jane's dress?

"Oh, Lizzy, pray, do not tease me so." Jane's cheeks colored. She pressed her hands to her face.

"What is wrong? You know I mean nothing by it."

"Still, I do not fancy you mocking me in that way."

"I was not mocking you. We have always played this game. What has changed?" Elizabeth set the brush aside and caught Jane's hands between hers.

Jane looked aside, as though unable to meet Elizabeth's gaze. "It seems foolish to say. I have only just met him. I am afraid I like him, though, more than I should, I think. Is it wrong to entertain hopes?"

"Hopes, so soon? Do you not think it very—"

"Unwise? Impulsive? Foolish? Silly?"

"I said none of those things. Pray, do not put words in my mouth."

Jane rose and wandered to the window casting a long shadow that reached all the way across the room. "I cannot explain it. I have never felt this ... convinced ... of anything."

Convinced? Were there dragons involved?

That was the only thing that made sense. But why would dragons meddle in the affairs of those who could not hear them? Certainly some enjoyed the sport, but Walker was the only dragon at Netherfield and certainly was not the type to make such efforts. No one at Longbourn would do so either, not with newly hatched chicks to protect.

Still, it was so unlike Jane.

"Just be careful. Do not attach yourself to him before you discern exactly what kind of man he is. You are apt to think well of everyone, but not all are so deserving of your admiration."

Jane drew a deep breath—was she covering up a sniffle? She pulled her shoulders back and lifted her head. "Of course, you are right, and I shall listen. It is unseemly for a woman to demonstrate her feelings to a man who has not declared himself. I will not allow anyone but you to know of my true feelings. You will be proud of my reserve."

Jane's smile was wan and thin, her eyes bright.

"And in return, I will hope for the best from Mr. Bingley, that your secret hopes—and now my own—might be fulfilled."

Jane blinked rapidly. "Thank you. I knew you would understand."

"Come now. Let me finish your hair before Mama entreats us to come downstairs."

Papa declined to accompany them to the assembly, as was his usual preference. The standing about hurt his feet and hips. Even the card room held little appeal when it was all he could do to hold the cards, unable to shuffle or deal in his turn. At least Mama did not argue as she usually did, probably counting herself fortunate that he did not insist she remain at home to tend her 'sick' daughter.

The past few days had been so intense, trying to meet the needs of the hatchlings and their new companions while keeping Mama and her sisters unaware. Had it not been for the persuasive powers of the dragons, it would have been impossible. Even Longbourn had to be called upon. He took up temporary residence in the cavern near the cellar and spent many hours inventing viable explanations for the odd sounds from the sickroom and even odder items which Elizabeth brought up from the kitchen.

Yes, a few hours away, lost in the music and dance steps was just what she needed.

Sir William Lucas greeted them at the door, wearing his 'Master of Ceremonies' sash. Since his visit to the assembly rooms at Bath, he had insisted upon wearing it at every assembly. He did so enjoy those subtle reminders of his importance as former mayor and only titled individual in the room. All told, it was a good thing that he was possessed of such a pleasant disposition or he might be insufferable.

Charlotte Lucas sidled up to her. "So you are here to see the legendary Mr. Bingley?"

"Indeed, why else would anyone attend?" Elizabeth chuckled.

Charlotte was her best friend for a reason. Few so

aptly understood Elizabeth's sense of humor.

"I have heard he rides a black horse and wears a blue coat. What new intelligence have you?" Charlotte's brows flashed up.

Though her features were universally regarded as plain, her wit was sharp and she did not hesitate to make her, sometimes unpopular, opinions known.

"Very little, I am afraid. We have only been in his presence once, when he and his friend called upon Longbourn. We found his manners very agreeable. He is in possession of a buff coat as well." Elizabeth's eye twitched in a little half wink.

"So then tales of his fortune must be true, if he is in possession of two fine coats."

"So my mother assures us."

"So which of your sisters has she claimed him for? Jane or Lydia? I will warn you, my mother has claimed him for me and Mrs. Goulding insists he will do for her eldest niece."

Elizabeth gasped. "You should not speak so!"

"Is it untrue? Does not every mother in the parish seek to claim him in some way?"

"True enough, but it is not safe to speak so out loud."

"Look there," Charlotte pointed toward the door. "I suppose I must curtail our conversation as the gentleman himself has arrived. With a party of friends as well—surely he will be the hero of the evening now. He brings another gentleman who may very well be as unmarried as himself."

Mr. Bingley, Mr. Darcy, two finely dressed women and a third gentleman slowly entered the rooms only to be accosted by Sir William. Given Mr. Darcy's expression, Sir William was anxious to introduce them to the entire room.

"He is unmarried, to be sure. Unpleasant, but un-married," Elizabeth muttered.

Why was Mr. Darcy even here? He had significant business to be about. Why was he wasting time at the assembly? Unless it was to try and garner further intel-ligence on the whereabouts of the missing egg.

But what could he discover in a public venue such as this? No wonder Papa was so put out with him.

Sir William approached with Mr. Bingley in tow. "May I present my daughter, Charlotte Lucas."

"Charmed to make your acquaintance, I am sure." Mr. Bingley bowed, all smiles, obviously ready to be well-pleased by all he saw.

Charlotte curtsied, blushing. It seemed even she was not immune to a charming man.

"Might I engage you for the first two dances, Miss Lucas?"

"Yes, certainly." Charlotte stammered a bit. Since her recent birthday—seven and twenty—fewer young men invited her to dance.

Good on Mr. Bingley for being so sociable. Still though, it was very obvious of Sir William—he almost demanded Mr. Bingley ask Charlotte to dance. Mama would call it intolerable conceit.

Jane appeared at Elizabeth's elbow. Where had she been?

Mr. Bingley looked past Elizabeth, to Jane, his eyes slightly glazed. "Ah, Miss Bennet, I am pleased to see you and your lovely sisters here tonight. Perhaps I may have the second set of dances with you?"

"I would be delighted." Jane's expression matched his.

Their slightly dazed expressions hinted that they

had already been at the punch, but it was too early in the evening for it. Neither were there dragons nearby to blame.

What was about with them?

"Miss Elizabeth, might I have the third set with you?"

She started and curtsied. "Thank you, sir, I would be honored."

At least she would have one dance this evening. With the women outnumbering the men, it could be the only dance she had. No, she should not dwell upon such gloomy thoughts.

Sir William ushered Mr. Bingley away and the introductions continued.

As the musicians took their places, Peter Long bounded up and requested Elizabeth dance the first set with him. He was gangly and a touch clumsy, not the best dancer in the room by far. But he was also lively and good humored, well-read and quite a conversationalist, so he would make a very tolerable partner indeed.

As the couples lined up for the first dance, Maria Lucas elbowed her and pointed with her chin toward Mr. Darcy.

"See the woman he is dancing with. She is Caroline Bingley, sister to Mr. Bingley. It is said she has a dowry of twenty thousand pounds! No wonder her dress is so elegant! I am quite certain it is silk. The sleeves, I saw them in the newest issue of *A Lady's Magazine*. She might have had it made just for this assembly. Can you imagine?"

Maria was quite correct both about the silk and the cut of the sleeves. So perhaps she was also correct about the amount of her dowry as well. It certainly made sense that Mr. Darcy would pay attention to such a woman. Not that he looked overly pleased about it, though. But his expression was generally so severe. He might not be able to look pleased about anything if he wished to.

Such a shame though, he was a well looking man—

No! Where had that thought come from? He was entirely disagreeable and that did not look well upon anyone.

The music began and Elizabeth lost herself in the music and movement. Three couples down, Bingley and Charlotte turned by the right hands and cast down the set. He was a graceful, energetic dancer, sure of his steps and easy to dance with. But his eyes remained fixed on Jane.

Two couples down, Jane danced with her partner, casting surreptitious glances at Mr. Bingley. While they were not nearly as obvious as Bingley's, anyone who really knew her would notice. Thankfully there were few here who truly knew Jane. Still, Bingley's actions would be enough to have rumors flowing by the end of the night. Pray Mama—

—it was too late, she had noticed. What else could the wave of her handkerchief toward the dancers mean? Mama bumped Mrs. Long's shoulder and turned to whisper something in her ear.

Poor Jane. She would not be able to escape Mama's machinations now.

The music ended and Peter Long escorted her off the floor. He bounded off to find his next partner.

Jane and Bingley came together and took their place on the dance floor. Without a partner, Elizabeth retreated to a corner. Usually it was a trial to be left a wallflower, but, at least for now, it was a boon, allowing her to observe her sister without attracting undue notice.

They danced together brilliantly, and insofar as that was the marker of a successful marriage, they were made for one another. Bingley's open temper suited Jane well. She needed a cheerful man. And there was certainly no objection as to his fortune or station in life.

How fortunate for her, her needs were so simple.

Oh, that was uncharitable, was it not?

Perhaps Elizabeth had become as cynical and jaded as Longbourn himself. Perhaps Papa's concerns that she had acquired too many of Longbourn's draconic traits were better founded than she had thought. At least she was not as disagreeable as Mr. Darcy, who stood not far from her, seemingly watching Bingley with the same interest she did Jane.

Did he think Jane not good enough for his friend? It would not be entirely surprising if he did.

The first dance of the set ended. Mr. Bingley slipped away from the dance floor, heading directly for Mr. Darcy.

"Come, Darcy," he said, "I must have you dance. I hate to see you standing about by yourself in this stupid manner. You had much better dance."

Darcy sniffed and edged half a step back. "I certainly shall not. You know how I detest it, unless I am particularly acquainted with my partner. At such an assembly as this, it would be insupportable. Your sisters are engaged, and there is not another woman in the room with whom it would not be a punishment for me to stand up."

"I would not be so fastidious as you are, for a kingdom! Upon my honor I never met with so many pleasant girls in my life, as I have this evening. There are several of them, you see, uncommonly pretty."

"You are dancing with the only handsome girl in the room." Mr. Darcy looked directly at Jane.

At least he could acknowledge Jane was pretty. That was a small point in his favor.

A very small one.

"Oh! She is the most beautiful creature I ever beheld! But there is one of her sisters sitting down just behind you. She is very pretty, and I dare say very agreeable. You have been introduced, so there is no impediment to you asking her to dance."

"Which do you mean?" and turning round, he looked for a moment at Elizabeth, till catching her eye, he withdrew his own.

Blast and botheration! He had seen her looking at him. Did he think she was eavesdropping on his conversation? While it was true she was, it would not do for him to be aware of it.

Or worse, did he think her pining after a dance with him? Oh, that would be insufferable.

Mr. Darcy's lip curled back. "She is tolerable; but not handsome enough to tempt me. I am in no humor at present to give consequence to young ladies who are slighted by other men. You had better return to your partner and enjoy her smiles, for you are wasting your time with me."

Mr. Bingley rolled his eyes and returned to Jane. Darcy squared his shoulders and wandered away.

Elizabeth's cheeks burned. She did not desire his attentions, not at all. What did his opinion matter? Even if it was very harsh?

Whilst it was entirely true that Jane was many times the prettiest of the Bennet girls, being so bluntly reminded of it was unpleasant at best. Had it been possible to think Mr. Darcy unaware of her presence, it would be easier to excuse his frankness. But he might as well have said it to her face.

The gall! The audacity!

With men like him about, was it any wonder that she should prefer the company of dragons?

The music ended, and Mr. Bingley ushered Jane off the floor to Elizabeth's side.

"Shall we have our dance, Miss Elizabeth?" Mr. Bingley extended his hand.

"If my sister is willing to part with her most eligible partner." Elizabeth took his hand.

"It will be but a brief parting, for I have already engaged her for another dance." Mr. Bingley bowed his head at Jane and escorted Elizabeth to the dance floor.

Jane was such an accomplished dancer that it was not unusual for her partners to request a second dance from her. It happened often enough, but tonight it felt particularly difficult.

The music started. The peculiar steps of My Lord Byron's Maggot distracted her pleasantly.

"How are you enjoying our little country assembly, sir?" Elizabeth asked during a pause in the dance.

"There is little I like more than a country dance, I assure you. Especially in the country as it were." He laughed, but stopped when he saw she did not do likewise. "I fear that you may have overheard my conversation with my friend."

Elizabeth flushed and looked away.

"It is as I feared. Please, accept my deepest apologies for his remarks."

"You have nothing to apologize for, sir."

"But I do. I provoked him into speaking what he is otherwise far too well-mannered to even think, much less say."

"Forgive me if I question his good manners after tonight." She cocked her head and tried to wink, but the expression was affected at best.

"Pray believe me. He is under much vexation of spirit at the moment. I should have known better than to try and cajole him into being sociable when it is not his long suit."

"The man you speak of bears little resemblance to the man I have seen. Are you certain we are talking of the same person?"

"You are not the first person to have made that observation, but perhaps the most civil. I am afraid he is known for giving offense wherever he goes."

"That is a serious indictment to his character, is it not? I am surprised that you should mention it so casually."

"It would be of greater concern if it were an accurate portrayal of his character." Mr. Bingley glanced over his shoulder toward Mr. Darcy who lingered near the wall, scowling at everything he saw.

"You maintain it is not?"

"Not at all, he is a great friend to me. I quite rely upon his judgement. One cannot have a greater friend than he, truly."

"If one can overcome being offended at every turn?" Elizabeth laughed a little, because it seemed she should.

"He does take some becoming accustomed to. But I pray you would excuse him tonight. He is dealing with some very bad news from home. It has him a bit out of sorts, I am afraid."

"Bad news? I am sorry to hear that."

The loss of a dragon egg was in truth bad news. And Mr. Bingley did have a point. It was a justifiable reason for ill-temper.

"I can see you are a gracious, compassionate creature, like your sister. I shall trust you to withhold judgement upon him until you can meet him in a more providential light."

The dance ended. He bowed to her.

"As you say." She curtsied, and he led her off the dance floor.

Perhaps he was right.

She glanced toward Darcy.

Bother, he was looking directly at her and caught her eye. His eyes narrowed and his lip curled back. He turned his back and walked away.

Then again, perhaps not.

Papa greeted them at the door and ushered them into the parlor, all inquisitiveness about the assembly. That was unusual enough, but the presence of hot cider and biscuits?

What was he about?

Certainly nothing could be wrong with the hatchlings. He would not be downstairs if that were the case. He must be seeking some sort of intelligence.

But why?

Hill took their wraps and served the cider. Lydia and Kitty sprawled on the sofa in a most unladylike fashion. Mama must be happily tired; she did not bother to correct them. Jane seemed little aware of it either, a dreamy expression in her eyes.

Mama threw her head back and pressed into her chair. "My dear Mr. Bennet, we have had a most delightful evening, a most excellent ball. I wish you had been there. Jane was so admired! Everybody said how well she looked. Mr. Bingley thought her quite beautiful, and danced with her twice. Only think of that, my dear! He actually danced with her twice! She was the only creature in the room that he asked a second time."

"Two dances? That is most notable." Papa glanced from Mama to Jane and back.

No, actually, it was not. It happened often enough. Why did Papa think it was now?

Mama fanned herself with her handkerchief. "First of all, he asked Miss Lucas. I was so vexed to see him stand up with her; but, with Sir William lurking about, introducing him here and there, what else could he do but ask her? He did not admire her at all. Indeed, nobody can, you know. He seemed quite struck with Jane when he entered the room, you know. So, he asked her for the two next. Then, the two third he danced with Lizzy, and the two fourth with Maria Lucas, and the two fifth with Jane again, and the two sixth with Miss King, and the Boulanger –"

Papa huffed and flicked his hand. "If he had had any compassion for me, he would not have danced half so much! For God's sake, say no more of his partners. Oh, that he had sprained his ankle in the first dance!"

Mama flapped her handkerchief at him. "How can you say that? I am quite delighted with him. I overheard him asked whether he did not think there were a great many pretty women in the room, and which he thought the prettiest? 'The eldest Miss Bennet beyond a doubt, there cannot be two opinions on that point.' He did not hesitate to say."

How many words could Mama utter on a single breath?

Jane blushed prettily and sighed. "He is just what a

young man ought to be, sensible, good humored, lively. I never saw such happy manners! So much ease, with such perfect good breeding!"

"He is also handsome." Elizabeth leaned back so she could see Papa and Jane at the same time. "Which a young man ought likewise to be, if he possibly can. His character is thereby complete."

"I was very much flattered by his asking me to dance a second time. I did not expect such a compliment."

"What could be more natural than his asking you again? He could not help seeing that you were about five times as pretty as every other woman in the room. No thanks to his gallantry for that. He certainly is very agreeable, though, and I give you leave to like him. You have liked many a stupider person," Elizabeth said.

Unfortunately, it was true. But she had never been so open about it before.

"Lizzy!"

Kitty and Lydia edged close to one another and tittered.

"You are a great deal too apt, you know, to like people in general. You never see a fault in anybody. All the world are good and agreeable in your eyes. I never heard you speak ill of a human being in my life. With your good sense, to be honestly blind to the follies and nonsense of others! And so, you like this man's sisters too, do you? Their manners are not equal to his." Elizabeth folded her arms over her chest.

Papa leaned forward, elbows on knees, studying Jane closely.

"Certainly not at first. But they are very pleasing women when you converse with them. Miss Bingley is to live with her brother and keep his house. I am much mistaken if we shall not find a very charming neighbor in her."

No doubt there were to be a great many good dinners and large parties hosted under her watch.

"I agree entirely, you know," Mama said, "His sisters are charming women. I never in my life saw anything more elegant than their dresses. I dare say the lace upon Mrs. Hurst's gown—"

Papa threw his hands up and waved them vigorously. "No discussion of finery and especially no lace!"

Mama sniffed and rolled her eyes. "If you do not appreciate that discussion perhaps you will find more interesting his friend's shocking abuse of our dear Lizzy. He quite refused to dance with her."

Papa's expression grew dark. "He insulted my Lizzy?"

There were unwritten rules governing the behavior of Dragon Mates to one another. Civility must always be extended, especially in public. If companion dragons became aware of a dispute, all manner of unpleasantness might ensue, not the least of which was their tenacity in making certain appropriate reparations were made. Major-dragons made things even more complicated.

Mama waved the question off. "Do not be troubled. I can assure you that Lizzy does not lose much by not suiting his fancy. He is a most disagreeable, horrid man, not at all worth pleasing. So high and so conceited that there was no enduring him! He walked here, and he walked there, fancying himself so very great! Not handsome enough to dance with! I wish you had been there, my dear, to have given him one of your set downs. I quite detest the man."

Lydia giggled and bumped shoulders with Kitty.

"Mrs. Long told me he sat close to her for half an hour without once opening his lips."

"Miss Bingley told me that he never speaks much unless among his intimate acquaintance. With them he is remarkably agreeable," Jane said.

"I do not believe a word of it, my dear. If he had been so very agreeable, he would have talked to Mrs. Long."

"I do not mind his not talking to Mrs. Long, but I wish he had danced with Lizzy." Jane sagged into her chair.

She was truly upset.

"Another time, Lizzy, I would not dance with him, if I were you." Mama waggled her finger toward Elizabeth.

Lydia and Kitty mimicked the gesture. How dear of them.

"I believe I may safely promise you never to dance with him. I would refuse him should he have the temerity to even ask."

"You might not want to be so quick to say such a thing, Lizzy. As I recall, it was you who sat out dances without a partner whilst Kitty and I danced every dance." Lydia snickered and launched into a description of her every partner during the evening.

Papa leaned back and chewed his lip. There was a great deal he was not saying, but clearly needed to.

He twitched his head toward the door and beckoned her to follow him.

She rose and curtsied toward Mama who was too engrossed in Lydia's conversation to notice.

Papa shut the study door behind them and locked it. This was a serious matter indeed. He gestured toward a chair near the fire, but he paced in his shambling way along the windows.

Moonlight poured through the glass, painting him with a cold grey-blue glow.

"You are troubled, what is it?" Elizabeth asked. "I cannot imagine something wrong with the hatchlings, or you would be upstairs with them."

"They are very well, keeping your aunt and sister constantly stuffing food down their gullets. They eat, they sleep, they preen, and they chatter—not entirely unlike a houseful of young daughters, I might add." He chuckled without mirth.

"I knew there was a reason you were so easy among fairy dragons."

He crossed back and forth before the windows three times. His steps fell in a tense, measured rhythm.

"Papa?"

He stopped and leaned on the windowsill. "What do you think of Jane?"

Would that he have asked anything else.

Lizzy hunched over, elbows on knees and heaved a heavy breath.

"You have noticed something too, then?" Papa stepped closer.

"I do not know what to make of it."

"Tell me what you see." He crossed the room and sat on the low ottoman near her chair.

"She has always been one to see the good and admire people freely enough. But usually she is far more reserved with her sentiments. Granted, it is true, she has liked a good many gentlemen, but none so quickly, or perhaps so much, as Mr. Bingley."

Papa chewed his upper lip. "I had come to the same conclusion."

"I do not know if I am glad for that or not. I should have liked it more to know that it was just me, and I could chalk the whole thing up to jealousy."

Botheration. That was not something she wanted to discuss, especially with him.

The creases alongside his eyes deepened and corners of his lips fell. He laid his hand on hers, warm and heavy. "You carry a difficult burden, my dear. I had always thought there would be a son to inherit Longbourn. One who would inherit my hearing as well as my estate. That would have left you free to follow your affections. I wish it could be so. I hope you understand that. I wish you did not have reason to be jealous of your sisters' freedom."

She looked away. If he caught her eyes now, he would know far more than she was willing to admit. "I should say it is well, and that you need not worry."

"But you are a very bad liar." He squeezed her hand. His veins stood out over the bent and knobby fingers. "You have been my strength, taking over for me as I have been able to do less and less. You are the true Dragon Keeper here, my dear. As much an honor as it is, it comes with a price."

"I know. Let us not speak of it for now. Jane is our current concern."

She felt his eyes on her, studying her. Would that he not do that! Could he simply accept her request?

He withdrew his hand and turned his eyes to the ceiling.

"It is possible that her attraction to Mr. Bingley is genuine, and we have no reason for concern." She forced her lips into something that should resemble a smile.

He tapped steepled index fingers along his lips. "As

much as I would like it to be so, it is not wise to rely upon that possibility. Not with dragon chicks about and a stolen egg said to be in our vicinity."

"You think the dragons might be involved with Jane and Bingley?" Elizabeth looked over her shoulder.

It was strange not to have April hovering close.

"It is one of the best explanations for their very odd behavior."

"But who would be inclined to such mischief? I had the same thought, I confess, but there is none I could point to as a culprit."

Papa clucked his tongue. "I know. The Longbourn house dragons are too concerned with the chicks to make mischief."

"And Mr. Darcy's cockatrice is far above such things. Besides, either one of us would doubtless have recognized his voice attempting to persuade Jane. His voice is very distinct. That leaves only Longbourn, who would hardly be bothered with such a game."

"True enough."

"So then, it cannot be dragon-wrought."

"There is another possibility."

A cold chill snaked down Elizabeth's spine.

He scrubbed his face with his hands. "Walker noted that an accurate accounting of the local dragons has not been kept. It is possible there is an unknown dragon in the vicinity."

"We know that there are wild fairy dragons and tatzelwurms in the woods. So certainly there are unknown dragons about."

"You know as well as I, they are unlikely candidates. On the whole, they are flighty and not willing to be bothered with something that should take so long to play out."

"Perhaps a cockatrice then?"

Papa pushed to his feet, resuming his track about the room. "With Rustle and Walker about, we would know about the presence of another cockatrice by now."

"A cockatrix then?" Elizabeth worried her hands together.

"We would have known about that even sooner. The females of their kind are so rare that their presence is always remarkable."

"Are you suggesting," she rose slowly, pulling on the back of the chair for strength. "That there may be a major-dragon unknown to any of us roaming the countryside? Surely that is not possible. A wild major-dragon—"

"Not necessarily wild, but perhaps a rogue, unattached dragon. There are estates in the kingdom abandoned by their dragons."

"Do your histories point to any possible culprits?"

"I have found none."

"Would not Longbourn be aware of it? I cannot imagine him keeping that kind of news to himself. Not to mention, he is so territorial, he would not tolerate encroachment on his land."

"It does seem unlikely. But I have no other explanation." Papa shrugged his bowed shoulders.

She pressed her hands to her cheeks. "A wild dragon would have made himself known by now. None of the villagers have gone missing, nor have we seen any odd disappearance of livestock, all sure signs of a wild dragon. And one unattached is equally unlikely. I do not like to disagree with you, but I simply cannot see it."

"Still, there must be some explanation."

"Can Jane not like a man because he is uncommonly agreeable?" Elizabeth shrugged. "I find that the most plausible explanation."

"Perhaps, perhaps."

Bingley's party returned from the ball in mixed spirits. Bingley declared he had never met with pleasanter people or prettier girls in his life. Everybody had been most kind and attentive to him. There had been no formality, no stiffness. With the most gracious help of Sir William, he had soon felt acquainted with all the room. And as to Miss Bennet—at this point in the conversation, it required all of Darcy's self-control not to stuff his fingers in his ears and begin reciting Pemberley's crop rotation schedule—Bingley could not conceive of an angel more beautiful.

Mrs. Hurst and Caroline Bingley allowed it to be so, claiming to admire and like her. More maddening, they also pronounced her to be a sweet girl, and one whom they should not object to know more of. No doubt that meant, Miss Bennet—probably the entire tribe of Bennets—would be invited to spend a great deal of time at Netherfield.

No, probably not the younger sisters whom all agreed were silly flitterbits. But impudent Miss Elizabeth Bennet would probably appear at Netherfield and remain a thorn in his side.

The social exertions of the assembly kept Darcy confined away from company for two days full. Though he shared a very steady friendship with Bingley, there was a great contrast in their characters.

Bingley had an easy, open ductility to his temper that made him a favorite in company. Bingley was sure of being liked wherever he appeared.

Darcy was continually giving offence—or so he had been told often. He was considered—according to Uncle and Aunt Matlock—haughty, reserved, and fastidious, and his manners, though well-bred, were not inviting. Gah! If only those same ones who judged him knew what he had to endure!

Company and crowds were an oppression to his spirit, weighing upon him, draining him like a wyvern drained its prey before consuming it. A few hours in company left him spent as a laborer in from an entire day's work. Every nerve was left raw and throbbing; his ears ached from the noise assaulting preternatural hearing; his skin prickled and burned from the unintended contact inevitable when too many people tried to share the same space.

He might as well drink an entire magnum of Madeira himself instead of attending a party. The hangover would be far less miserable.

On the third morning after the assembly, Darcy rose early, took to his horse, and invited Walker to join him. A morning ride—a long one—would do a great deal toward setting his soul to rights once again.

It had to. He had to focus on the task at hand. He had six, maybe seven weeks before the egg hatched.

If it did so without human presence, he would have no choice. He would have to turn from Dragon Keeper to Dragon Slayer. The sword he secreted in his horse's stall in the barn would taste dragon blood. It was the only way to preserve the fragile peace between the species. But it would cost him everything.

The Blue Order would expel him. That he could live

with. But no dragon would tolerate his presence after he killed one of their own.

Even if it was necessary.

Walker would leave him, and he would have destroyed the greatest legacy of the Darcy family. The Darcy line would end with him. The dragons would ensure that, one way or another.

Fitzwilliam Darcy, the last of the Pendragon D'Arcys.

His horse broke into an easy trot along the bridle path. Stray branches slapped against Darcy's shoulders, spraying him with still fresh morning dew. Morning smelt the same everywhere; fresh, new and hopeful.

He needed hope.

Walker flew lazy circles overhead. Wings outstretched, silhouetted in the morning sun, he was a magnificent creature.

"You should not have insulted Elizabeth."

And an impertinent one.

"How would you know anything of that?"

Walker swooped low overhead. "You cannot imagine I would allow you into the public forum without keeping some watch over you. One can hear a great deal from the attic rafters. You were insupportably rude."

"I never asked you for your opinion." Not that it mattered. Walker never held his tongue.

"You should. I know a great deal."

"If you know so much, then tell me where our egg is, so we can be done with this affair and return to Derbyshire." Darcy gritted his teeth.

He had best watch his tone. Walker was as tense as he. If the cockatrice got offended—

"She would be of great help, if you had not

offended her."

"How would she help? She knows nothing of eggs and hatchings and firedrakes. What would she do? Is she a sleuth capable of ferreting out—"

Walker squawked a sharp admonition. "She knows more about hatching than you do. The eggs on their hearth hatched a se'nnight ago. The house is a-flutter with new chicks."

"Fairy dragons that you deem useless bits of fluff and nonsense. I am surprised you consider their hatching worthy of notice."

New dragons at Longbourn? Perhaps he should call. He had never actually seen a baby dragon of any kind. Walker had hatched into Father's hands well before Darcy had been born.

But no, Bennet was not likely to welcome him, particularly if he knew how he had spoken about Miss Elizabeth.

Damn cockatrice was right again. But Darcy did not have to admit it aloud.

"Their heads are full of gibberish and noise, I grant you, but they are observant little pests and can be useful for garnering information. Information which you clearly need." Walker swooped a little closer. "Mind the horse. He will bolt if you scare him."

"You need a better horse. Get that Bingley fellow to help you find a colt. He has a good eye for horseflesh. I will help you train it properly."

"And what shall I do with this one?"

"Eat it."

Darcy shivered at the bloodlust in Walker's tone. "I need this beast, thank you. Go and dine on a deer. They are roaming the woods."

"I need Longbourn's permission. They are his."

"Then go and ask. You have never been shy about such things before."

"He likes Elizabeth, and I do too. You offended her."

He liked her? Surely Darcy misheard.

"I doubt she has told Longbourn such petty concerns. But I dare say, if you are so fond of his favorite, he will grant you hunting privileges simply for appreciating her."

"You should apologize." Walker circled low, over Darcy's head.

"I have nothing to apologize for. You, however, are not helping me at all in our quest and that should be your bigger concern."

"There is something else you should know. I hear a voice. At least I think I do."

Prickles scoured Darcy's face and he swallowed hard. "What kind of voices? There are fairy dragons all about. They chitter constantly."

Walker snorted and shook his head, glaring dangerously. "I would not bother about those. No, this voice is something different, something I have not heard before."

"You have spoken with every kind of dragon in England, even a few foreign visitors."

"That is what troubles me. I have not heard this kind of voice before. And it is very, very old."

Very old meant very powerful. And very smart. And very persuasive.

Dragonfires!

Old, powerful and persuasive usually equaled cranky, cold, and difficult. Very difficult.

Maybe dangerous.

"Are you certain?"

"No." Walker hopped from one foot to the other, his serpentine tail lashing around the branch so fast it whistled through the air. "I can barely hear the voice, so I am not certain."

"And that is not good?"

"No, it is worse. My uncertainty makes me more certain."

Unknowns amongst the dragons were almost certainly dangerous, if not deadly for human and dragonkind alike.

"Can you tell anything about it?" Darcy drew the back of his hand across his mouth.

"It is not hungry, it is bored."

Darcy squeezed his eyes shut. A bored dragon was many times more dangerous than a hungry one. "Have you any idea what kind of dragon you are hearing?"

Walker peered into the woods. "A wyrm of some kind, I think. Perhaps a lindwyrm, but I am not certain."

Darcy cursed under his breath. Horses were the lindwyrm's favorite prey. Did his mount smell a lindwyrm? That would explain his horse's general unease.

"You know the militia will encamp in Meryton soon. Yesterday I saw troops arrive to build the barracks, they came with wagons of wood, already cut, barrels for nails, and enough men to make quick work of the process," Walker said.

"You believe that party might conceal Pemberley's egg?"

"It would not be difficult among all the paraphernalia they carried. But there is a fair chance that he will think the situation very safe and that the egg will not be as well guarded."

"So much the better for us then. We can be done with this business and be home."

"You know, wyrms of all sorts prey upon dragon eggs, too."

Darcy clutched his forehead. "Go to Longbourn, and tell him I request an audience."

"He would be more likely to see you if Elizabeth made the request."

"Just do as I ask."

Walker screeched and flapped away. At least he was being cooperative.

Of course that was a bad sign, too. Only the deepest of anxiety over the egg would keep him from his favorite sport—taunting Darcy.

4
Chapter

Walker's entreaties to Longbourn fell on deaf ears. For a se'nnight he paid daily visits to the wyvern, pleading with him to accept a visit from Darcy, but he was as intractable as his Keeper, Bennet.

So, Darcy was reduced to skulking about the countryside like some highwayman stalking the militia's building crew. With Walker's help, he investigated every wagon, every barrel, every crate—anything that might conceal a dragon egg. They even investigated the stables and outbuildings of the public houses and taverns the troops inhabited. Walker detected traces of egg-scent in several places, but none held the egg.

Either the men or their equipment had been in contact with the egg. But it did not travel with the advanced party.

Damn and bloody hell!

If only he could go straight to the regiment itself. But Matlock insisted any direct approach would draw too much attention and risk exposure. He was probably right. There was little to do but wait for them to arrive. Then he could contrive to get an invitation to visit and search without drawing notice—or at least not so much that Walker could not create a persuasion against it.

At least listening to the building crews' conversations turned up the news that the regiment would be split between Meryton and Ware, so the efforts were not wholly misspent.

Perhaps that information would have some value to Longbourn. Darcy dispatched Walker to make one more attempt with the wyvern.

Darcy finished his morning ablutions and dismissed his valet. How much longer would Walker take? He stalked from one side of the spacious room to the other. The deep burgundy paper hanging was entirely free from dust and cobweb. The mahogany furnishings, masculine and heavy, were polished to gleaming. Housekeeper Nicholls certainly did manage an excellent staff. Miss Bingley had not been resident here long enough to take credit.

He sat at the writing table near the window and stared into the horizon.

At last! A dark figure, winging his way toward the house.

Walker landed on the window sill and shook his head. He hopped from Darcy's window to the mirror on his dressing table and flapped his wings. "I have never seen a creature so stubborn!"

The mirror bobbed forward and back. Apparently Walker had forgotten it was not fixed like the one at home. He squawked and fluttered his wings, but the mirror would not come to rest.

"That means a great deal coming from you." Darcy steadied the mirror and swallowed back a laugh. Walker hated to be laughed at.

Walker regained his balance and lifted his chin. "I am not so easily daunted, though. I have a plan."

Darcy winced. Walker's plans were not always mindful of local law. He did not seem to understand one must not offend the local constabulary. Hopefully he did not intend for Darcy to steal a sheep or other delicacy to bribe the recalcitrant dragon.

"Miss Elizabeth intends to pay a visit to Longbourn today. You should ask her to introduce you to him."

"I would rather steal a sheep."

"Pardon me?" Walker leaned far over the mirror to peer almost nose to nose into Darcy's eyes. The mirror tipped forward.

"I will not ask that woman for any favors, especially concerning the estate dragon."

"You are as stubborn as Longbourn. But I expected as much. I have an alternative. You may follow her to Longbourn's lair and wait until she leaves him. I will then present you to Longbourn and, assuming you do not immediately offend him in some way, we might be able to speak to him."

"I do not relish the idea of stalking Miss Elizabeth like hunting a fox out of season, but with less than a month—"

"You do not need to recount to me the urgency of our mission. You need to hurry and get out as she has probably left the house by now."

Darcy grabbed his hat and hurried downstairs without excusing himself to his host. "How exactly then are we to follow her?"

Walker chirruped something that sounded insulting. "I will follow and come back to lead you to her. I know the lair is on the sunset side of the estate, head in that direction. I shall find you directly."

Walker flew off.

The plan was sound, if degrading. Sneaking about like some poacher. The very thought was galling. But then, what about the current situation was not?

Darcy stalked down the westward footpath.

It seemed as though everything in Hertfordshire was designed to reinforce the humility of his position. He was subjected to Caroline Bingley's constant attentions and attempts at flirtations. She was well mannered and proper, to be sure, but she was also obvious and nigh on intolerable. She had not an original thought in her head nor had read anything since leaving the insipid girl's seminary she had attended. Her twenty thousand pounds would be a welcome way to replace Georgiana's dowry, but at what cost? Far better to mortgage some part of the estate and not live with the constant prattle and mindless chatter.

All that paled in comparison to the weight of the lost egg, though. Would he ever live down the ignominy?

At least Uncle Matlock had contacted only Bennet about the situation, not all the Keepers between Meryton and Derbyshire. And Bennet seemed too lazy to gossip. Perhaps the Darcy and Matlock reputations might be spared once it was recovered.

If Miss Elizabeth kept her peace.

And if the egg was recovered.

If only Father had been more cautious. But Wickham had deceived them all. He was so convincing, so easy to like. Much like Bingley.

Oh, that was a thought to give one pause.

Darcy grimaced.

But no, Bingley was not at all like Wickham, not in essentials. Bingley was honest and cheerful to a fault. Those traits were not affectations.

Wickham's were.

They had all thought Wickham heard dragons, but he was only an accomplished charlatan. And for that, Darcy was reduced to scampering about the countryside in hopes of demanding an audience with a lesser dragon who wanted nothing to do with him.

Oh, Father, such a legacy!

Walker screeched and circled overhead. "I have found them. Follow."

Darcy squinted into the bright sky and jogged after him.

Half a mile into the woods of Longbourn estate, Walker slowed and landed high in a tree. He pointed with his wing to an overgrown hillside. Brambles and thorny vines—probably berries of some kind—grew wild from the top of the hill, reaching over the hillsides. At the base, equally thorny undergrowth sprang up, thick and leafy. A ray of sunlight penetrated the heavy tree canopy, enough to light the hill enough for the bushes to grow … and to warm the stony ground sufficiently for dragon basking.

Darcy inched nearer, peering through a break in the underbrush. The scrapes and divots in front of the hillside suggested a dragon used that spot frequently. He hunkered down to watch and wait.

Miss Elizabeth, with an entourage of companions, ambled up to the hill. As usual, the little blue fairy dragon flitted circles around her. On her shoulders were puffs of red and pink fluff—the dragon chicks? Three fairy dragons in her company at once?

That much prattle-chatter could make him go distracted in a matter of minutes.

An exceptionally large tatzelwurm wove around her ankles and between her feet, purring loud enough for Darcy to hear quite clearly. The tabby-stripe fur on its feline front was brushed to glistening and its tail scales showed signs of recent oiling. The creature seemed to worship the very ground she walked on.

What was it about her that dragons found so very endearing?

She stood on a patch of ground worn clear of undergrowth.

Scratches and rumbles boomed from inside the hill. Dragon-sized sounds.

The fairy dragons chittered and hid in the particularly generous hood of her green cloak, almost as if it had been designed for the purpose. The tatzelwurm ducked between the cloak and her skirt.

"Good day, Longbourn," she called, hands cupped around her mouth.

A loud snort and the vines parted ahead of a great scaly head and a body to match.

An estate dragon, no matter what kind, was a fearsome sight, even if it were only a wyvern.

The creature stood ten, perhaps twelve feet tall, if it stretched fully upright on its two clawed feet. But it did not; it crouched to put its face on her level, like an adult bending down to address a child.

Stiff, angular ridges extended from the top of his head to the end of his tail. The thick, lashing appendage added at least six feet to its length, all covered in grey-green-brown scales. The thick, horny scales were dusty, but patches gleamed, vaguely metallic, in the sunlight. Someone must brush and oil his hide regularly.

The body was sleek, not fat and lazy as he would have expected. Well-nourished, but not overfed. Streamlined leathery wings folded neatly over its back, resting against the spine ridges. What kind of a wing-span did it have? Enough for flight, or just for show?

Its face was largely square—sharply masculine, with large, glittering gold eyes and whiskers that gave the impression of a long mustache and eyebrows. Somehow, he brought Bennet to mind.

That was a bit unsettling.

Fangs and talons resembled polished ivory, gleaming and sharp, ready to be put to use. Was that a drop of ochre venom on one fang? Venomous wyverns were rather uncommon. Did this one only bite, or had it learned to cast its poison in a breathy cloud as well?

Best assume the latter.

Longbourn shook his head and roared.

Walker flapped his wings to regain his balance against the dragon-thunder. The crashing tones penetrated Darcy's chest, rattling his ribs. It was easy to forget just how loud a dragon could be.

Miss Elizabeth covered her ears with her hands and waited.

After far too long, the bellowing and rumbling ceased and the wyvern stared at Miss Elizabeth, ochre foam bubbling on his lips.

"Are you quite finished with your temper tantrum now?" She planted her hands on her hips and tapped her foot.

"No."

She stepped back in a half-bow and extended her hand. "Pray continue then, I should hardly suspend any pleasure of yours."

Longbourn stomped, flapped and snorted for several more minutes, sending a rain of leaves cascading from the hillside vines, and a cloud of dust rising from the ground.

It really was an impressive show. Had Darcy encountered it without Miss Elizabeth, he would probably have left. Longbourn did not seem to want visitors.

"Are you finished now?" She crossed her arms over her chest and glowered at him with a decidedly maternal stare.

Longbourn huffed a breath through his lips, sending foam spraying.

Miss Elizabeth jumped back. "That was uncalled for."

"You have stayed away for a full se'nnight. That was uncalled for." Was it possible for a dragon to pout?

Darcy blinked and shook his head. The wyvern had transformed from towering dragon to petulant child.

"Oh, you silly, silly creature." She opened her arms and crossed the distance to the wyvern.

It stretched its neck toward her. She embraced the huge scaly head and scratched behind his right ear with both hands.

Dear god, the creature wagged his foot just like a dog. How undignified.

How astonishing.

"Oh, there, yes. Exactly there." A shiver rippled down the spine ridges until Longbourn's tail thumped the ground.

The unsettling display continued as she ministered to his other ear and under his chin.

"There now, am I forgiven?" She asked, planting a

kiss—a kiss!—on the rugged snout.

Longbourn snuffed and sniffed. "I suppose." A long forked tongue snaked out and lapped her face.

No. That was entirely too much! How had she reduced a dignified dragon to something more akin to a slavering lap dog?

"Thank you, dear one."

"I missed you. I hope you had a good reason." Longbourn stretched out full length on the ground, spreading his wings.

She inspected them. "You need a thorough oiling—"

"And brushing. I want my wings brushed, they itch." His wingtips fluttered.

The ensuing breeze rustled the nearest branches.

"Indeed they do. And you shall have it, I promise. I shall return this afternoon and bring Mary with me."

"She scratches good."

"I know she does." She scratched the back of his wing.

"Why does she not come more?"

"Because you frighten her, you great oaf! If you did not relish your show of being a dragon so much, she might come more often."

Another snort raised a cloud of dust. "You are not frightened."

"I used to be." She picked her way around the wing to stand beside his head and scratch the base of the first head ridge. "Until I discovered it is all puff and nonsense. You are really just a soft, itchy bundle of scales and snuff."

Longbourn cuddled into her waist, nearly knocking her off her feet as he pulled her into his shoulder.

Dragons did not cuddle.

This was just so wrong. Entirely, completely wrong.

"Are you jealous?" Walker whispered in his ear.

When had he left his high perch?

"It is undignified. Rosings would never behave that way," Darcy hissed.

"She would if she met Elizabeth. She knows how to scratch." Walker's shoulders twitched.

He was always itchy there. But he was very particular about who touched him.

"Dare I ask how you would know?"

"No. It is not your business. You do not like her." Walker turned his face aside.

Darcy pressed thumb and forefinger to his eyes.

"I have important news for you, a great deal of it." Her voice was sweet and cajoling, the way one talked to a petulant child.

Darcy's stomach churned. Someone needed to teach her about draconic dignity.

"I do not like news. News is always inconvenient."

That sounded exactly like what Bennet might say.

"Now you are just being difficult in the hopes of getting a treat. I will bring you one, but you must listen and behave properly first."

"Mutton?"

"Is that what you want?"

"I like mutton. A great deal." Longbourn flicked his tongue across his lips.

"Then you shall have a sheep tonight."

"I like mutton."

"Now, if you want mutton, you must listen carefully to me and not act the big scary estate dragon."

Longbourn pouted again.

Dragons should not pout.

"Very well."

Miss Elizabeth placed a kiss along one of his brow ridges.

No, no! The tip of his tail wagged.

She stepped back to look into both his eyes. "We have admitted new members into our Keep. It is time for you to greet them—and promise not to eat them."

Longbourn snorted. "I want a snack."

She huffed and tapped her foot. "You have an entire herd of deer roaming your lands. There is no reason for you to be complaining about snacks."

"Oh, very well. Show me these creatures. I promise I shall not eat them." He closed his eyes and rolled his head to the side.

"Now or ever?"

The dragon snuffled. "Now or ever."

"On your honor?"

He picked up his head and stared down at her. "Upon my honor as a wyvern and ancestral estate dragon of Longbourn, I shall not eat whatever annoying little creature you present to me. Are you satisfied?"

"I am." She looked over her shoulder into her hood. "Did you hear? You are safe, Longbourn shall never harm you."

"I never said that, I only said I would not eat them."

"Longbourn!"

"Oh, all right, I won't harm a scale on their pretty little bodies."

"Or hair or feather?"

Longbourn stomped. "I want two sheep."

"Promise me, and you shall have two." The look in her eye suggested that had been her intention all along.

"I promise."

"You can come out now. You have nothing to fear." She flicked the edge of her cloak back and stepped aside to reveal the tatzelwurm.

It stepped forward, stopping just in front of her, cowering just a little. She crouched and stroked its neck.

Longbourn slid his head along the ground to inspect the cat-like dragon. "I know you."

"I used to live in the wood here. Now I live in the house." The tatzelwurm extended a thumbed paw and touched the wyvern's snout.

"He is now part of the Keep and under your protection. His name is Rumblkins." She scratched the tatzelwurm with one hand and the wyvern with the other.

Rumblkins? What kind of a name was that?

His purr filled the woods, excessively loud for his size.

"I like rats. They are very tasty." Longbourn blinked almost flirtatiously.

The tatzelwurm looked up at Miss Elizabeth.

"It would be very appropriate for you to bring him one, now and again. Hill would hardly notice you bringing one less to her."

"I can do that." Rumblkins voice was deep and almost furry. The tip of his tail flicked.

Longbourn licked his lips. "Then you shall be very welcome here."

Rumblkins rubbed his head against Longbourn's snout. Longbourn licked the top of Rumblkins' head.

Real dragons did not accept one another so easily. What was going on here?

"Perhaps you might go in search of one now?" Miss Elizabeth said.

Rumblkins mrowed and scampered away.

"He is not the only new arrival. We have had a

hatching of fairy dragons."

Longbourn rolled his eyes.

At least there was something Darcy agreed with him on.

Miss Elizabeth reached into her hood and withdrew three colorful fluff-balls. "You know April. These are Heather and Phoenix."

Longbourn sniffed at them. Small wonder he did not snuff them up his nose.

"A male?"

The red puff cheeped, its voice almost too high for Darcy to make out.

"As much as you." Phoenix jumped up and hovered between Longbourn's eyes.

"You might pick the mites off his head ridges." She pointed.

Phoenix obeyed, soon joined by the pink and blue fairy dragons.

"Oh, yes, there, just there." Longbourn purred and wagged his tail.

This was disgusting.

"I forgot how much I like fairy dragons. You will bring them when you come with Mary?"

"I will. Thank you, I know they appreciate your welcome."

The pink and red fluffs lit on Longbourn's snout, just between his eyes, squawked something, then curled up into sleeping balls. The blue one—April was it?—settled between them, a wing over each.

How domestic.

"Since you will be so well cared for by your Keep, you will have no need to disturb the militia that is coming to camp in Meryton."

Longbourn's lip curled back. "Militia? A large

number of men and beasts are coming to invade my territory?"

"Not invade, dear one. They will be training here for a time, then move on. There is no reason to trouble yourself." She edged around to scratch his ear again.

Longbourn snorted, disturbing the sleeping chicks. April pecked his snout and scolded.

The sight would have been comical had it not been likely to result in the quick demise of the fairy dragons in a single gulp.

"I do not like militias. Remember what they did to—"

Miss Elizabeth's shoulders sagged. "Yes, I cannot forget my great aunt's story. But eating her assailant did little to restore her honor." She wrapped her arms tightly about her waist.

Longbourn inched forward and wrapped his neck around her.

She leaned into the dragon. "I promise we shall be very, very careful."

"I will eat anyone who hurts you or any of my Keep. Slowly, one tiny bite at a time."

Darcy shuddered. That was not a threat to be taken lightly.

"I would not ask you to do otherwise. You are, after all, an estate dragon. You must protect your Keep. But pray, do not harass the militia." She pressed her face to Longbourn. "It would be very bad for the Keep if the soldiers were to be meddled with."

"As long as they do not harm what is and who are mine, I will keep the peace ... but I want another sheep."

"You shall have one for each se'nnight they are here."

"I like that."

"I hoped it would make your forbearance worthwhile. I must ask an important favor of you whilst they are here."

"More? Is it not enough that I do not bother them?"

"It should be, I know, but this is very, very important to all of dragonkind."

Longbourn craned his neck to look at her. "The missing firedrake egg?"

"You know of it?"

"All the major-dragons know."

"Why did you not tell me?" Her eyes grew wide.

So did Darcy's.

"It is a dragon matter. I would have consulted you if necessary."

The whole of England knew of Pemberley's trial? Darcy pressed his fist to his mouth.

"I have met the Keeper of the missing egg."

Longbourn rose, slowly enough not to disturb the sleeping fairy dragons. Slowly enough to be threatening and ominous.

He looked directly at Darcy. "Is that why you have brought that man here?"

Miss Elizabeth jumped and whirled around. "What man? I brought no one here."

Walker launched and landed lightly beside her. He bowed, beak to the ground. "Forgive us, Laird Longbourn. I know we have trespassed, but our errand is dire. We desperately need your assistance."

"Come forth, trespasser." Longbourn bellowed and stomped.

The fairy dragons squawked and sped into the trees.

Darcy gulped and stood. One did not ignore a major-dragon's commands. Squaring his shoulders, he stepped through the undergrowth, approached Long-bourn and bowed, knee to the ground.

Longbourn stepped closer and rose to his full height as Miss Elizabeth and Walker jumped aside. The huge head shadowed over him, breath so hot it burned on his face. His nose wrinkled against the pungent, acrid notes of venom. Perhaps that was what burned against his skin.

"You have offended me." Longbourn breathed heavily through his words.

Darcy bit his lip. Of course he had. He expected it with people, but how had he offended a dragon he had not even met?

"Pray forgive me, Laird Longbourn. It was done in ignorance. Pray tell me how I have offended. I shall make reparations to you and your Keep."

"Apologize to her and dance with her at the next ball."

"What?" She and Darcy exclaimed together.

"Her offense is mine. Apologize to her." Long-bourn twitched his head toward Miss Elizabeth.

"I told you." Walker flapped and hopped close enough to her to touch his wingtip to her skirt.

"This is absurd! How would you know about that?" she asked, looking from Longbourn to Walker to Darcy.

"You did not tell them?" Darcy's brow knit.

"Hardly. How do you know?" She planted her hands on her hips.

Longbourn twitched his brow ridges.

The fairy dragon?

"I do not need draconic interference—"

"Protection." Longbourn snorted.

She stomped, nearly on Walker's tail. "Interference.

I do not need it in every facet of my life. Mr. Darcy might have been abominably rude to myself and the entire community, but that is no reason to suggest he should be eaten by the local Laird."

His face burned. His neck burned. His chest burned. Humiliation seared deeper than mere dragon breath.

"I am still offended." Longbourn stared at her. She glowered back.

Darcy cleared his throat. "I thank you that you think my error not a capital offense, but pray accept my apologies for slighting you."

She turned her glower on him, potent as wyvern venom.

No one, save a dragon, had ever looked at him that way.

She was stunning.

And a little frightening.

Longbourn coughed. "And?"

No. Really? A dragon cared about dancing?

No, he cared about Miss Elizabeth, passionately.

"And … may I request your hand for the first two—"

Longbourn growled.

Overbearing, interfering lizard!

"For the supper set at the ball Bingley is planning to host at Netherfield?" Darcy bowed.

"What ball at Netherfield?" she asked.

"The one to be held at full moon next month." Longbourn blinked slowly.

"What would you know about that?"

Longbourn shrugged his wings. "Accept the dance."

"I do not wish to dance."

The dragon stomped and huffed.

She returned the gesture.

A low rumble grew in Longbourn's throat, rattling Darcy's bones. "I did not ask you if you wished to dance. Reparations must be made; the codes of dragon honor must be satisfied. You will dance with him."

Something in the dragon's tone changed, no longer playful and affectionate. This was a dragon in charge of his Keep.

"Very well. Sir, I thank you for your offer. I shall dance that set with you." She rolled her eyes and looked away. "Are you satisfied now?"

Longbourn licked her face.

Never had his offer to dance been accepted thus. It was offensive, degrading … and quite possibly deserved.

"Is there further reparation you require, Laird Longbourn?" Darcy asked.

"Do not offend her again."

Walker chirruped something that sounded like agreement.

"As you say." Darcy bowed again.

"Your business?" Longbourn settled back on his haunches.

"I came to this county in search of a dragon egg stolen from Pemberley Keep. I have reason to believe it is concealed among the militia yet to arrive. I am convinced that it is not among the troops already here."

"You wish help in recovering it?" Longbourn cocked his head. "It is not as though I can march into the camp and demand it. Well, I could. It would be satisfying. But it would be against the Accords and nearly as much of a problem as a firedrake hatching wild."

Hot, vaguely venomous breath etched Darcy's face.

He coughed into his handkerchief. "I do not ask your help, only your permission to be in your territory during my search."

"I do not take kindly to trespassers, but for such an errand, I will grant permission."

Darcy started to bow, but Walker hopped and flapped, bowing to the wyvern. "That is not all, Laird Longbourn."

Elizabeth gasped and crouched beside Walker and offered her arm as a perch. "What is it?"

He hopped up and she lifted him toward Longbourn. The wyvern dropped his head to look him in the eye.

"Speak, small one."

"There is something amiss in this territory." Walker said.

Longbourn flexed his wings. "Tell me."

"I hear a voice of a kind I do not know. I think it may be a lindwyrm."

Elizabeth stifled a cry with her hand. "Papa has been concerned there might be an unattached dragon—"

Longbourn roared and drowned out her words. "My territory is under my control. There are no trespassing dragons about."

"Forgive me, Laird, but a lindwyrm would present an unspeakable danger to an egg—" Darcy said.

Longbourn stomped toward Darcy. "I said my territory is secure. There is nothing unknown in my borders. Any egg here is safe. I will not have my dominance questioned."

A drop of venom glistened on his fang.

Darcy bowed. "We meant no offense, Laird Longbourn."

"I am offended." Longbourn snorted and stomped back into the hillside cave.

Darcy, Walker and Elizabeth stared at one another.

"He is known to be capricious, but this is odd even for him." She stared into the darkness.

Perhaps she expected him to reappear. But he did not.

"That was an utter waste of time." Darcy muttered, kicking a small stone.

Miss Elizabeth rounded on him, eyes wild. "Well, forgive us poor country folk for not living up to your expectations. Good luck in your endeavors. Perhaps you can manage not to destroy the entire kingdom in the process."

She spun on her heel and stalked off. Three colorful blurs streaked from the trees to catch up. The blue one veered off toward him, streaked past his head, nipping his ear as it went past.

Darcy's jaw dropped.

Stunning, simply stunning in her fury.

"You are a total cock up, Darcy. Bollocks for brains," Walker squawked and flew off.

The hillside was empty and eerily quiet.

Rumblkins trotted up with a large rat, still wriggling, in his mouth. He mrowed a question, and Darcy pointed into the cave. Rumblkins rubbed against his leg, tail flicking in a gesture of thanks and he trotted inside.

At least someone was happy with him.

5
Chapter

The following day, the ladies of Longbourn waited on those of Netherfield to celebrate the end of Mary's and Aunt Gardiner's 'extended convalescence.' Heather and Phoenix were well beyond their need for hourly feeds by then, but Papa had insisted on the extra time. It would be best to give the new companions as much time as possible to become acquainted with each other. Not to mention it gave April and Rustle and Rumblkins more time to persuade Mama of how much she liked caged 'birds.' Even one as susceptible to persuasion as Mama could require some convincing when asked to accept something that might push her limits.

That forenoon, after they returned from their visit, Uncle Gardiner made a show of presenting Mary and Aunt Gardiner with a 'present.' Each received a 'hummingbird' in a pretty cage, a gift he said, from a 'business partner' in London.

Most likely the cages came from someone of the

Blue Order who made them especially for Dragon Mates. None of the dragon-deaf members of the family seemed to notice that the cages latched from the inside.

Mama sniffed at the addition of yet another 'bird' to the family party. But after nearly a se'nnight for persuasion, she was also convinced that the pretty birdsong was well worth the fuss and bother of another 'pet.'

Jane seemed a little jealous, but Kitty and Lydia were happy—probably with a little dragon assistance—that it was Mary, not them, who would have the bother of a creature to tend.

The Gardiner children, particularly Anna, were entranced with their new pretty companion. Though they could not hear clearly yet, the children obviously recognized there was something unique and special about Phoenix. They treated him with special care and respect even without their parents' reminders.

All told, the fairy dragons' introduction into family life went very well indeed.

The women of the Bingley party visited Longbourn the next day. Elizabeth dodged the fairy dragons as they zipped upstairs into the safety of their cage-havens when Miss Bingley entered the house.

There were some people that dragons seemed to like and some they did not. Miss Bingley was definitely one of the latter. The tiny dragons had excellent judgement and very good taste.

If only Elizabeth could have joined them upstairs. But, no, decorum, and Mama, insisted she appear in the parlor instead.

The 'superior sisters' as the dragons called them, clearly found Mama intolerable. It was quite a good name for them, superior sisters.

Botheration! Now she had heard it, she would have

to be very careful not to speak it as well.

Whilst the Bingley sisters—there, she noted them correctly, perhaps it would not be so difficult—were entitled to their own opinions, it was poor form to allow it to show so obviously in their supercilious treatment of nearly the entire Bennet family. It seemed there was little at Longbourn house that could please them.

The visit was not without some bright spots. Though they did not address a single remark to Kitty or Lydia, they had the good graces to be attentive to Jane and herself, though Elizabeth loathed admitting the latter. It was pleasing that they desired to be better acquainted with Jane, but it would have been far more pleasing to Elizabeth if she could have declined her share of the favor.

Perhaps their kindness to Jane, such as it was, had a value, as arising in all probability from the influence of their brother's admiration. It was generally evident whenever they met, that Bingley did admire Jane and equally evident that Jane was happily yielding to the preference. They seemed to be very much on their way to being in love.

For Jane's happiness, Elizabeth would learn to tolerate those who might soon be Jane's sisters.

Somehow.

Eventually.

At the end of the customary quarter of an hour, the superior sisters—Confound it!—departed. The rest of the afternoon was spent reliving those minutes as Mama picked them apart and examined them for every possible nuance.

The next day, the full militia company arrived in all

their pomp and circumstance. At last, Papa, with Uncle Gardiner's assistance, could finally actively work to recover the missing egg. With any luck, they would soon find it and the querulous Mr. Darcy would be on his way back from whence he came.

Several evenings later, Papa wandered into the parlor, where Mama gathered those daughters of hers who were already prepared to depart for Lucas Lodge. To Mama's chagrin, Lady Lucas issued the first invitations for a gathering in honor of the militia.

"Lizzy, come to the study and help me with my cravat." He beckoned her to follow and disappeared.

"I do not understand why he needs you for such a task. Certainly my brother could assist—" Mama fluttered her handkerchief toward the door.

"I do not mind." Elizabeth ducked out and hastened toward the study.

Uncle Gardiner closed the door behind her.

Regardless of what Mama might say, Papa's cravat was a mess. She went to right it.

He lifted his chin. "Do not strangle me with your knots, now, though I know you will not be pleased with what I have to say."

"Whatever do you mean?" She loosed the remnants of the knot and smoothed out the creases.

"I know you would rather enjoy this party with your friends. But, it is essential that somehow we extract an invitation from the colonel—"

"Mail coach knot or barrel knot?" she asked.

"I prefer Napoleon style," Papa muttered.

"That is far too casual. Mama will insist she retie it if she sees you that way. You always complain that her knots strangle you."

Uncle Gardiner snickered.

"Do a barrel knot then. It is less confining than the other." Papa sniffed. "As I said—"

"This is not a social engagement, but an assignment direct from the Order itself. We are to get close enough to the colonel such that one of us extracts an invitation to visit the encampment. And we must rely upon our wits and wiles alone, as we will have no dragons with us to craft any persuasions. I well understand our purpose." She straightened the ends of the cravat and tucked them into his waistcoat. "Mama will approve now."

"I am sure she will." Papa's voice softened, and he caught her elbow. "I am sorry that you have not the luxury of socializing and delighting in meeting new company as your sisters do."

A knot, tighter than the one she tied for him, lodged in her throat. She turned aside, swallowing hard. "It is a small price to pay for the company I am privileged to keep."

She lifted her chatelaine from her waist. The embossed seal of the Order caught the first beams of moonlight. Though it was not fashionable to wear such a practical piece with a dinner dress, she never went anywhere without it. "Few societies so readily welcome young ladies as equal partners in their business."

Uncle coughed. "I think the dragons are more accepting than the men."

"They usually are." She flashed him a tight smile.

"That reminds me. I had a letter from my cousin, Collins. He shall arrive in just over a fortnight. He expressed special delight in the opportunity to come to be acquainted with you and your sisters face to face."

She dropped her gaze and studied the faded carpet. Large dragon eyes peered up at her, cleverly woven into the background of the floral pattern. Had papa ever noticed them there?

Uncle Gardiner crossed the room toward them in heavy, almost angry steps. "Do you know anything about this man?"

"We know he is heir to Longbourn estate, I am heir to its Keeper, and Longbourn insists that we marry. What more need we know?" Elizabeth fought to keep her voice light and shrugged. "A great many marriages have been built upon even less a foundation than that."

"I do not like this. How can you insist upon her marrying him when we know not the first thing about him?" Uncle loomed over her shoulder with an expression he might have learned from Longbourn.

"Longbourn must have a say in the next Keeper. My eldest daughter is as dragon-deaf as your sister. So it falls to Lizzy." Papa folded his arms across his chest. "It is his right according to the Pendragon accords."

Elizabeth bit her lip. Pray this conversation would stop, preferably immediately.

"Your plan is a good one where nothing is in question but keeping a dragon happy. If Elizabeth were determined to get a rich husband, or any husband at all, I dare say you should proceed as you are. But these are not Elizabeth's feelings."

No, they were most definitely not.

"Feelings play little role in the matter." Papa glowered at her. "It is the way things have been done amongst the Keepers for centuries."

Did he think she had put Uncle up to broaching the topic?

"But it is not the way they are done now. Dragons must accommodate the changes in human philosophy and society. Do they not? If she were to act by your design, not even certain of the plan's reasonableness, what chance is there for success? Is not her contentment also essential for Longbourn's?"

"Please, Uncle." She laid a hand on his forearm.

He covered it with his, holding it there. "She has no knowledge of him. She has read—what, parts of four letters you have shared with her, perhaps less? She has never danced with him, never dined in company with him. This is hardly enough to make her understand his character."

"Not as you represent it. Still four letters may do a great deal." He waggled his eyebrows at her as though asking for agreement.

She drew breath to speak, but Uncle cut her off.

"Yes, these four letters have enabled her to ascertain that they both like Vingt-Un better than Commerce. But with respect to any other leading characteristic, I do not imagine much beyond that has been unfolded."

Papa folded his arms over his chest. "You make me sound as if I were some ogre from the previous century! I wish Elizabeth success and happiness in marriage with all my heart. But in truth, I am convinced that if she were married to him tomorrow she has as good a chance of happiness as if she were to be studying his character for a twelvemonth. Happiness in marriage is entirely a matter of chance. If the dispositions of the parties are ever so well known to each other, or ever so similar before-hand, it does not advance their felicity in the least. They always contrive to grow sufficiently unlike afterwards to have their share of vexation. It is better to know as little as possible of the defects of the person with whom you are to pass your life."

The mantel clock chimed eight times and Mama's voice wafted through the closed door. "It is time, Mr. Bennet, it is time."

Elizabeth screwed her eyes shut and bit her tongue. Papa's views on marriage were so very convenient for him, but would he say the same to Jane?

Uncle grunted. "It is not sound, even if shaped by your own experience. I would never act in this way nor counsel any of my children to do so. I do not consider this discussion over."

"But I do." Papa strode from the room.

The six Bennet women rode in the carriage whilst Papa and Uncle rode their horses alongside. Fortunately, Papa could still manage that, at least for a short distance, when he had someone to ride alongside of him. It would be a difficult day when he lost that ability as well.

Would that she had the option of being alone with her thoughts as they did. At least Mama's effusions and raptures over the opportunity to meet the officers provided sufficient entertainment to distract her from dwelling on deeper concerns.

The Bennet carriage pulled up to the door of Lucas Lodge just behind Bingley's carriage. The superior sisters made a great show of their exit, shaking out their skirts and fluffing their feathers. Did they not understand how to dress appropriately for an evening party in the country? On second thought, they probably did, but chose to dress above the rest of the company to demonstrate their superiority.

Elizabeth bit her tongue. She must bring those thoughts under control before she joined the rest of the company.

Mr. Darcy followed the ladies into Lucas Lodge. Why was he here? His company was even less desirable than the ... Bingley sisters'.

But of course Mr. Darcy would be there. He needed the colonel's assistance as much as they did.

One more reason to relish this evening.

At last the Bingley carriage pulled forward, and the Bennet coach took its place. The driver handed them out. She took her place in the parade, behind Jane and before Mary.

Papa pulled her aside. "Keep Darcy from the colonel as much as possible. We do not need his bumbling to hamper our efforts."

"He did determine that the egg was not with the building party. That is something, is it not? Perhaps his energies—"

"Elizabeth! Now is not the time to discuss his competence. It is better that your uncle and I handle this matter now. Just do as I have asked."

"He has no very good opinion of me. How am I to accomplish this?" She crushed the edges of her cloak in her fists.

"You are a clever girl, I have faith in you. Many a stupider woman has managed a man she did not care for. I am certain you are up to the task." He patted her shoulder and went inside.

Vexing, annoying, impossible man! At times like these, Mama's complaints about him seemed entirely accurate.

How was she to accomplish such a task without even a dragon to assist? It was not as though she had their persuasive powers.

If only she had not needed to leave April at home.

What if Mr. Collins was deaf as Jane and could not

share even dragon companionship with her? A cold shiver coursed down her back and she shuddered.

"Come in now, Lizzy!" Mama bustled out to her. "One would think you do not wish to enjoy the Lucases' society! Besides, the night air is not good for you." She grabbed Elizabeth's elbow and propelled her inside.

Sir William and Lady Lucas greeted her at the door with genuine smiles and enthusiasms. They knew her far too well to take offense if she was slow to enter.

She scanned the room. Jane sat with Mr. Bingley and several other young ladies who clearly wished for his attentions. No doubt they would call the evening a disappointment as his attentions were clearly fixed on Jane.

A familiar laugh caught her attention. Charlotte beckoned her from across the room. She stood with a tall, well-looking man whom Elizabeth had never seen before. He towered over her, broad of shoulder and chest, a little peacockish with his long, narrow nose slightly in the air.

"Colonel Forster, may I present my friend, Miss Elizabeth Bennet," Charlotte said.

He bowed. "Delighted to make your acquaintance. One of the famed Bennet sisters, I expect?"

"Indeed, sir I am. But I can hardly consider us famed." Elizabeth curtsied.

"A family of five girls all with beauty equal to yours? Of course that is notable." His eyes drifted toward Jane.

It was a kind, even polite thing to say, but his meaning was clear.

"So sir, are you here to protect Meryton from the invading French?" She smiled as prettily as she could.

"Clearly you think the danger unlikely—a testament to your faith in our efficacy, madam. I accept the compliment on behalf of the regiment." He dipped his head.

At least he had a sense of humor. Always an agreeable trait in a man.

"Since the town appears quite secure, I feel at leisure to pursue the other part of my mission. My men are in great need of training."

Lydia sashayed up, an unfamiliar young man in tow. "And his officers in need of entertaining."

"Lydia! Pray pardon her, sir, she is full young—"

Lydia tossed her head and rolled her eyes. "La! I am quite old enough to be out in company. I am far more interesting than you. See, I have already been introduced to all the officers."

Charlotte's lips pressed in a tight smile. No doubt she feared her sisters would be following Lydia's lead.

"I must find someone to play for us. We must have a dance. It is a shame you came too late for this month's assembly. We could have had many lively dances then. Where has Mary gone to?" Lydia hopped off.

Colonel Forster watched Lydia depart. "Do not worry. Her lively energy is most welcome among us."

Apparently only her two prettiest sisters possessed the traits necessary to capture his attention.

And now Mr. Darcy was approaching!

Lovely, exactly what she wished for.

"So now that you have come among us sir, you know the properest course of action, do you not?" Elizabeth batted her eyes.

How did Lydia do that without becoming dizzy?

Why was Darcy staring? Was it not enough that she

had to play-act the coquette? Why must he be in the audience?

Charlotte stared at her as though she were a complete stranger.

"Tell me if I am incorrect, Charlotte, but I believe the whole of Meryton expects you to host a ball."

One that she might offer to assist in planning, which would of course require spending time near the militia. Hopefully Papa would approve.

"A ball, you say?" Forster thumbed his lapels.

"That is a singularly good idea, Lizzy." Charlotte eyed her narrowly.

"My Harriet does love to dance."

"Harriet?" Charlotte asked.

"My betrothed. We are soon to be married."

A betrothed man should not spend so much time looking at pretty girls not attached to himself.

Charlotte clucked her tongue. "So that is why you took Willow Cottage instead of rooms at Mrs. Parson's. My mother had been wondering if we were to wish you joy soon."

"She is a very observant woman, your mother. I will pay her my compliments—"

"Pray excuse me." Sir William ambled up, Papa and Uncle Gardner at his sides. "Permit me to introduce the master of Longbourn estate, Mr. Bennet."

Papa dismissed her with a nod, and she faded back, Charlotte with her.

Not a moment too soon! Perhaps he could secure an invitation in a way that would not result in her arranging a ball for the officers to host.

Mr. Darcy joined the conversation with Colonel Forster. Papa did not appear pleased.

"You are staring, Lizzy." Charlotte tapped

Elizabeth's elbow with her own.

Elizabeth looked away. "What did Mr. Darcy mean by listening to my conversation with Colonel Forster?"

"That is a question which only Mr. Darcy can answer. Perhaps he would like another opportunity to refuse to dance with the ladies of Meryton." Charlotte chuckled under her breath. "I cannot believe he could say such a thing about you!"

Elizabeth shrugged. The tightness in her throat would not allow words to pass. What did his opinion matter?

Consarn it! Darcy balled a fist behind his back. If only he had moved more quickly, but how did one break into a conversation one was not invited into?

Sir William seemed to have no difficulty, easily interrupting to introduce Mr. Bennet and his brother Mr. Gardiner to the far too gregarious colonel. To his credit, Lucas was courteous enough to include Darcy in the introductions. At least now he could in all propriety speak with the colonel—no it was lieutenant colonel.

If the colonel himself were here it would be easier. He had known Viscount Clarington since they were boys. He had even attended the reception that had made Clarington Lord Lieutenant of the county. Darcy could have approached him with ease. But no, Clarington was off taking leave.

Nothing could be easy.

Bennet's left eye twitched as he pointedly ignored Darcy's presence. "How are you finding Hertfordshire?"

Forster clapped his heels together. "Capital, capital. The barracks are quite adequate for our encampment and there are many excellent venues for them to train upon. My officers and I are excited to begin our exercises. We will have a review for Meryton in a fortnight or so."

"I should think your encampment quite a sight to behold." Gardiner thumbed his lapels.

He wore a signet ring with a blue stone, engraved with the symbol of the Blue Order. Landless, but able to hear dragons. Perhaps he was the companion to the cockatrice Walker had mentioned encountering in Longbourn's woods. Here to help Bennet, no doubt.

"Indeed they are. I have heard that the Hertfordshire regiment has recently come short a field officer."

"Indeed they have, their lieutenant colonel has taken too ill to serve, dropsy of the heart I have heard." Forster rocked back on his heels. "Is it possible you are considering stepping up to the office?"

Bennet shrugged, "There is something to be said for the exclusive company of men when one lives in a house of six women."

Liar. The man was a bold-faced liar. A Keeper would never abandon his dragon voluntarily.

"I find it rather a smart business, truth be told. Certainly a welcome change from the drudgeries of land management. Perhaps you gentlemen would enjoy a closer inspection of the regiment as we settle in and prepare for the review?"

"I would most gladly take you up on the offer. My cousin is a colonel in the regulars," Darcy said.

Whilst Bennet might be a manipulative liar and the colonel a short-sighted fool, an opportunity was an opportunity.

"I have no such fortunate relations, but we should welcome your invitation, nonetheless," Bennet said through gritted teeth.

What would Bennet do if he found the egg before Darcy? Surely he would not try and withhold it from its proper Keeper, would he?

No, Bennet would not take that chance. Not when Darcy was this close.

"Tomorrow then, after the morning drills?" Forster was a proud one. Clearly he enjoyed all this attention from the local residents of quality.

What kind of yeoman farm did he come from? He had little bearing, coarse manners, and an unpolished tone in his voice that would have Walker hating him immediately.

"Thank you, we will look forward to seeing you then." Bennet glanced at Gardiner, who nodded.

"Indeed." Darcy bowed and allowed Gardiner to pick up the threads of a new conversation.

He would be there shortly after dawn tomorrow, well before Bennet could arrive.

He slipped back, out of the conversation and surveyed the room.

With Walker's help, he could begin a thorough search of every inch of the territory the four companies occupied. Pray it would be among them. Otherwise he would have to create some reason to visit Ware. Perhaps the pretext of seeking to visit Clarington, who would conveniently not be there?

Disguise was his abhorrence, but what choice did he have? No one here knew he thought Clarington a simpering dolt whose company he would ride miles to avoid.

Best not think of that now. There was still some

good that might be accomplished this night. He scanned the knots of people dotting the room for Wickham. Matlock's intelligence said he was friendly with Forster and likely to be in the lieutenant colonel's shadow. Moreover, he was not the kind to relinquish such an opportunity, relishing few things more than the opportunity to amuse himself with young ladies.

Where was he?

Did he think the egg so near hatching that he dare not leave its presence? Or did he not feel secure enough in its hiding place that he could not leave it unguarded? That was more likely. He might be a selfish, undisciplined opportunist, but he was no fool.

That could be to his advantage. If it were not well hid, then perhaps Walker could discover it, and they could make short work of recovering it without drawing the attention of the militia or the locals.

Except for Bennet. No doubt he would find out. If nothing else, those irritating fairy dragons would report everything.

Troublesome little gossips.

Miss Elizabeth stood against the far wall conversing with the eldest Lucas girl. His face heated. Just an hour ago, in the carriage ride here, he had heartily agreed with Miss Bingley's assessment that Miss Elizabeth had hardly a good feature in her face.

It was not true. Far from it.

Her features were uncommonly intelligent, especially because of the beautiful expression of her dark eyes. Granted, there was more than one failure of perfect symmetry in her form, but her figure was light and pleasing. Her manners were certainly not those of the fashionable world. But was that truly unforgivable? Their easy playfulness appealed to many, including the dragons. She was indeed pretty, far from 'not handsome enough' to dance with.

He never should have spoken those words. It was beneath him. Walker was right, he needed to make amends.

He made his way toward them. Miss Lucas noticed immediately and welcomed him with a curtsey.

"How are you enjoying the party, Mr. Darcy? Have you found the company agreeable?"

"Thank you, I have been most grateful for the invitation." He dipped his head.

"Do you enjoy music, sir? I am going to open the instrument, Eliza, and you know what follows." Miss Lucas' eyebrows rose, and she cocked her head.

"You are a very strange creature by way of a friend! Always wanting me to play and sing before anybody and everybody!" Miss Elizabeth's cheeks colored. "If my vanity had taken a musical turn, you would have been invaluable, but as it is, I would really rather not sit down before those who must be in the habit of hearing the very best performers."

"You play very prettily, Eliza, and I must insist. It is your duty to take your turn at the pianoforte and display as all of us shall."

"Very well. If it must be so, it must." She curtsied and followed Miss Lucas to the far side of the room.

Her performance was pleasing, though by no means capital, but her manner was easy and unaffected. Her voice was lighter than he expected, clear and sweet. Her cheeks colored prettily as she sang, and her dark eyes shone. After a song or two, and before she could reply to several entreaties that she sing again, her sister Miss Mary, eagerly succeeded at the instrument, apparently impatient for her turn to display.

Darcy gritted his teeth through her entire performance. She had neither genius nor taste, playing with a pedantic air and conceited manner, which would have injured a higher degree of excellence than she had been privileged to reach. What a relief when the long concerto gave way to her younger sisters' demands for music they might dance to.

Two or three officers eagerly joined in dancing at one end of the room. But Wickham was not among them either.

Darcy clasped his hands behind his back and muttered under his breath. What a torturous way to pass an evening when he had far more important concerns to attend to.

Miss Bingley approached, a vaguely predatory look in her eye.

Why her?

She stepped far too close, her nearness prickling his skin. "I can guess the subject of your reverie."

"I should imagine not."

"You are considering how insufferable it would be to pass many evenings in such society. I am quite of your opinion. I was never more annoyed! The insipidity, the noise! The nothingness and yet the self-importance of all these people! What would I give to hear your strictures on them!" She fluttered her feathered fan before her face.

If only he might share his strictures on her, but that would be insupportable. "Your conjecture is totally wrong, I assure you. My mind was more agreeably engaged. I have been meditating on the very great pleasure which a pair of fine eyes in the face of a pretty woman can bestow."

She followed his gaze toward Miss Elizabeth and

sniffed. "I am all astonishment. How long has she been such a favorite? Pray when am I to wish you joy?"

He pinched the bridge of his nose. "A lady's imagination is very rapid. It jumps from admiration to love, from love to matrimony, in a moment."

"You will have a charming mother-in-law, indeed, and of course she will be always at Pemberley with you."

Miss Bingley lingered long over the topic, clearly enjoying her little tease.

But what would Pemberley be like under the care of a mistress like Miss Elizabeth? It was an interesting mental exercise indeed.

6
Chapter

Three days of near torrential rain delayed Darcy's visit to the militia encampment. That alone would have been enough to drive him stark mad—so close to his objective and yet it remained impossibly out of reach. But coupled with the company of Hurst and the Bingley sisters—it was nigh on intolerable.

Was there an hour of day Hurst was not inebriated? It was not hard to believe that his wife encouraged it to keep him pacified. His temper was nearly as disgraceful as his opinions were ignorant. Not that his wife's were much better, but at least she had better manners.

Miss Bingley was a problem though. Since her taunting remarks at the Lucas' party she hovered at his shoulder like a fairy dragon. Her prattle certainly sounded like one, only slightly less high-pitched. Walker warned that she was seeking a mate.

Desperately.

But if that were the case, why did she keep bringing up Elizabeth Bennet? It made no sense.

Bingley warned him not to encourage her. How did one not encourage a woman when one was not certain what encouraged one in the first place? Did he mean it was wrong to even talk to her?

Gah, this was exactly why he hated London and the marriage mart there. If he could find other Meryton lodgings, alone, he would. But it would open him up to questions and attention he did not need.

In the meantime, avoidance seemed the best alternative. But doing so when one was confined inside a house, even one as large as Netherfield, was a task beyond his powers.

The end of the rain could not have been more welcome. Darcy rose before dawn, penned a note for Bingley regarding his plans—or at least what Bingley should know of them—and left.

There was little need to hurry since no one but him kept country hours, but still, the rush—to finally be doing something!—was invigorating.

The bracing air revived his spirits. His man would not appreciate the state of his coat and boots when he returned splashed with a substantial layer of mud. But delaying until the roads dried would drive him to Bedlam. The militia's barracks rose before him.

Walker flew high overhead, surveying the encampment from his unique vantage point. With any luck, he would spot the most likely hiding places in the surrounding countryside, making their search a brief one.

His horse, though nervous on the best days, was difficult to manage. The creature had never much liked Walker's presence and became skittish when the cockatrice was near. But this was extreme. Could it be the horse smelt a dragon egg? That was a heartening thought indeed.

Walker screeched and dove at something in the bushes ahead. Terror slithered down Darcy's back.

Even knowing Walker's voice, his shriek still raised a visceral response. Had Walker found their quarry?

Darcy urged his horse into a trot, but it balked.

Damnable creature!

He leapt down and tied the horse off on a tree branch.

Ahead, the bushes rustled and growls—deep, dangerous, dragon growls—resounded.

Bloody hell, what had he found there? He sprinted for the sounds.

"No!" A female voice screamed.

Not a scream of fear, but of authority.

Miss Elizabeth.

Of course, she would have to be here.

He broke through the undergrowth into a small clearing overhung with heavy branches.

On the ground between two large trees, Walker and another cockatrice faced each other. Wings extended, necks outstretched, they hissed and clawed the ground, churning up dead leaves and debris. The other cockatrice was slightly smaller, rather shabby by comparison, but his courage was to be commended. Not every dragon would stand up to one clearly its superior.

Miss Elizabeth, a lumpy market bag slung on her shoulder, jumped between them, arms outstretched, holding her cloak open to make herself as big as possible.

How did she know to do that?

She dragged her feet in the dirt, mimicking the

dragons' clawing and flapped her cloak enough to give the impression of wings. "Both of you cease this behavior at once. I will not have it. You are civilized creatures and will act that way immediately." She looked from one dragon to the other. "Now take two steps back. Both of you, now do it. I will drop my cloak and introduce you properly and politely. No more shrieking and hissing out of either one of you."

The two dragons backed off, slowly, hesitantly, but they did obey. She lowered her arms, allowing them to see one another again. Both cockatrices extended their wings, beaks snapping, but they did not shriek.

"Much better." She slid back a bit and curtsied to both dragons. "If I may introduce you—"

Both snorted.

No doubt they would rather fight.

She cleared her throat. "That was not a question. I will introduce you, and you will accept the acquaintance, just as Longbourn has accepted both of you as visitors into his Keep."

Walker, then the other dragon, flipped his wings to his back, but kept his head lowered, still ready to fight.

"Walker, companion to Mr. Darcy of Pemberley, may I present Rustle, companion to Mr. Gardiner of Gracechurch Street, London."

The cockatrices eyed each other warily, heads bobbing as they circled Miss Elizabeth.

She stood her ground as though unaware of the danger she put herself in.

A dragon less civilized and well-mannered than Walker might well injure her or worse for forcing an introduction upon him.

She growled deep in her throat—a draconic sound she must have learnt from Longbourn. The hair on the back of his neck prickled.

Both cockatrices stopped and stared at her.

So did Darcy.

"I have neither time nor patience for this posturing. Enjoy your dragon pomposity later. We all have the same errand today, and it is more important than your pride." She waved the two dragons together. "Go on now. Now I say."

Her tone carried all the authority—and confidence—of a major-dragon.

The cockatrices met in front of her and bowed to one another. Rustle bowed lower. Walker plucked a scale-feather from the back of his head. Rustle yipped and Walker gulped the scale down, cawing softly.

Dominance was established with no bloodshed.

And Walker seemed satisfied. How was that possible? He always wanted a taste of blood first.

Miss Elizabeth crouched and reached down to them. They hopped toward her, craning their necks toward her hands. She scratched them simultaneously, and they rolled their heads into her hands.

"That is much better, much better." She looked up at Darcy. "Good morning, sir. I imagine we are on the same business?"

"Walker?"

Walker contorted himself to look at Darcy whilst contriving to remain under Miss Elizabeth's ministrations.

"That is undignified," Darcy muttered under his breath.

"She knows where to scratch." Walker closed his eyes.

Rustle pressed his head into her hand, but looked at Darcy and growled.

She pulled away. "No, that is Mr. Darcy. Papa and Longbourn have recognized him. There is no need for that sort of display."

Rustle scowled but stopped.

After one more scratch, Miss Elizabeth rose and straightened her cloak.

"You should not be here." Darcy offered Walker his forearm as a perch.

"Why precisely is that? We share the same concern and the same directive from the Order."

"You do realize you are skulking about outside an entire camp full of soldiers." Darcy gestured toward the distant barracks with his free arm.

"Indeed, I thought I was outside my favorite millinery shop." She adjusted her bonnet.

"This is not a joke, madam. I cannot imagine your father would condone the danger you put yourself in."

She looked away. "I have Rustle here with me. I am far from unguarded."

Apparently Bennet had odd ideas of what was appropriate for a young woman, even in the company of dragons.

"But you have not brought the fairy dragon. No doubt you do not wish to endanger her. Does that alone not tell you something? Pray, does Longbourn approve of this?"

Walker chirruped something that sounded like support.

"He does not know."

Something about the look on her face suggested she did not like keeping secrets from Longbourn.

"You are then aware of the very great risk you are taking, not only with yourself, but with Longbourn and even Rustle, and probably Walker as well. If, god

forbid, anything were to happen, it is quite clear—" –
dangerously, alarmingly clear— "—that your friends
would be intolerant of the offense and respond in the
most dragonesque of ways. It will be difficult for even
a pair of adept cockatrices to persuade over three hundred men that their companions were not dragon
casualties."

She hung her head, shoulders bowing. Rustle edged
back against her legs and extended one wing around
her.

"You see how uncomfortable they are." Darcy
lifted Walker a little higher, so he could look her in the
eye. "They were listening when Longbourn mentioned
an aunt—"

She lifted her hands as if to push him away. "Mr.
Darcy, that is quite enough. I am entirely aware of my
family's history. I am not insensitive to Walker's and
Rustle's concerns. But desperate times require sacri-
fices of us all, do they not? No doubt you can see, my
father is unable to actively search himself, and my uncle
is required to attend the colonel with him. The Order
has demanded we assist you. What other choices are
there?"

"You are a young lady alone!"

"There is only one solution," Walker chirruped.
"You must work together in this matter."

"No, the solution is for her to return to her home
and cease this improper cavorting about."

She dodged around Rustle and stood nearly toe to
toe with Darcy. "You think this cavorting, that I am
here for pleasure and flirtation? That this is my idea of
sport?"

Her eyes burned with mesmerizing intensity.

Darcy edged back. "I misspoke; it was a poor choice

of words."

"Indeed it was. I take my responsibilities to dragon-kind quite seriously."

"And you imply I do not?"

She rose up on her toes. "I am not talking about you at all. Only what the situation requires. And in that case, Walker is quite correct. We are both here to search for the missing egg. We can do so more effectively if we work together and cease these petty arguments."

"And if we are caught together, your reputation will suffer. It is not right for us to be together without a chaperone."

"You think I want to be compromised? By you?" She rolled her eyes. "I am promised and all but betrothed to a cousin, the heir to Longbourn, so you have nothing to worry about, sir. I have no need to seek a husband."

Something about the tone of her voice—resignation mixed with regret. What kind of man was this cousin?

What did it matter to him?

"Besides, Walker and Rustle are adequate chaperones, well able to convince any who we may encounter of the propriety of our company." Her shoulders fell a little.

Would it have been so disagreeable to be caught with her? She was the only woman he had ever met who not only heard dragons, but had the heart of one herself.

He shook his head. Where had that thought come from? He glanced at the cockatrices, but they were engaged in conversation with one another in a language reserved for their kind alone. Besides, Walker was above playing that sort of game with him and the other would not be capable of influencing Darcy so easily.

"I have a task to accomplish, and I had best return to it. Am I to proceed alone?" She stepped away.

"No." Walker blocked her path. "Darcy, if you do not go with her, I shall."

Darcy huffed. It did not help that Walker was right. "Very well."

The cockatrices chirped and lifted their beaks into the wind.

"There is egg scent in the air," Rustle said.

"That means it is here, does it not?" Miss Elizabeth asked.

"Perhaps, but we only know for certain that something here has been in close contact with an egg." Walker snorted. "It is strongest on this side of the camp. Near that hillside." He pointed with his wing.

The dragons took to the air and Darcy and Miss Elizabeth followed. She picked her away around the rocks and up the steep path, ignoring him when he offered his hand.

Obstinate, headstrong girl. Proud as any dragon!

Walker would probably blame him if she fell, and Longbourn would certainly hold him accountable for any mishap.

"Pray allow me to assist you." He extended his hand again.

"Take his hand," Walker squawked. "Do not argue, and do it now." He swooped a little lower over their heads.

She huffed and took his hand in a surprisingly strong grip.

Just over the rise of the hill, Rustle landed in front of an opening in the stone outcropping. An arm span wide and slightly shorter than Miss Elizabeth in height, it was an ideal place to secrete something valuable.

The cockatrices, with their keen night vision, hopped in first.

A moment later Walker called, "Come in."

Darcy removed a bit of touch paper, flint and steel from one pocket and a candle from the other. He struck a quick spark that lit the touch paper and then lit the candle from that. Miss Elizabeth took it from him while he snuffed the touch paper and returned the items to his pocket.

Taking the candle back from her, he led the way into the hillside cavern.

Just inside they paused, allowing their eyes to adjust to the candlelight.

Darcy could not stand upright inside. The cavern smelt of cold stone, stale and lifeless. The jagged ceiling sported low hanging rocks that threatened to seriously injure the unaware. Stones from the size of his fist upwards to small boulders littered the floor, probably fallen from above. The dirt around them showed evidence of boot prints and trails of items dragged into, and probably out of the cavern. Perhaps this hiding place had been used before, perhaps often.

They followed the caws of the dragons deeper in, beyond the reach of the sunlight. The flickering candle flame bathed the walls in eerie dancing light.

"There—" Miss Elizabeth pointed half a dozen steps beyond.

A stack of crates and several barrels lay just behind a large pile of stones. The dragons perched on the topmost crate.

"I smell egg." Walker scratched at the crate.

"No, it is this one." Rustle jumped down onto a

large barrel.

Miss Elizabeth opened the market bag and withdrew a small pry bar. The way she held it suggested she knew how to use it—probably would not be afraid to make a weapon out of it if forced to it.

Uncommonly well prepared for such an uncommon assignment.

"Sir, what are the physical properties of the egg? Size, weight?" She asked, rolling the barrel away from the crates.

He handed her the candle. "It would just fit in the barrel, I believe. Perhaps five stone in weight?"

"How much does that barrel weigh, another stone perhaps. So, if it contains the egg, it should weigh just more than six stone?"

"Half of what it would weigh full of brandy. Clever." He squatted and wrapped his arms around the barrel. He grunted and lifted it, contents sloshing. "No, that is far too heavy." He replaced it.

"Then the crates perhaps?" She handed him the pry bar with a look that said she could have managed happily on her own, but was humoring him for the sake of the dragons, or possibly his pride—it was difficult to discern which.

They lifted the lids on the crates, but found only tea, tobacco and one with French lace. After restoring it all as they found it, they hastened away from the cave.

"I wonder if Clarington is aware he has smugglers attached to his militia," Darcy muttered.

"That is not your business, Darcy. Do not become involved in it." Walker perched on Darcy's forearm and stared him in the eye. "I know you are awfully committed to such human conventions, but this is neither the time nor place for your quaint moralities.

There are much bigger concerns to contend with."

"As much as I do not like to side with lawlessness, explaining how we came upon the goods of free-trade men would be difficult at best. I fear it might cause widespread searching—" Miss Elizabeth looked over her shoulder.

"That could see the egg, if it is here, uncovered by the wrong people." Darcy clutched his forehead and grimaced. "You are right. The excise men can wait for their victory until Pemberley is safe."

Miss Elizabeth bit her lip. "It seems that the egg is either in the hands of smugglers or of one who is doing business with smugglers, perhaps using them to transport the egg along with smuggled goods."

"The regiment was just on the coast, well situated to receive goods from France." Darcy bounced his fist on his chin.

"Could someone be trying to remove the egg to the continent?" Her face lost a little color.

"No, I am quite certain that is not the case."

"How do you know?"

"Walker, are there other caches like this one?" Darcy turned his shoulder to her.

"Several and they all smell of egg. Come." Walker launched. Rustle followed not far behind.

"I asked you, how do you know smugglers are not trying to take the egg from England?" She crossed her arms over her chest, brows drawn low over her eyes.

"We should follow them." Darcy hurried down the stony hillside, leaving Elizabeth to find her own way down.

Walker and Rustle uncovered four further hoards of smuggled goods, all of which had been in contact with

Pemberley's egg. The egg itself though remained stubbornly absent. Walker insisted the traces could not have been over a fortnight, perhaps just a se'nnight, old. So, it had likely parted ways with the goods when the building parties separated from the regiment, one to Meryton and the other to Ware.

But the hillsides were full of small crevices and caverns, some deep enough to impede Walker's sense of smell. They could not consider their search complete until they had scoured them all, a task that would take days, even weeks. All the while, the egg might be with the company at Ware.

Even the cockatrices agreed, the expedient thing was to part ways. Miss Elizabeth and Rustle would continue their efforts in the hillsides farther removed from the encampment. Rumblkins and April would join her. They would watch for wayward soldiers and persuade them away from her. Hardly ideal, but it was better than nothing.

Tomorrow he would ride for Ware. It was only common courtesy to pay his old friend Clarington a call. And if he was not actually in Ware with his regiment, so much the better.

Elizabeth gripped the banister for support as she trudged downstairs for breakfast, groggy and sore, despite having slept far later than usual. Though several days had passed since her last foray into the hillsides, the days of fruitless searches still took their toll. Who knew there were so many caverns, grottos, cavities and fissures in the hillsides? Was it possible they had searched them all?

Hardly.

Perhaps Mr. Darcy had been wise when he gave up his search in favor of seeking out the other militia company.

Shins, feet, legs, back, all screamed that she had done too much. But that could not be true. The egg had not been recovered. Nothing could be considered too much until it was.

Hopefully, Mr. Darcy's latest efforts were yielding more fruit.

Papa and Uncle Gardiner were already in the morning room, conversing in hushed tones that the dragon-deaf family members would be unlikely to make out. She slipped in and closed the door behind her.

Cool sunbeams, filtered through heavy clouds, barely made their way through to light the room in a dull glow that turned the blue-green walls muddy and dreary. She rubbed her hands over her arms. Though not actually cold, a chill settled over her shoulders.

An empty cup with the dregs of willow bark tea sat beside a freshly steeping cup. That did not bode well for Papa's humor.

Coffee fragrance wafted from the table—it was too early for tea to be set out. Hill never brought it until Mama made her appearance. Some cold meat and rolls, a bit of butter and jam lay untouched in the center of the table. Was it still too early to eat? What time was it?

The mantel clock revealed it half past ten, not too early to eat. Was Papa's appetite ruined by his discomfort or by their recent failures?

Given his current expression, probably the latter.

"If I never see a militia encampment again as long as I live, it will be too soon." Papa huffed and snapped the newspaper open. "I declare I know it better than my own house now."

Just as she knew the grounds surrounding the encampment better than Longbourn's gardens. Was it selfish and wrong to wish he might take notice of that as well? Usually he was far more considerate.

A sign of his anxiety, no doubt.

"Feigning interest in joining up was a brilliant excuse, to be sure." Uncle smirked, just a little.

"So will be the bout of gout I will claim when this whole affair is put to rest. I suppose it was far too much to expect that the egg would be so easily recovered." Papa sipped his willow bark tea.

"Rustle is convinced the egg is no longer with the militia company." Elizabeth slid into her seat.

"All we know is that it had contact with those—ah—free-trade goods within the past fortnight." Papa set aside his paper. "That is not to say it is no longer in the vicinity. Perhaps we should resume the search of the countryside. Concealment deeper underground could cover the scent. I cannot help but think some hiding place has been overlooked."

"We have no way of knowing at what point the egg may have come into contact with the militia or where it might have parted company with them—if, as your father suggests it even did so. We have so little to go on, I am afraid that we are in even a worse situation than we were before. Closer to the hatching, but no closer to finding it," Uncle said.

"I spoke with Walker—"

"I have no very good opinion of Mr. Darcy. Why are you communicating with his companion?" Papa drummed his fingers on the table.

"Hear her out. She does not deserve your spleen." Uncle offered her a conciliatory look.

Papa smiled tightly. "You are right, of course. Forgive me, Elizabeth, I do not mean to denigrate your efforts in this matter. Pray, what did the fine cockatrice have to say?"

"Walker was certain the contact had been within a fortnight, perhaps coinciding with the regiment separating into its two divisions. He and Mr. Darcy have gone to Ware to see if it might be with the other division."

Papa huffed and chewed his lip. "And why have you not mentioned this to me sooner?"

"Because," Uncle leaned forward on his elbows, "you have been consumed with searching every nook and cranny of the encampment here. You have not had dinner at home this last se'nnight, dining with the officers instead. Nor have you been accessible for a conversation. We should be glad that Darcy is following up another lead, particularly in light of our lack of success."

"Darcy is the last person we need finding that egg." Papa's lip curled.

"He is the egg's Keeper, Papa." Elizabeth kept her eyes on the tablecloth.

"One clearly not worthy of the name or the task. I have been studying the histories and this situation is ripe for disaster even if he finds the egg. The dragonet can hear all the talk around it and will know what has happened—and resent Darcy for it. I say it is best to see him replaced now, before the only alternative is to allow the dragon to eat him and choose a replacement. Have you any idea what chaos that would cause?"

Elizabeth gulped. "That has not happened in nearly five hundred years. Such things do not happen anymore. Dissatisfied dragons hibernate—"

Papa rapped the table with his knuckles. "It has not happened because the Blue Order has been careful to keep watch on Keepers and dragons and intervenes before the situation escalates to such extremes. But I fear the Order itself is now tainted—"

"Just because Darcy's uncle is head of the Order does not mean that there is favoritism about." Uncle sipped his coffee. "I like to think most of us realize that maintaining peace and order between our species far outweighs the ties of family."

"One would like to think so, but stupider decisions have been made. I cannot take it lightly when such a threat to the Pendragon Treaty looms so close. If one dragon turns on its Keeper, even with sound reason, a dangerous precedent is set."

"Could it really erupt into full dragon war?" Elizabeth whispered.

"Perhaps not if Pemberley replaced its Keeper. Such an event might be managed. But if the egg is not found before hatching? What choice is there but to hunt it down before it can ravage the countryside? And if man kills dragonkind—"

"But it cannot come to that. Surely it would not be good for the dragons either, they would act—"

"They are loath to kill their own, especially a royal dragon. Perhaps they would step in somehow, but even that would not be without consequences more far-reaching than I want to consider. Remember the Pendragon Treaty keeps peace between the various strains of dragonkind as much as between our species. Should a wyvern or a wyrm kill a wild-hatched firedrake, war between those species might ensue."

"Even if it were necessary to preserve the treaty?" She swallowed hard, hands clasped tightly in her lap.

"When so few major-dragons are born, the unnatural death of any of them has the potential to trigger war."

Uncle dabbed his face with his napkin and served himself from the platters. "There, there, it is not useful to dwell on such negatives. We must focus on the positive. We have at least three, possibly up to seven more weeks in which to act. I feel certain—"

Chattering voices in the hall silenced their conversation. The door swung open and Mama, Kitty and Lydia bounded in. Jane and Mary followed.

"Aunt Gardiner asked me to say she was still helping the children with their breakfast in the nursery, and that she will be down later." Jane slid into her place beside Elizabeth.

"I am surprised you have joined us, Mary." Mama accepted Papa's assistance into her chair. "You and sister Gardiner seem to spend all your time with the children—and those birds of yours. If I did not have reason to think otherwise, I would be convinced that it is more the birds than the children you wish to keep company with."

"Oh Mama, what a terrible thing to say." Jane pouted just a little.

"Oh just as well," Mama waved her napkin as she tucked it into her lap. "At least it has kept Elizabeth's little bird out of mischief, has it not? Perhaps you might consider offering it to your Aunt and Uncle when they return to London. Mary, you too. I think it would be—"

"No." Elizabeth, Mary, Papa and Uncle declared simultaneously.

Mama jumped. "Very well then, as you will." She rang the bell for Hill to bring tea. "So then, Lydia,

Kitty, you were in town yesterday?"

"Indeed we were, Mama," Lydia bounced in her chair, cheeks and eyes bright. "We sat with Aunt Phillips for a full hour, I dare say. There was so much to talk about!"

Kitty leaned into Lydia's shoulder, and they giggled, "So many officers!"

"We have learned ever so much of them." Lydia bit her lip, but grinned anyway.

"Have you now?" Papa leaned back in his chair. "Do tell what sort of intelligence have you managed to unearth?"

What was Papa about? He never attended to Lydia and Kitty.

Kitty and Lydia tittered.

"Go on, girls, do answer him. Your father is interested, and he must be satisfied." Mama sat up a little straighter in her chair. Did she think Papa had suddenly come around to her way of thinking?

Mary looked aside and rolled her eyes while Jane tried to smile pleasantly. They had not missed Papa's behavior. Apparently they did not like the way he subtly mocked Mama any more than Elizabeth did.

"Well, we have learned all the names of the officers quartered in Meryton. Colonel Forster, you know of course, he has gone off now, to be married. He will be back very soon though, and has invited us to call upon his new wife." Lydia ticked off the point on her finger.

Half an hour later, they were still hearing the details of the names and lodgings of the officers of the regiment's Meryton division. Papa and Uncle listened intently. They probably would have been taking notes if it would not have aroused Mama's curiosity.

"And that is all you have learned?" Papa buttered a

bun and scooped on a spoonful of jam. Did he notice it was blackberry jam—the kind he detested with all the little seeds?

"Oh, hardly!" Kitty bumped shoulders with Lydia, and they dissolved into another fit of giggling.

"Before he left, Colonel Forster said that he expected another several wagons full of supplies to be coming in soon, just after he was set to return with his bride." Lydia batted her eyes.

"He says those supplies will keep his men well fed and happy for the next several months. I don't suppose it is more than a load of food and grog—" Kitty added.

"But he did say it would allow him to throw a ball, just like the regiment should."

"No, it was not the supplies, you feather-pate, it was who was in charge of the supplies." Kitty wagged her finger at Lydia.

"Oh, well, I suppose you are right. He said that there were three more officers with those supplies—"

"Did he say why they were not with him now?" An impatient edge tinged Papa's voice.

Lydia stopped and looked up at the ceiling, brow knotted. "Do you remember if he said? I surely do not."

"He said something about the wagons needing repair or some such, I think. They broke wheels, or axels, or something like that perhaps, and had to remain behind for repairs. But that is of little matter. The important thing is that there shall be more officers, very soon!" Kitty grasped Lydia's hands. "Oooh! Officers!"

"There now girls, that is a very good thing. I think we must plan some sort of party to welcome them into the neighborhood." Mama rose as Hill trundled in with the tea things. "A tea party may be just the thing."

"I cannot imagine they would enjoy something like that, Mama." Lydia harrumphed. "A dinner party would be much better, for we know men like to eat."

"Lydia is right." Kitty nodded vigorously. "You are known for the fine dinners you host. Perhaps you would be willing to invite Mr. Bingley and his party, too!"

"Oooh! Mr. Bingley!" Lydia squealed. "That would make Jane very happy, I suppose."

Jane gasped and blushed.

Mama happily picked up the topic, though, and waxed on about Mr. Bingley's suitability and wealth for several long, very long, minutes. Lydia and Kitty chittered like fairy dragon chicks, agreeing and adding to everything she said.

Papa leaned back in his chair, grumbling under his breath. "From all that I can collect by your manner of talking, you must be two of the silliest girls in the country. I have suspected it for some time, but I am now convinced."

There was the old Papa back.

Kitty stopped mid-sentence and appeared entirely disconcerted, but made no answer to him. Lydia chattered on with perfect indifference expressing her admiration of Captain Carter, and her hopes of seeing him when they went to Meryton later in the day, as he was going the next morning to London.

Mama was prevented replying by Hill's entrance. "A note just come for Miss Bennet, and the servant what delivered it is instructed to wait for an answer." Hill trundled the note over to Jane.

"Well, Jane, who is it from? What is it about? What does he say? Well, Jane, make haste and tell us; make haste, my love." Mama all but bounced in her seat.

Jane unfolded it with the same care she took with all things. "It is from Miss Bingley, she says:

"My dear Friend,

"If you are not so compassionate as to dine to-day with Louisa and me, we shall be in danger of hating each other for the rest of our lives, for a whole day's tête-à-tête between two women can never end without a quarrel. Come as soon as you can on the receipt of this. My brother and the gentlemen are to dine with the officers. Yours ever, Caroline Bingley."

"With the officers! I wonder Aunt Phillips did not tell us of that." Lydia parked her elbows on the table, her lips screwed into a pout.

"The gentlemen are dining out? That is very un-lucky." Mama looked toward the ceiling, chewing her lower lip.

No, that was her thinking face. It never boded well.

"Can I have the carriage?" Jane asked.

Mama waved her finger at Jane. "No, my dear, you had better go on horseback, because it seems likely to rain. Then you must stay all night. That will give you opportunity to see Mr. Bingley in the morning."

"That would be a good scheme, if you were sure that they would not offer to send her home." Elizabeth pressed her temples hard.

Poor Jane.

"The gentlemen will have Mr. Bingley's chaise to go to Meryton. They cannot send her home."

"Pray, Mama, I had much rather go in the coach."

Mama smiled far too sweetly. "But, my dear, your father cannot spare the horses, I am sure. They are wanted in the farm, Mr. Bennet, are not they?"

"They are wanted in the farm much oftener than I

can get them." What was that odd glint in Papa's eye?

"If that is the case, surely you can spare them once more." Elizabeth glanced at Jane.

"No, Lizzy, I am afraid your mother is entirely correct. I cannot spare the horses. Jane, you must decide if the weather warrants you staying home or taking a risk and riding horseback."

Jane glanced out of the window. She did not wear her disappointment well. "I cannot decline their kind offer, so I suppose it would be good to have the horse readied."

"I will see to it. Elizabeth, come with me, I have a letter I need you to write for me." He rose, and she followed him to his study.

Once inside and behind closed doors she turned to him, "Pray allow Jane the carriage, Papa. I fear if she gets caught in the rain she might become ill again. You recall what happened last winter."

"I do, child, and I am heartily sorry for this, but with the intelligence your sisters have brought us, this situation has just taken a turn in our favor. We cannot miss any advantage we can take."

"I do not understand."

"There are additional men and supplies set to arrive at the regiment, soon. Given what your sisters described and what Darcy's cockatrice reports, it appears they were separated from the main body at about the right time for them to still have the egg with them. I require you go to Netherfield Park and stay with your sister."

"Forgive me, sir, but you are not making any sense at all. I was not invited. How am I to join Jane there?" Best not add that she had no desire to spend time in the company of the superior sisters. "I do not understand, what has Netherfield to do with any of this?"

"I had not recalled until just now, but two generations ago, the owner of Netherfield was something of an eccentric." Papa shuffled to his bookshelf and scanned the volumes. "There, on the third shelf from the top, the green volume."

Elizabeth hauled the library ladder to the shelf and retrieved the dusty, oversized volume. Papa shoved piles on the desk to make space and opened it to a fantastically detailed—and accurate—map of Longbourn estate, even including Longbourn's cavern!

"Netherfield's old master had a passion for cartography. He did this one of our estate, without permission, but Longbourn knew and persuaded him to feel guilty enough to gift it to my great grandfather along with detailed descriptions of our holdings. He had a remarkable eye for detail."

"You think there are more maps like this one?"

"Great-grandfather once mentioned the man was obsessed with his maps and spent much of his life making comprehensive maps of all the hillsides and caverns between here and Ware. It is likely that any hiding place the smugglers may use will be on those maps. They could help us determine where the egg might still be hidden or where it might yet be hidden if it arrives with the supplies."

Elizabeth bit her tongue. It would have been nice to have known about those a se'nnight ago. They might have enlisted Mr. Darcy's help—no, Papa would hardly have condoned that. Still, whilst it might not have been pleasant to work with Mr. Darcy, it might have improved their chances at success. As it was, Papa's protracted resentment could undermine their efforts.

"And how precisely am I to get to Netherfield, much less manage to search potentially every room in the manor, known and unknown for maps made two generations ago?" For all they knew, there could be some sort of secret chamber—

"I will have Gardiner send Rustle to Netherfield to convince Jane she has come down with a serious cold and her hostesses that she is far too ill to come home. Dutiful sister that you are, you will go to attend her and be invited to stay throughout the duration of her illness. Bring April with you. She can assist you in your search. Though not as convincing as Rustle, she will no doubt be able to assist with any necessary persuasions."

"There is so much duplicity in this, Papa. Would it not be far better to inform Mr. Darcy of the situation and recruit his assistance?"

"He is not even at Netherfield now according to your report, so it is a moot point. Even if he does return whilst you are there, there is no need for you to discuss your errand with him."

"I hardly agree—"

"Lizzy, do not interfere in business you do not understand. It is times like these that I question the Order's willingness to involve women in such weighty matters."

Why did he not just slap her in the face? It would be far kinder. Granted, allowances should—must—be made for the desperateness of the situation, but still, it would be far better should he keep such opinions to himself.

7
Chapter

As expected, rain—dreary, drenching November rains—began shortly after Jane left the house and continued throughout the evening and well into the night. Somehow, the clouds exhausted themselves before morning, and the sun made its regular appearance at dawn.

Whilst the family was still assembled in the morning room, Hill delivered Elizabeth a note from Netherfield.

"I am sure it is from Jane." Mama nearly trembled with excitement. "I can hardly wait to hear of her success. Read it aloud for us, Lizzy."

It would not do to roll her eyes, so Elizabeth unfolded the note and cleared her throat. "She writes: My dearest Lizzy, I find myself very unwell this morning, which, I suppose, is to be imputed to my getting wet through yesterday. My kind friends will not hear of my returning home till I am better. They insist also on my seeing Mr. Jones—therefore do not be alarmed if you should hear of his having been to see me. Excepting a sore throat and headache, there is not much the matter with me."

No, there was probably nothing the matter with her at all, save draconic influence.

"Well, my dear," Papa removed his napkin from his collar and set it aside. "If your daughter should have a dangerous fit of illness, if she should die, it would be a comfort to know that it was all in pursuit of Mr. Bingley, and under your orders."

It was quite unfair of him to tease her so when it was all his doing in the first place.

Mama waved him off. "Oh! I am not at all afraid of her dying. People do not die of little trifling colds. She will be taken good care of. As long as she stays there, it is all very well. I would go and see her, if I could have the carriage."

Papa raised an eyebrow at Elizabeth.

"I am sure the horses are still wanted on the farm, Mama. I shall go to her for I am quite willing to walk to Netherfield." She could not bring herself to meet Mama's gaze.

"How can you be so silly as to think of such a thing, in all this dirt! You will not be fit to be seen when you get there."

"I shall be very fit to see Jane—which is all I want. The distance is nothing, when one has a motive; only three miles."

"Oh very well, if you must. You are a very stubborn girl. Be certain you pay all proper civilities to Miss Bingley and Mrs. Hurst. If all goes as I plan, they shall be your sister's sisters and in a way to set you in the paths of rich young men."

Elizabeth rose, carefully avoiding both her parents' eyes. "I shall keep that in mind, Mama."

Mary followed Elizabeth out, Heather half hidden in the knot of hair pinned low over her neck. It was a most becoming—and convenient—style for them both.

"How long do you think you will be gone?" Mary grasped the banister and started up the stairs.

"If it were up to me, I would be home by dinner, but I cannot imagine Netherfield will give up its secrets so easily. I may be away for several days."

"But Longbourn will—"

Elizabeth laid her hand on Mary's shoulder. "I know. Longbourn gets cranky when I am away. You must step in and tend him while I am at Netherfield. Explain to him the nature of my errand and that Papa requires it—oh, and bring the pot of oil I have in my closet and the stiff brush. A sound application of both will leave him quite content. He has told me he likes the way you scratch."

Mary chuckled. "He does enjoy that. But Heather—"

"He promised not to interfere with her when I introduced them. You may remind him of that if he seems to have forgotten."

Heather peeked at Elizabeth and cheeped.

"I know Longbourn is frightening, little one." Elizabeth stroked the top of her head with a fingertip. "But he is fiercely protective of his Keep, and you are part of that now. He may bluster, but that is merely draconic pride, to which he has a right as Laird of this Keep. Treat him with respect. If you pick the scale mites from his brow ridges, he might even share his mutton with you."

"I don't like mutton." Heather snorted.

"Of course you don't. But you do like beetles, and there are plenty in his cavern. He does not like the scratchy noises they make. I am sure you may eat as many of those as you wish, and he will welcome it." Elizabeth scratched under Heather's chin.

"I want to see Longbourn." Heather rubbed her head along Mary's ear.

"You see, the problem is solved."

"You make it seem far too simple." Mary tilted her head to cuddle Heather.

"And you make it far too complicated. You and Longbourn will get on fine. Invite Rumblkins with you as well. Phoenix too, if Aunt will part with him. It is good for all the dragons of a Keep to enjoy society together."

"I have never seen that in the Order's instructions."

"Those tomes are useful, to be sure, but not exhaustive. I have written a great deal down in my own commonplace book. You may peruse it whilst I am gone if you wish." Elizabeth beckoned Mary into her room and closed the door behind them.

She unlocked a drawer in her bedside table with a key on her chatelaine and withdrew a thick, blue bound journal.

"Here. On this page is a list of Longbourn's favorite things—and what he hates most. A recipe for his favorite scale oil. How to make a proper scale brush. Many bits and bobs I have observed. Take it, see if there is anything you might find helpful."

Mary clutched it to her chest. "This is amazing! Something useful at last. The Order's books with all their histories and genealogies and territory maps have hardly a practical insight from beginning to end."

"That is because they were written by men, my dear, upon whom the government of men places the authority of law. So that is what they write about. However, Providence has put us in the place to care for hides and hearts. So we must keep our own books."

"Might I share this with Aunt Gardiner?"

"Of course. April has taught me so much. There are pages and pages of my ramblings about fairy dragons there, too."

Mary hugged her hard. "You are truly the best of sisters."

A quarter of an hour later, she left the house, April hiding in the hood of her cloak. Best avoid the discussion of whether her 'pet' ought to accompany her on a visit.

The recent ugly weather made the usually pleasant walk a soggy slog through puddles and fields that more resembled swamp rather than meadow. When at last Netherfield rose before her, her half-boots were soaked, her stockings and hems laden with mud and her barely-recovered ankles aching and sore.

And cold.

Though the day was reasonably warm for November, the mud and puddles were uniformly cold and just simply miserable.

Nicholls, the housekeeper, showed her into the breakfast-parlor, where all but Jane were assembled, and where her appearance created a great deal of surprise. Somehow, that she should have walked three miles so early in the day, in such dirty weather, and by herself, was incredible to Mrs. Hurst and Miss Bingley. April disapproved of them whole-heartedly and began softly convincing them of their concern for Jane and how very ill she was.

Mr. Bingley immediately gushed with solicitude toward Jane.

He was awfully susceptible to dragon persuasion, just as Papa had thought. At least it might work in her favor now. She would worry about the other implications later

Mr. Darcy—when had he arrived back from Ware?—watched the entire conversation without comment himself. He looked away when she met his eye, probably embarrassed that she had caught him staring at her hood, listening to April's determined discourse.

No doubt he would inquire about that later. What was she to tell him? Papa's plans did not consider the possibility of his presence here. Even if she told him nothing, Walker would have it out of April in a trice. Then what?

Miss Bingley showed her to Jane's room. The poor dear had slept ill and was very feverish. Certainly not well enough to leave her room, or so Miss Bingley said, and left her to her sister.

Jane looked very ill indeed, but a hand to her forehead confirmed the fever only a draconic persuasion. Jane's relief at her arrival only deepened the creeping guilt that one entirely unaware of the situation at hand should have to suffer so for it, even if the sufferings were effectively imagined.

At least she could suffer in comfort. The guest room was well appointed with sumptuous bed linens and feminine paper hangings. A generous fire crackled in the fireplace. Her hostess was certainly sparing no expense for her comfort.

Not long after, Mr. Jones the apothecary came. About that time, Rustle perched on the railing just outside Jane's window. He and April whispered constantly, and the apothecary agreed that Jane had caught a violent cold, and promised her some draughts.

After Mr. Jones left, Jane's feverish symptoms increased, and her head ached acutely, solidifying Elizabeth's resolve to make quick work of her errand here. Even imaginary suffering was unpleasant.

The Bingley sisters called upon Jane and sat with them for some time, quickly succumbing to Rustle's suggestion that they invite Elizabeth to stay and attend to Jane.

A servant was dispatched to Longbourn to acquaint the family with her stay, and bring back a supply of clothes. All was settled exactly as Papa had wished for.

That, of course, was the easy part.

Darcy dismissed his valet and stared in the mirror. Starched white cravat at a time like this? He had far more important business to be about than dining with Bingley and his houseguests. But without daylight, he could hardly be off and about looking for anything. Besides, where would he look? He and Walker had investigated everything that smelled of egg. Now they were reduced to aimless wanderings in hope of finding a potential hiding place.

What were Miss Elizabeth and that flying blue flutterbob doing here, convincing everyone her sister was far too ill to be moved?

Walker flew in through the open window and landed on the edge of the dressing table, assiduously avoiding the unstable mirror.

"Have you ascertained what Miss Elizabeth and her

dragon entourage are doing here?" He buttoned his waistcoat.

"I do not like this, not at all. She is keeping the fairy dragon very close to herself—away from me. I have not been able to talk to her at all. I have already promised them both that no harm will come to the tuft-of-fluff from me. There is no reason at all for them to avoid me." Walker preened the edge of his wing.

"And what of the cockatrice?"

"He had little more to say, only something about her father and the Blue Order—oh, and he does not much like you." A loose feather drifted to the floor.

The cockatrice or Bennet? Probably both.

"I will keep that in mind, thank you ever so much. But that is of no help. Could you truly get no more information out of him?"

"Bennet wants his daughter here for some reason that probably has to do with the egg. But more I cannot say. You will have to talk to her yourself."

"You know I cannot do that." Darcy tugged his cuffs to show just below his jacket sleeves.

"More like you will not. You well know you can do nearly anything you want—at least anything I am willing to help cover for you. Tell her what happened at Ware. That should dispose her to share her secrets with you. You need her help."

"You said that at the militia camp, and I dare say it all came to naught." Darcy turned his back and wandered toward the open window.

"Hardly naught. You learned a great deal in the time you spent searching with her."

"Nothing that I have not heard before."

Walker launched himself toward the window and landed on the sill. "Reading it in the tomes of the Order is not the same as hearing it from someone who has experienced it firsthand."

"She keeps a wyvern, not a firedrake. And a most peculiar one at that. How does her experience apply? Not at all. Merely amusing anecdotes to pass the time. Nothing I would call a worthy education in dragon keeping."

"She is pretty, and you like to look at her."

"What has that to do with any of this?" Darcy clutched his temples. Walker was truly annoying—and right—which made him all the more annoying.

"I like her."

"So much the better for you. Why do you not ask her what she is about? With your great affinity towards each other, I feel certain she would tell you."

"That is a good idea. I will." Walker chirruped and flew off.

Headstrong creature.

Perhaps he would be able to extract the puzzling truth from her and save Darcy the effort. It was not as if dinner or drawing room conversation would allow him much useful discourse with her in any case.

Dinner was a dreary affair with solicitude toward the absent Miss Bennet taking up the better part of the conversation. While Bingley sounded sincere, his sisters swung from fawning to indifferent, depending on whether the little fairy dragon was whispering from her perch behind the curtains or not.

After dinner, Miss Elizabeth returned to her sister rather than accompany them to the drawing room, ending any opportunity to ask her anything directly.

The drawing room furnishings and appointments were what were to be expected of a country house of this magnitude, showing enough taste to be comfortable, but not nearly so much as to be in any way personal. A large fire crackled on one side of the drawing room. A great many candles brought light to the rest of the room. More than truly necessary. Miss Bingley was no doubt making a demonstration, probably for his benefit.

Darcy settled into a marginally comfortable chair near a table bearing a few books.

Miss Bingley perched on the overstuffed settee across from him. "I cannot say that I am disappointed in the loss of Miss Elizabeth's company. Her manners are quite intolerable, a mixture of pride and impertinence. She has no conversation, no style, no taste, no beauty. She has nothing, in short, to recommend her, but being an excellent walker. I shall never forget her appearance this morning. She really looked almost wild. Why must she be scampering about the country, because her sister had a cold? Her hair so untidy, so blowsy!"

"Yes and her petticoat. I hope you saw her petticoat, six inches deep in mud, I am absolutely certain." Mrs. Hurst raised her eyebrow, the corners of her lips crooking just so.

Bingley drew a chair near his sisters. "Your picture may be very exact, Louisa, but I thought Miss Elizabeth looked remarkably well, when she came into the room this morning. Her dirty petticoat quite escaped my notice."

"You observed it, Mr. Darcy, I am sure." Miss Bingley turned to him with a far too familiar gaze.

He dodged it before she could meet his eyes.

"I am inclined to think that you would not wish to see your sister make such an exhibition."

"Certainly not."

"To walk three miles, or four miles, or five miles, or whatever it is, quite alone! What could she mean by it? It seems to me to show an abominable sort of conceited independence, a most country-town indifference to decorum." Mrs. Hurst played with her bracelets.

"It shows an affection for her sister that is very pleasing," Bingley said.

Miss Bingley batted her eyes. "I am afraid, Mr. Darcy, that this adventure has rather affected your admiration of her fine eyes."

"Not at all, they were brightened by the exercise." Darcy rose and paced the length of the room.

Silence descended.

Perhaps that would be the end of—

"I have an excessive regard for Jane Bennet." Miss Bingley wandered to the fireplace, close to his walking path. "She is really a very sweet girl, and I wish with all my heart she were well settled. But with such a father and mother, and such low connections, I am afraid there is no chance of it."

"I think I have heard you say, that their uncle is an attorney in Meryton," Mrs. Hurst said, almost as if they had rehearsed the conversation.

"Yes, and they have another, who lives somewhere near Cheapside."

The sisters laughed heartily, the same high pitched, tittering laughter that hinted of a little too much wine at dinner and a bit too little good sense at other times.

"If they had uncles enough to fill all Cheapside, it would not make them one jot less agreeable." Bingley slapped the arm of his chair as if that settled the veracity of his point.

"But it must very materially lessen their chance of marrying men of any consideration in the world." Darcy clasped his hands behind his back and continued pacing.

Silence again.

"Cards, anyone?" Bingley waved at Hurst to help him set up the card table.

Half an hour later, with everyone playing at loo, Miss Elizabeth entered the drawing room.

"Pray join us, Miss Elizabeth." Bingley rose and reached for another chair.

"Thank you for the invitation, but I may need to return to my sister should she call for me. I would not want to disrupt the game, so I shall amuse myself with a book."

Mr. Hurst looked at her wide-eyed. "Do you prefer reading to cards? That is rather singular."

"Miss Eliza Bennet despises cards. She is a great reader and has no pleasure in anything else." Miss Bingley laughed, but it had a bit of an edge.

"I deserve neither such praise nor such censure. I am not a great reader, and I have pleasure in many things."

"In nursing your sister, I am sure you have pleasure. I hope it will soon be increased by seeing her quite well." Bingley returned to his seat.

"You are very gracious, sir. Thank you." Miss Elizabeth walked towards the table with the only books in the room.

"If you do not find any of these to your liking, pray help yourself to any you find in the house. Netherfield seems to be filled with books. There is a dedicated library upstairs, Nicholls will show you if you wish. But there are books in nearly every sitting room, parlor, and closet. I dare say, if they were all collected together in a single place, the collection might be rather considerable."

Miss Elizabeth's countenance brightened, far more than might be explained by being a great lover of books.

"What a delightful library you have at Pemberley, Darcy!" Bingley said.

"Speaking of Pemberley," Miss Bingley leaned forward, a little too much, "is Miss Darcy much grown since the spring? Will she be as tall as I am? How I long to see her again! I never met with anybody who delighted me so much. Such a countenance, such manners, and so extremely accomplished for her age! Her performance on the pianoforte is exquisite."

"It is amazing to me how young ladies can have patience to be so very accomplished as they all are." Bingley shook his head and chuckled. "They all paint tables, cover screens, and net purses. I am sure I never heard a young lady spoken of for the first time, without being informed that she was very accomplished."

"The word is applied to many a woman who deserves it no otherwise than by netting a purse, or covering a screen. But I am very far from agreeing with you in your estimation of ladies in general. I cannot boast of knowing more than half a dozen, in the whole range of my acquaintance, that are really accomplished." Darcy glanced at Miss Elizabeth.

She cocked her head, and her eyebrow rose as if to meet his challenge.

"Nor I, I am sure," said Miss Bingley.

"You must comprehend a great deal in your idea of an accomplished woman." Miss Elizabeth stared directly at Miss Bingley.

The air between them crackled with electric tension.

"I do comprehend a great deal in it. A woman must have a thorough knowledge of music, singing, drawing, dancing, and the modern languages, to deserve the word. Besides all this, she must possess a certain something in her air and manner of walking, the tone of her voice, her address and expressions, or the word will be but half deserved." Miss Bingley folded her hands on the table before her. Everything in her countenance suggested she believed the air, manner of walking, address and expression of her current company sorely lacking.

Miss Elizabeth drew breath to speak, but Darcy cut her off. "All this she must possess, and yet she must add something more substantial, in the improvement of her mind by extensive reading."

"I am no longer surprised at your knowing only six accomplished women. I rather wonder now at your knowing any." Miss Elizabeth turned to Bingley and curtsied. "Thank you for welcoming me into your libraries, sir. I believe I shall go and select something now and return to my sister. Good night."

They watched her leave and shut the door behind her.

Too bad he could not go after her. A book would be far better company than Bingley's superior sisters.

"Eliza Bennet is one of those young ladies who seek to recommend themselves to the other sex by undervaluing their own, and with many men, I dare say, it succeeds. But, in my opinion, it is a paltry device, a very mean art," Miss Bingley muttered and fanned the cards in her hand.

Darcy cleared his throat. "Undoubtedly, there is

meanness in all the arts which ladies sometimes conde-
scend to employ for captivation. Whatever bears
affinity to cunning is despicable."

Miss Bingley stared at him blankly and batted her
eyes.

The next morning, shortly after breakfast, the Bennets—or rather the female Bennets—descended upon
Netherfield like some sort of plague. No doubt the
apothecary would follow soon behind them.

No, that was ungracious and beneath him. But only
a little.

As soon as their carriage rolled up, Walker took to
his wings and disappeared. If only Darcy had the same
liberty. As it was, the Bennets were ushered into the
narrow breakfast parlor, after they first saw to Miss
Bennet, giving him nary an opportunity to escape.

"My dear Mrs. Bennet." Bingley rose and bowed.
"How do you find Miss Bennet this morning? I hope
she is not worse than you expected."

Miss Elizabeth helped her mother to sit down, just
two places from Darcy. How very thoughtful of her.

The breakfast parlor was definitely too small to accommodate so many people—so many ladies, all
talking at the same time. All the places at the oblong
table were taken, and surely all the oxygen in the room
must be used up with so many words flying so fast.

"Indeed I have, sir. She is a great deal too ill to be
moved. Mr. Jones says we must not think of moving
her. We must trespass a little longer on your kindness."

No, it is not time for her to go. She must not be removed.

What? Darcy cast about the room. The little blue
fairy dragon perched on the top of the floor-to-ceiling
curtains, hiding in their folds.

Why was that little featherpate involved? What manner of trickery was this? He glowered.

Talk to her, she will make you understand. It is necessary.

Darcy huffed and frowned.

This is not about your dragon-deaf friend. It is for Pemberley.

Pemberley? Darcy squeezed his eyes shut and pressed them with thumb and forefinger. What was Miss Elizabeth playing at?

"Removed! It must not be thought of. My sister, I am sure, will not hear of her removal." Bingley waved his hand for emphasis. He was such a gudgeon—especially when dragons were involved.

"You may depend upon it, Madam." Miss Bingley sat up a little straighter, her tone as cold as the morning's mid-November frost. "Miss Bennet shall receive every possible attention while she remains with us."

Mrs. Bennet made a show of dabbing her eyes with her handkerchief. "I am sure, if it was not for such good friends I do not know what would become of her, for she is very ill indeed, and suffers a vast deal, though with the greatest patience in the world—which is always the way with her, for she has, without exception, the sweetest temper I ever met with. I often tell my other girls they are nothing to her. You have a sweet room here, Mr. Bingley, and a charming prospect over that gravel walk. I do not know a place in the country that is equal to Netherfield. You will not think of quitting it in a hurry, I hope, though you have but a short lease."

How quickly the topic turned when the fairy dragon stopped her whispering. Did that Bennet woman ever stop for breath?

Bingley laughed. "Whatever I do is done in a hurry, and therefore if I should resolve to quit Netherfield, I should probably be off in five minutes. At present, however, I consider myself as quite fixed here."

Miss Bingley rolled her eyes. She was right, this woman bordered on insufferable—nothing like either of the eldest daughters.

"I cannot see that London has any great advantage over the country for my part, except the shops and public places. The country is a vast deal pleasanter, is not it, Mr. Bingley?"

"When I am in the country, I never wish to leave it. And when I am in town it is pretty much the same. They have each their advantages, and I can be equally happy in either."

Netherfield ball.

What was that consarned fluffbit whispering about now?

"You know, Mr. Bingley," the youngest Bennet girl—was it Lydia?—batted her eyes, "those four and twenty families we dine with are frightfully bored right now. And you did promise a ball. Do you recall? It would be a shameful thing indeed if you failed to keep your promise."

Bingley's forehead knit as he took on a faraway look.

"A ball, you say?" Miss Bingley asked. "I can honestly say this is the first I have heard of such a thing."

Not it is not. It has been discussed for quite some time now— since you took the lease.

Bingley's brow knotted. "I recall now, yes, indeed I do. I am perfectly ready, I assure you, to keep my engagement, and when your sister is recovered, you shall, if you please, name the very day of the ball. You surely would not wish to be dancing while she is ill."

Lydia clapped softly. "Oh, yes! It would be much

better to wait till Jane was well, and by that time most likely Captain Carter would be at Meryton again. And when you have given your ball, I shall insist on their giving one also. I shall tell Colonel Forster it will be quite a shame if he does not."

"Two balls this season, what great fun is that!" The other younger sister bumped her shoulder to Lydia's.

What was the girl's name?

"Indeed you are correct, Kitty. Is he not a fine example of true gentleman-like behavior?"

Miss Elizabeth cringed. Who could blame her?

With one further round of effusions of thanks for their care of her eldest daughter, Mrs. Bennet and her younger daughters departed. Miss Elizabeth escorted them out, the fairy dragon discreetly departing with them.

Neither returned to the breakfast parlor. No doubt she was mortified at her family's display. Any rational creature would be.

The Bingley sisters did not hesitate to offer their own observations, all at Miss Elizabeth's and Miss Bennet's expense. Darcy excused himself. There were questions he needed answered, and those answers would not be found in the breakfast parlor.

Where would she be? He stalked to the front hall and listened for female voices.

"She is upstairs in the small library on the sunrise side of the house." The fairy dragon hovered just in front of his face.

He jumped back. "You are aware that is a most annoying habit …"

"April, my name is April. It would serve you well to remember it, if we are to work together."

"And why precisely will we be working together?"

She zoomed closer and nipped his ear.

Darcy shooed her away. "I will not have that. Stop it at once."

"Then you might want to stop saying very stupid things indeed." She buzzed back and forth in front of him. "Well, get on with you, upstairs now. There is no one else with her. You will be able to talk freely."

She took off toward the stairs. Darcy jogged along after her.

"Why are you convincing the house—"

"She will explain it all. This way."

Darcy grumbled under his breath, but she was right. Miss Elizabeth would provide much quicker answers. It might take hours to get a straight story out of a fairy dragon.

She led him to a smallish room in the public wing of the first floor, near the guest rooms. With east-facing windows, it was still dim and cool with morning light. Bookcases lined three walls and comfortable chairs for reading clustered near the center of the room.

What a delightful place to retreat. Why had Bingley not shown him this room sooner? It would certainly have made his evenings here more pleasant.

Miss Elizabeth stood three rungs up on the library ladder, scanning the topmost shelves of the little library.

"I have brought him." April flew up to Miss Elizabeth.

"Oh, very well, I suppose you are right. Pray excuse me a moment, Mr. Darcy." She picked her way down the ladder and approached him.

"Are you going to explain that fairy dragon's performance this morning?" Darcy folded his arms over his chest.

Miss Elizabeth shrugged and took a seat near the book shelves. She gestured for him to do likewise. "Will you not tell me of your trip to Ware?"

They stared at one another.

The clock chimed.

April chirruped and scolded, flying from one to the other, nipping both their ears.

Darcy yelped and grabbed the side of his head. "Where did she acquire such an appalling habit?"

"Longbourn taught her."

Darcy clutched his forehead and groaned.

"It seems we are both in possession of information the other needs. Though my father does not agree, it seems in the best interest of the Order for us to work together in this instance."

"Am I to understand your father—"

"Is not privy to this conversation. In this case, he is my problem, not yours. Let us put the dragons' interest above our own. I assume that your trip to Ware was not as profitable as you hoped?"

"No, it was not. Clearly the egg has not been recovered." He drummed his fingers along his arm.

"But you have returned here, which implies—"

"Yes, I still believe the egg might arrive here. There are several wagons of supplies—"

"That are yet on their way here. We have come by the same information, sir." She met his gaze with a steady confidence few men possessed.

"But that does not explain why you are inserting your presence at Netherfield."

"My father is not convinced we have done all that is possible to find the egg. He thinks it is here already. But even if it is not, as we discovered, there are far more hiding places than we imagined. He recalled that the previous master of Netherfield was an amateur cartographer, obsessed with mapping every crevasse and cranny of the surrounding area. Papa believes that there are maps somewhere in the house that will point us directly to the most likely hiding places for the egg. I am here to find those maps."

Darcy leaned back in his chair and stared at the ceiling roses. "I must say, this is the first truly welcome news I have had in quite some time."

"If we find them."

"Did your father have any insight into where they might be found?"

"Sadly no, and it does not seem that Netherfield's last owner had a great penchant for organization. I have yet to find rhyme or reason behind the placement of anything here." She glanced at the bookshelves behind her.

Darcy threw up his hands. "Naturally."

"It is entirely possible that they are not even in a library—and, by the way, there are at least two other rooms with sufficient quantities of books to bear the name as well. It is as Mr. Bingley said last night, there are books strewn about in every room I have looked in. No doubt the rest of the house is similar. And there are closets, trunks, boxes and attics to be considered." She dropped her face into her hands.

"Can the fairy—that is, April—can she read human script?"

"I am right here, you may speak directly to me," she snipped.

Of course he should, that had been rude.

"Are you able?" he asked.

"I have never learnt."

"But could you identify maps?" He stalked toward the globe in the corner of the room. "Like this, but flat, spread on a single sheet of paper."

April landed on the globe and looked down on it. She hopped off and perched on the table and studied it. "I think I could."

"Perhaps, if you are willing, you and Walker might assist in the search. You could start in the bedrooms and closets and the like. Places it would be difficult for us to explain our presence. If you could simply identify those rooms that contain maps—"

"Yes, yes," Miss Elizabeth knelt beside the globe and looked into April's eyes. "That is a very good idea, as long as Walker will agree to help. She is far too small—"

Darcy rose and opened the nearest window. He unfastened his watch fob and raised it to his lips. The whistle was shrill and thin, something only dragons or those who heard them could detect.

Elizabeth covered her ears and winced.

She was right, it was a dreadful sound.

Walker swooped in and perched in the window frame. "Are they gone?"

"Yes, the callers have left."

"You mean my mother and sisters." She offered Walker a scratch. "It is all right, I know few dragons can tolerate them with equanimity."

Walker leaned into her hand, all but cooing.

Darcy scratched his head. He had almost become accustomed to Walker's odd ingratiating behavior whenever Miss Elizabeth was about. He explained their plan.

"Work with the flutterbob? The sky toned, fluffy-pate with nary a lick of sense—"

April shrieked and flew at him, yanking a feather from the top of his head. "You will stop your whining and do as you are asked. You proud, arrogant, unfeeling creature."

Darcy tensed to intervene. Walker might well injure or even kill the little dragon for her attack.

Miss Elizabeth gasped and covered her mouth with her hand.

Walker pulled his head back, turned it to the side and peered at her with a dragon version of a smile. He bobbed his head in a bow. "As you say Lairda April. We shall join our efforts in search of these maps."

April cheeped and her eyes glittered. She hovered very close to Walker and touched her cheek to his.

Darcy pinched the bridge of his nose. What game was Walker playing, applying a courtesy title to a fairy dragon?

Did it really matter until they found the egg?

Walker flew out of the window, whilst April zipped into the hall, in search of maids to persuade to open windows for him. Darcy left for the sitting room on the opposite side of the house, said to contain a considerable book collection.

At least Miss Elizabeth brought some useful occupation in her wake, far preferable to simply waiting about for the militia to arrive.

8
Chapter

Mr. Darcy's suggestion to involve the dragons in the search had been a good one. So good, it was embarrassing that Elizabeth had not come up with it herself. The Bingley sisters must be getting under her skin more than she realized. Jane's 'illness' still required Elizabeth's attendance; far too much of her time was spent keeping company with Jane and her hostesses.

April and Walker made a surprisingly good, if querulous team. Even their quarreling seemed more for sport, at least from Walker's side, than true animosity. Amidst all their bickering, they were effectively able to rule out a number of rooms that Elizabeth and Darcy would have had to otherwise search themselves.

Though Papa would not appreciate Mr. Darcy's interference—as he would call it—without it, she would hardly be able to search the manor in less than a se'nnight, probably more like a fortnight. Maddening as the man was, he was maniacally focused on whatever might help them locate Pemberley's egg. The energy he brought to the task was truly remarkable.

Dinner called a halt to their efforts, requiring them to dress and pretend they were merely guests thrown together largely by chance for an evening. At least she pretended. Mr. Darcy scarcely exerted the effort to be civil. He was nearly silent, bordering on taciturn throughout.

Odd, Mr. Bingley hardly seemed to take note. Could it be possible this was Mr. Darcy's normal mode in company?

How insupportable.

After dinner, she checked in on Jane, then joined the party in the drawing room.

Shortly after, a servant appeared with a letter for Mr. Darcy and two for her. Papa and Mary had written.

Thankfully, the loo table did not appear, allowing her to curl up in relative privacy with her missives. Little surprise that Papa would be inquiring about the success of her efforts. Aunt Gardiner had written it for him—how sweet of her to be his hands whilst she was away. No doubt Papa would not have considered that inconvenience when he sent her to Netherfield.

Would it be better to write back to him or send April with the message? No, the dear little flit would inevitably get something wrong and cause him to worry. Perhaps she could call Rustle to her room later tonight. He could carry word straight to Papa, leaving no chance for Mama to get hold of the letter by mistake or machination. Yes, that would be best.

Mary's letter detailed her visit to Longbourn. Heather and Rumblkins had joined her. Together, they distracted him from his displeasure at Elizabeth's absence. After a thorough oiling and brushing, he seemed quite content with Mary's company. Perhaps there was some good in forcing Mary to visit alone. While Longbourn could be intimidating, he was hardly as fearsome as Mary made him out to be. Mayhap this was just what they needed to break the ice between them.

Across the room, Mr. Darcy was writing, and Miss Bingley, seated near him, was watching the progress of his letter, distracting his attention by requests to include messages to his sister.

Was he even writing to his sister? His uncharacteristic posture, hunching over his letter, suggested otherwise. As did the bits of blue sealing wax, from the letter he had received, strewn about the writing desk.

"How delighted Miss Darcy will be to receive such a long letter!" Miss Bingley craned her neck, an obvious attempt to try and read over Mr. Darcy's shoulder.

He turned his back a bit more, blocking her view.

"You write uncommonly fast."

"You are mistaken. I write rather slowly."

Miss Bingley fluttered her fan in front of her face. "How many letters you must have occasion to write in the course of the year! Letters of business, too! How odious I should think them!"

"It is fortunate, then, that they fall to my lot instead of to yours."

"Pray tell your sister that I long to see her."

"I have already told her so, as you requested just a moment ago."

Mr. Darcy gritted his teeth loud enough to make Elizabeth wince.

This was truly rich, almost enough to leave her feeling sorry for him. The woman was every bit as tenacious as Mama and as flirtatious as Lydia, though a touch more refined in her efforts. The poor man was being driven to distraction.

Probably a fitting penance for his solemnity at dinner.

"Tell your sister I am delighted to hear of her improvement on the harp, and I think her playing infinitely superior to Miss Grantley's."

Elizabeth clenched her fists. She must not laugh aloud. Did he even know the Miss Grantley to whom Miss Bingley referred?

"Will you give me leave to defer your raptures until I write again? At present I have not room to do them justice." He returned his pen to its box.

"Oh, it is of no consequence. I shall see her in January. But do you always write such charming long letters to her, Mr. Darcy? It is a rule with me, that a person who can write a long letter with ease, cannot write ill." Miss Bingley stood and glanced about the room. "Charles writes in the most careless way imaginable. He leaves out half his words and blots the rest."

Mr. Bingley threw his head back and laughed heartily. "She is right, I fear. My ideas flow so rapidly that I have not time to express them, which means my letters sometimes convey no ideas at all to my correspondents."

"I think it displays a pleasing desire to ensure no correspondence is left unfinished." Elizabeth refolded her letters.

"I appreciate your compliment, Miss Elizabeth. My friend is quite sure I am simply impetuous and my ideas ill-conceived." Mr. Bingley's smile grew even broader—something that hardly seemed possible.

"I am by no means convinced you are heedlessly rash." Mr. Darcy turned to face them. "I think it just as likely if, as you were mounting your horse, a friend were to say, 'Bingley, you had better stay till next week,' you would probably do it—and, at another word, might stay a month."

"So your friend is not nearly so impetuous as he is obliging?" Elizabeth glanced from Mr. Bingley to Mr. Darcy. "To yield readily—easily—to the *persuasion* of a friend is no merit with you."

Darcy blinked at the word.

Did he suppose Mr. Bingley weak-willed for his susceptibility to dragon persuasion? Would he think the same of Jane? Did he truly understand what kind of will was required to withstand the determined inducement of a dragon? Barely one man in a hundred had it.

"It appears you allow nothing for the nature of the influence itself. You must agree that there are some requests that veritably demand yielding to, without waiting for arguments to reason one into it. I am not particularly speaking of such a case as you have supposed about Mr. Bingley, of course," Elizabeth said.

Mr. Darcy's brow rose. "Will it not be advisable, before we proceed on this subject, to arrange with rather more precision the importance of the request, as well as the nature of the relationship subsisting between the parties?"

She sat up a little straighter and pulled her shoulders back.

"By all means, let us hear all the particulars, not forgetting the comparative height and size of those involved, for that will have more weight in the argument, Miss Bennet, than you may be aware of." Mr. Bingley snickered. "I assure you that if Darcy were not such a great tall fellow, in comparison with myself, I should not pay him half so much deference. I declare I do not know a more awful object than Darcy."

He had certainly not met a dragon, especially an angry one. Even an irate fairy dragon could be far more awful than Mr. Darcy, even in high dudgeon. No wonder Mr. Bingley could not oppose any dragon suggestions.

"I see your design, Bingley. You dislike an argument, and want to silence this," Mr. Darcy said.

"Perhaps I do. Arguments are too much like disputes. If you and Miss Bennet will defer yours until I am out of the room, I shall be very thankful."

"What you ask is no sacrifice on my side. I am sure Mr. Darcy had much better finish his letter," Elizabeth said.

He took her advice, folding and sealing his letter—with blue wax.

Was it possible he had found something that he did not share with her? What would be worth reporting to the Order—or his uncle, which in some ways were one and the same? Dare she ask him?

Miss Bingley moved to the pianoforte, and Mrs. Hurst joined her there to sing.

Why was Mr. Darcy staring at her, with that odd inscrutable gaze of his? What fault did he find with her now?

After playing some Italian songs, Miss Bingley launched into a lively Scottish air.

Mr. Darcy drew near. "Do not you feel a great inclination, Miss Bennet, to seize such an opportunity of dancing a reel?"

She stared at him. No, nothing could be farther from her mind, but...

Dance. A reel would be pleasant. You should dance with him.

The voice was not familiar. She closed her eyes and

listened carefully. Silence. Had there been anything there but her own thoughts?

"Would you care to dance?"

She opened her eyes to Mr. Darcy staring into her face. "I am not certain I wish to dance a reel at all. But I think perhaps I will, despite my inclinations. And now despise me for my ductility if you dare."

"Indeed I do not dare." He bowed to her and escorted her to the center of the room.

Mr. Darcy proved himself a good dancer, and their two dances in the Netherfield drawing room were exceedingly pleasant.

But disquieting.

No doubt he was simply being contrary, finding a subtle way to demonstrate his powers of persuasion over lesser beings like herself and Bingley.

Bah and botheration! Dragons she understood, but men she did not. And Mr. Darcy was even more puzzling than most.

The following day, with April and Walker's help, they completed their search of the attics and servants' rooms. The dragons turned up several maps, but they seemed to be freshman efforts in a study of cartography. Blotted and wobbly-lines crisscrossed the maps, illustrating Netherfield's grounds, and not very well at that. But they did suggest the detail with which the map-maker imbued his creations. If they could find countryside maps—if they even existed—they could prove invaluable.

Instead of easing her mind, though, the teasing only left her irritable and prickly. Not a good frame of mind with which to endure the superior sisters' company. At least she had the excuse of Jane's illness to make an early retreat from the drawing room. Especially welcome as Mr. Darcy was looking at her so peculiarly.

She rose with the sun the next morning. There were several promising rooms she might be able to search before the Bingley party rose.

April led her, via a servants' corridor, to a small room at the end of the hall in the family wing of the house. What a very convenient way for their companion dragons to traverse the house without worry of drawing the attention of its occupants. Too bad Longbourn house was not grand enough for such architecture.

Scuff marks along the floor resembled tatzelwurm tracks and marks along the beams resembled claw marks. Not all estates had dragons attached, especially those not part of a titled seat. Had Netherfield once been occupied by a Dragon Mate, who kept multiple small, companion dragons? Neither Papa nor Longbourn had ever mentioned it. It seemed as though they would have. Usually a county's Dragon Friends always knew one another fairly well.

April hovered in front of the door. "There is no one within, Walker is waiting for us."

Elizabeth pushed the door open with her shoulder and peered inside.

A smaller, masculine style bedroom, paneled, not papered. The burgundy drapes, heavy and plain, were made of a very fine wool. Sunlight crept around the edges, casting just enough light to make out Walker's form perched on the foot of the bed. She entered and shut the door behind her.

"So where is this treasure you wish me to see?"

April zipped across the room and perched on a dull, brass door handle. "In here, in here, hurry, you must see!"

Walker's face contorted into a draconic version of mirth. "I do not read human script, but I agree, it does look promising." He hopped along beside her toward the door.

It led to a smaller room with a large window, covered by a white sheet. With no fabrics or wall coverings, only a large desk, chair and trunk, there was little to protect from the fading powers of the sun. Sunlight filtered through, leaving the room pleasingly bright. Her footsteps echoed off the walls, hinting that perhaps she was not welcome.

Walker stood on the edge of the desk and tapped a large book with his beak. "Here."

Underneath the book lay a large, half drawn map depicting the road from London to Meryton. The paper beneath it was blank.

She yanked the desk drawer open, revealing several more half-finished maps. Her heart thundered. This must be the room in which the map-maker pursued his craft. Surely it would be here!

She sorted through, leaf by leaf.

Blast and botheration! Nothing more than half-hearted efforts.

Perhaps the bedroom!

She ran to the bedroom shelves.

"Walker, April, I cannot reach those. Can you—"

Walker squawked and flapped up to the top shelf, dust flying in his wake.

"Under the bed!" April shrieked.

Elizabeth dropped to her knees and peered under the bed. The maids had been taking short cuts for certain. Some of those dust clods might be alive.

There were myths of dust-dragons …

A portfolio! She shoved forward on her toes and caught the corner with her fingertips.

Dragging it out raised another cloud of dust that sent them all into sneezing fits. Between spasms, she forced the buckle open and peeled up the flap. A quire of foolscap at least!

She sat back on her heels, blood pounding in her temples, and pulled the portfolio into her lap. April landed on her shoulder, Walker on the floor beside her. The paper fought her, but finally relented and slipped from the case.

Maps! Two dozen of them. Amazingly detailed, but impossible to read. The hand was unlike anything she had seen before.

Walker walked from one side to the other, peering and chittering. "By my brood mother's blood, that is dragon script!"

Elizabeth's limbs prickled and ran cold. "So the writer was a Dragon Friend of some kind? Perhaps even a Keeper?"

"No other human might know dragon script. But the signet mark, there," Walker pointed with his wing to an odd character on the bottom left of the map, "I do not recognize it. Darcy must see this."

"Yes, yes, of course. Do you think I would keep it to myself? It is far too important." She rose and dusted her hands on her skirt.

"Of course, I meant no offense, Lady." Walker bobbed his head.

"I am no Lady, and you know that. Why flatter me? You should know if there is something you need you have only to ask it of me."

"I do not flatter you, I only please myself. I see a Lairda and a Lady. I shall call you both such, regardless of what anyone else might say."

Who—what had Mr. Darcy been saying about April and herself?

"You are most gracious." She curtsied to Walker. At least he deserved the courtesy. "Pray keep watch here in the unlikely event anyone else should approach. I shall find Mr. Darcy."

She hurried away, her chest a mass of conflict and tensions.

What was on those maps? What did they say? Were the maps they needed yet among the artifacts in that room?

What sort of calumny was Mr. Darcy speaking against her in the privacy of his rooms, or even with his friends?

Downstairs, Nicholls directed her to the northern gardens to where she had seen Mr. Darcy depart with Miss Bingley.

The northern garden contained a labyrinth: tall box-woods, trimmed into a formidable hedge reaching well over the top of her head. Of course, there were multiple entrances. At least she could hear low conversational tones filtering from within the hedges. Mr. Darcy and Miss Bingley were within.

Perhaps it would be better to simply call out to them.

Miss Bingley would surely mock her for such brash behavior, though, and then it would be hard to extricate themselves from her company.

It could not take long to find them properly. She trotted through the nearest entrance. After a few steps she paused and listened. They were close.

She followed the narrow path through the shrubbery. Close, but not close enough. The voices grew louder, but they did not appear around the next corner.

"I hope you will give your future mother-in-law a few hints, when this desirable event takes place, as to the advantage of holding her tongue."

Dragon's blood! That was Miss Bingley.

"If you can compass it, do cure the younger girls of running after the officers. And, if I may mention so delicate a subject, endeavor to check that little something, bordering on conceit and impertinence, which your lady possesses."

His lady? His lady! The presumption! How dare she?

"Have you anything else to propose for my domestic felicity?" Mr. Darcy asked, flat-toned and acerbic.

"Do let the portraits of your soon-to-be Uncle and Aunt Phillips be placed in the gallery at Pemberley. Put them next to your great-uncle, the judge. They are in the same profession, you know, only in different lines. As for your Elizabeth's picture, you must not attempt to have it taken, for what painter could do justice to those beautiful eyes?"

"It would not be easy, indeed, to catch their expression, but their color and shape, and the eyelashes, so remarkably fine, might be copied." No doubt what sounded like a compliment must be made a cut by the facial expressions she could not see.

Mr. Darcy and Miss Bingley burst through an opening in the hedges.

"I did not know that you intended to walk." Miss Bingley had the good graces to look shocked, even a little horrified. "You used us abominably ill, not telling us that you were coming out. We would have been happy for your company with us here."

She was not a good liar.

"This walk is not wide enough for our party. We had better go into the avenue." Mr. Darcy brushed past them both and out of the maze.

Miss Bingley hurried after him, leaving Elizabeth to trail them both.

A few steps into the open, Miss Bingley stopped and fiddled with her bonnet. "I thank you for the walk, Mr. Darcy. I pray you both will excuse me, though, I must meet with Nicholls over the menus." With a quick curtsey, she dashed away, cheeks flushed.

Perhaps it was something in her favor that she could feel shame—or at least appeared to. Still it made little material difference.

Darcy turned to Elizabeth, looking ready to say something, but she cut him off.

"While you have been keeping our hostess occupied, we have found something worth looking at. Pray come." She turned sharply and dashed away. He could follow if he wished, but if he did not, her duty was amply discharged.

Heavy footfalls trailed after her. She took him by way of the servants' door. Perhaps the great Mr. Darcy had never taken such a humble path before. If he objected, he could find his own way.

Sparkling conversationalist that he was, he said nothing as they made their way upstairs. He did open the door she indicated and held it for her. Some little gallantry, perhaps to soothe his conscience?

Walker greeted them at the door. "Dragon script, there is dragon script written here."

Darcy sprinted to the portfolio, nearly running over April.

April squawked and dove for his ears. He tried to cover them, but she was faster and drew blood along the left one.

"Apologize, Darcy," Walker snapped.

Darcy looked over his shoulder and nodded. "Pray forgive my clumsiness. Now, the dragon script?"

Elizabeth shouldered her way through the dragons and laid out the half dozen sheets bearing the scratchy, faint figures Walker called dragon script. "Can you read it?"

"No, I recognize it, but I am unable to read it. My uncle might be able to—"

"And my father, I believe he has studied it and reads it as well."

"Your father? I hardly think—"

"That he is honorable enough or learned enough or high ranking enough to have learnt? He is Historian of the Order, after all."

"I said none of those things."

"But you clearly thought them. My father, for all you think him insufficient, is a dragon scholar, a very fine one."

"Anything in dragon script is critically important to the Order and must be delivered up to them at once."

"It is most properly delivered by way of my father."

"And how long then would it take to arrive at the Order? This cannot be delayed. You do not understand the implications here."

"Pray tell, why do you assume that?" She planted her hands on her hips.

Walker and April squawked and flapped, standing on a large trunk in the opposite corner.

"Look here!" April screeched. "I have peered through the keyhole. There are more in here."

Darcy crossed the room in four long strides and knelt before the trunk. He tried the lid, but it was locked.

Naturally.

"I think I saw a key in the other room." Elizabeth raced to the desk.

She rooted through the desk drawers. Yes!

Darcy stepped aside to allow her to fit the key into the lock. It took her both her hands to force the key to turn, but it did. They lifted the lid together, sneezing through the cloud of dust the lid left in its wake.

"There! Look, I recognize the gorge where the militia is encamped!" She grabbed the topmost sheet.

Ochre dust exploded from the page, hanging like mist in the air, acrid and smelling like old death.

Her eyes watered and burned. Her chest tightened, hard and sharp, too tight to draw breath as a bitter, rotting taste coated her tongue.

Darcy coughed and sputtered, clutching at his throat.

"Out! Get out! It is poison!" April shrieked and dove at Elizabeth.

Her vision grew fuzzy and her knees soft as she pulled herself toward the servants' door.

Walker grabbed Darcy's coat and yanked hard. "Come now, come now!"

They staggered into the servants' corridor, choking and gasping. Elizabeth leaned against the wall and sank to the floor, head on her knees, struggling to force air into her scorching lungs.

April hovered around Elizabeth's head. "Cough hard and spit, do not try to contain it."

"She is right," Walker flapped fresh air into their faces. "Cough it out."

Elizabeth pitched forward and coughed as hard as she could, bile and spittle splattering the floor. Darcy retched painfully beside her.

At last the searing pain subsided enough for her to draw a sufficient breath. "What was that?"

Darcy sat back on his heels and pressed his head against the wall. "Dragon venom of some kind. I am not sure which. Someone dried it to a powder and coated the maps or perhaps the inside of the trunk with it, so that it would become airborne when opened."

"Who dabbles in dragon venom?"

"That is a very good question. The practice has been outlawed for not less than a century, perhaps two now? I cannot quite think straight, but it has been for all of our lifetimes."

"But nothing in that room is that old."

"No, it is not. I do not like the implications." He raked his fingers through his hair.

"Nor do I." She dragged in another jagged breath. "I must tell my father. The Order must know."

"All of those documents must make it into the Order's hands."

"But how? I do not think it safe to even enter the room right now, and we need those maps."

"There must be some way." Darcy rubbed his eyes with his fists. "I shall send Walker with enquiries to the Order. There must be one there who knows some means of neutralizing the poison."

"My father may know something, we should consult him directly."

Darcy groaned.

"You are so prejudiced against him that you would not even ask?"

"I said nothing. Feel free to ask him, there is little else you can do here at Netherfield."

"Is that to say you are throwing me out, sir?"

Maria Grace

He peered at her, blinking hard. "We must get ourselves to rights. Come, the best remedy now is fresh air."

They made their way down the stairs and into the garden.

Once they were able to breathe properly again, they parted company and went to their respective rooms.

Darcy forced himself to the small writing desk near the window, but his hands still shook and his eyes watered too much to focus on the paper. Walker ushered him into bed where he fell into a deep slumber until his valet came to dress him for dinner.

He cleared the grit from his eyes. Each breath still scorched his lungs and his face and hands stung as though scalded. The airborne venom was nothing to be toyed with. Had their dragons not recognized it for what it was, it could easily have killed them both.

Why would maps be guarded with such wards? What secrets were contained in the dragon script?

Walker had warned him not to brave another foray into the map room. Already weakened as he was, he would be more susceptible to the venom. Moreover, since it was already airborne, it would affect him even more quickly. Chances were good it would be lethal.

He hurried through dressing and dismissed his valet. Just enough time for a quick note to the Order.

Far from the neat hand Miss Bingley had lauded him for, but it was enough to communicate the relevant facts. He sealed it and fitted it into a small leather satchel. Walker lifted his head for Darcy to fasten the straps around him.

"I will follow the main road towards Norfolk to see if I locate the remaining militia wagons. If so, I shall try and smell for the egg. I will ask Rustle to accompany me, that I might send word back with him as to my success."

"I thought you did not approve of him."

"He improves with exposure. Besides, the situation calls for it." Walker picked at the straps with his beak. "That one is too tight."

Darcy adjusted it. "Do you think Rustle will agree to fly with you?"

"He will when he learns of what happened to Elizabeth. Warn her not to tell Longbourn, not yet. His protectiveness might overwhelm his good sense." Walker flexed his wings.

"Good sense? I thought you said his reputation—"

"He is lazy and complacent, to be sure, but his judgement is as sound as any major-dragon's. Of course where Elizabeth is concerned, he could be very rash indeed. I will return as quickly as I can." Walker dove through the open window and into the sunset.

The mantel clock chimed the dinner hour. His stomach roiled. Perhaps he should send his valet downstairs with his regrets. But no, that would give Miss Bingley reason to turn her hospitality on him. That he could well do without.

He ate little at dinner. How convenient that Miss Bennet's appearance captured the bulk of the conversation. Better still, the ladies withdrew together from the dining room for the first time in days.

The conversation among the gentlemen was hardly improved without the ladies present. Rather, it gave Hurst the opportunity to share his favorite ribald stories. Bingley laughed as he always did. Darcy allowed his attention to drift inward.

Miss Bingley's teasing this morning had been irritating at best, but to have Miss Elizabeth wander into it was wholly unsupportable. Was Miss Bingley unaware that few places in a large house were truly private and that one must always guard their words carefully?

Especially when one had secrets as large as dragons to keep.

Had Miss Bingley ever entertained hopes of a union with Darcy, her indiscretions this morning ended them entirely. It was a stretch to consider any woman who could not hear dragons. One who was crass and insensitive to boot, no, that was entirely impossible.

It was a shame that Miss Elizabeth did not come from better stock, better connections. Everything else about her was entirely suitable. Her connection to dragons was uncanny—

"Darcy, Darcy?" Bingley peered into his face. "Are you there, old fellow?"

"Oh, yes, forgive me." Darcy blinked hard. His eyes were gritty again.

"What say you we join the ladies now?" Bingley led the way out.

Miss Bennet was ensconced near the fire, well-guarded from the cold and attended by the Bingley sisters. Miss Elizabeth sat slightly to the side, gazing absently through the window. Her complexion was pale, and her eyes did not have their usual sparkle.

Lingering effects of dragon venom, no doubt.

Near the ceiling, April hid amongst the plaster work, eyes focused on her Dragon Mate. The little flitterbob seemed worried. That was probably not a good sign.

Miss Bingley's eyes instantly turned towards him. She was at his side, nattering, before he had advanced three steps into the room. She guided him toward Miss Bennet, where he was able to pay a tolerable address and bow before Miss Bingley propelled him to the table for tea.

Bingley, though, took Miss Bingley's abandoned seat and offered salutations full of joy and attention. He spent not less than half an hour piling up the fire, lest Miss Bennet should suffer from the change of room. Then, he insisted she remove to the other side of the fireplace that she might be farther from the door and its draughts. At her new station, he pulled a chair close and sat down by her, talking scarcely to anyone else.

Mr. Hurst hinted that the card table might be brought out, and Darcy made good his escape from Miss Bingley's pointed attentions. Whilst the rest of the company decided they did not wish to play cards, he found a book and a chair near the fire. Not that his irritated eyes and pounding head would actually permit him to read. The appearance of it was all he needed right now to keep the rest of the company at bay.

Mr. Hurst settled on the far sofa and fell asleep while Mrs. Hurst joined her brother and Miss Bennet. What was Miss Bingley doing, walking toward the book table? The woman did not read—with her mean opinions it was easy to wonder whether she could. But no, she selected a book and a chair near Darcy's and settled in.

Heavens above! She had chosen the second volume of the book he had. Did she intend to—

"Do you find the hero's speeches a bit ... pedantic?"

She blinked at him over the edge of her book.

"Hardly, I consider him insightful." He forced his eyes back down to the open pages. The words were still blurred by dragon venom.

She leafed through several more pages and chuckled. "I think you will enjoy the speech he makes to the heroine. She is so ill-mannered." Miss Bingley's eyebrow rose just so and her eyes drifted toward the corner Miss Elizabeth occupied.

"I find her impertinence provides a foil to the superciliousness displayed by the secondary antagonist."

It probably was not right to enjoy the blank look on Miss Bingley's face quite so much. But it did stop her questions. Perhaps she might actually read the book and discover who the secondary antagonist actually was.

Perhaps.

"You cannot be serious, Mr. Bingley!" Miss Bennet hid a smile behind her hand.

"Absolutely, Miss Bennet! I told your youngest sister, she could name the date of the ball once you had sufficiently recovered." Bingley grinned and leaned forward, elbows on knees, clearly enjoying Miss Bennet's pleasure.

"Charles," Miss Bingley threw aside her book and leaned over the back of her chair to look at him. "Are you really serious in hosting a dance at Netherfield? I would advise you, before you determine on it, to consult the wishes of the present party. I am much mistaken if there are some among us to whom a ball would be rather a punishment than a pleasure."

Bingley waved her off. "If you mean Darcy, he may go to bed before it begins, if he chooses, but as for the ball, it is quite a settled thing. As soon as Nicholls has made white soup enough, I shall send round my cards."

Darcy peeked at Miss Elizabeth, who kept her eyes toward the window. What would Bingley think to know he had already engaged her for the supper set of that ball?

Miss Bingley sniffed and began a turn about the room. Her figure was elegant, and she walked well. No doubt many hours had been spent walking with books on her head at her fancy girls' seminary.

So that was her use for books!

Darcy coughed over his snicker and turned the page.

"Miss Eliza Bennet, let me persuade you to follow my example, and take a turn about the room. I assure you it is very refreshing after sitting so long in one attitude."

Elizabeth lifted her hands and began to protest. Miss Bingley took her arm, effectively silencing her. They proceeded along the length of the room.

Miss Bingley sported an elegant, columnar silhouette. Next to her, Miss Elizabeth seemed short and unrefined with her soft curves and definite steps, though they seemed weaker than usual.

Darcy closed his book. The comparison was not fair, though. With Miss Bingley it was all affectation. When the next fashion came through, she would abandon this and chase after that without a second thought. But Miss Elizabeth was genuine, everything about her was real, fashionable or not. She would be the same tomorrow as she was yesterday.

There was something reassuring in such steadiness.

"Pray join us, Mr. Darcy," Miss Bingley called over her shoulder.

"No, I think not. I can only imagine but two

motives for you to walk up and down the room together. My joining you would interfere with either of them."

"What could he mean?" Miss Bingley leaned close to Miss Bennet as if sharing a great confidence. "Pray, do you understand him?"

"Not at all, but depend upon it, he means to be severe on us, and our surest way of disappointing him will be to ask nothing about it." Miss Elizabeth turned her face aside, away from Darcy's view.

"I require that you explain these two possible motives, sir, for I cannot fathom your meaning at all."

Darcy rose and leaned against the back of the chair. "Either you chose this method of passing the evening because you are in each other's confidence, and have secret affairs to discuss."

Of course that was patently untrue. Miss Elizabeth knew his hearing to be as acute as hers. She would know better than to attempt to share secrets in his presence. Nor did she have affection enough for Miss Bingley to share secrets with her.

"—or because you are conscious that your figures appear to the greatest advantage in walking. If the first, I should be completely in your way. If the second, I can admire you much better as I sit by the fire."

Miss Elizabeth gasped softly and pressed a hand to her cheek.

"Oh, shocking! I never heard anything so abominable. How shall we punish him for such a speech?" Miss Bingley clutched Miss Elizabeth's arm tightly.

She pulled back a bit to meet Miss Bingley's eye with a pointed, narrow gaze. "Tease him. Laugh at him. Intimate as you are, you must know how it is to be done."

Darcy winced.

Miss Bingley pressed her hand to her chest. "But upon my honor I do not. I do assure you that my intimacy has not yet taught me that. Tease calmness of temper and presence of mind! No, no, we will not expose ourselves by attempting to laugh at such a subject as Mr. Darcy."

"Mr. Darcy is not to be laughed at? That is an uncommon advantage, but one I cannot admire as I dearly love a laugh." Miss Elizabeth removed her arm from Miss Bingley's grasp.

"Do you? In some circles it is thought inadvisable to be so prone to mirth." Miss Bingley's eyes narrowed. If she had had fangs, they would have been exposed.

"I hope I never ridicule what is wise or good. Follies and nonsense do divert me, I own, and I laugh at them whenever I can. But these, I suppose, are precisely what you are without, Mr. Darcy." Miss Elizabeth's eyes were almost fever bright as she turned them on him.

"Perhaps not, but it has been the study of my life to avoid those weaknesses which often expose a strong understanding to ridicule." He clasped his hands behind his back.

"Such as vanity and pride."

"Yes, vanity is a weakness indeed. But pride, where there is a real superiority of mind, pride will always be under good regulation."

Elizabeth bit her lip and turned aside.

"I am perfectly convinced that Mr. Darcy has no defect." Miss Bingley smiled her predatory smile.

For one who certainly did not know dragons, she had many of their expressions perfected.

"No." Darcy stepped toward them. "I have made no such pretension. I have faults enough, but they are not, I hope, of understanding. My temper I believe too unyielding—certainly too little for the convenience of the world. I cannot forget the follies and vices of others so soon as I ought, nor their offences against myself. My temper would perhaps be called resentful. My good opinion once lost is lost forever."

"That is a failing indeed! Implacable resentment is a shade in a character. But you have chosen your fault well. I really cannot laugh at it." The corners of Miss Elizabeth's lips turned down.

Was she disappointed in him?

Why did that knot his stomach? Or was that the effect of the venom?

"There is, I believe, in every disposition a tendency to some particular evil, a natural defect, which not even the best education can overcome." He shrugged.

"And your defect is a propensity to hate everybody." She cocked her head and lifted an eyebrow.

"And yours is willfully to misunderstand them."

She opened her mouth to make a response, but Miss Bingley cut her off.

"Do let us have a little music." She proceeded to the pianoforte for no less than five songs, none of which were fit for dancing.

Just as well. Miss Elizabeth was far too intriguing to risk another dance with.

9
Chapter

The next morning over breakfast, Jane declared she was much improved, enough so that she need no longer impose upon her friends' hospitality. Miss Bingley did not hesitate to offer her brother's carriage to convey them back to their home.

Perhaps it was a good thing no one thought to ask Elizabeth her feelings on the matter. Had they, she would have been forced to say she hardly felt well enough for the ride home, regardless of how much she wished to leave Netherfield. But since she was not consulted, she said nothing, gritted her teeth through the process and leaned heavily on Mr. Bingley as he handed her up into his well-appointed carriage.

"Oh, Lizzy, such manners and solicitude. I am so grateful for my dear, sweet friends. Have they not been everything friends should be?" Jane leaned into the side glass and watched Netherfield disappear behind them.

Elizabeth pressed her head into the squabs. She

barely ate at breakfast in hopes that she would not succumb to the urge to cast up her accounts. Pray let them stay where they were.

Her head throbbed with a residual ache that had lodged itself firmly in place since their dragon venom encounter. Breathing still burned, with an occasional sharp, tearing sensation through her ribs. Each step she took felt as though she carried a dragon-weight on her shoulders, joints protesting with each effort. If only she might go straight to bed and not wake up until the egg was recovered and Mr. Darcy was long gone. Yes, that was a very good idea indeed.

"Have you been taken by my cold?" Jane peered into her face.

"I think perhaps I have." Elizabeth threw her arm over her eyes.

Oh, that felt better. The darkness and the pressure on her eyes eased the ache in her head.

"Perhaps we should have stayed then? We must get you to bed as soon as we get home. You have been so good to me these past few days. I am glad I shall be able to return the favor." Jane tucked Elizabeth's cloak around her snugly.

Elizabeth closed her eyes and drifted off until the carriage rolled to a stop.

Mama met them half way up the walk, less than pleased at their return. She had meant for Jane to stay a full week complete. Somehow it was Elizabeth's fault that Jane had recovered too soon and did not require several more days' convalescence. Yes, yes, it was unfortunate that Elizabeth was feeling poorly, but really, she should have found some way to do so whilst remaining at Netherfield.

Kitty and Lydia met them in the front hall, prattling

about their newest gossip from Aunt Phillips—several of the officers had dined recently with Uncle Phillips. A private had been flogged, Colonel Forster had been married, and more officers were due any day now.

That latter piece of information seemed like it should be important somehow. Certainly it reminded her of something she had once thought important. But it was all so unclear.

The hall wavered, and her knees melted.

"Lizzy, dear? Lizzy?"

Elizabeth forced her sandy eyes open. Afternoon sunlight streamed through her window. She was in her bed, but how had she gotten there? Her normally soft sheets rasped like sand against her skin. The bountiful pillows seemed to be filled with rocks. She might as well be sleeping in Longbourn's lair.

Was there anything that did not hurt?

Aunt Gardiner walked across the room and opened the window. A rainbow of fairy dragons zoomed through the window and hovered around Elizabeth.

"She needs rest." April chirped and flew to Aunt. "You must keep her meddling mother at bay, and see that she rests."

Phoenix snorted. "I shall keep her away."

Elizabeth raised a hand for him to perch. How sharp his tiny toes were! "You are a very dear little fellow." She stroked his head, and he cuddled into her hand. Even his downy feather-scales prickled and scratched today.

Heather landed on her shoulder and nestled into her neck, trilling.

"Please, dear, not just now. I should like to stay awake for just a little while longer."

Mary sat beside her on the edge of the bed. When had Mary come in?

"What happened, Lizzy? You really do look a fright."

"It is good to know that no one will be mistaking me for hale and hearty today." Elizabeth encouraged Heather to perch in her hand with Phoenix.

"Do not make light of it." April landed on the pillow beside Elizabeth. "It is a serious matter. They ought to know."

"What happened?" Mary whispered.

"It is a little difficult to believe. I hardly believe it myself. I think I have been poisoned by dragon venom in one of the rooms at Netherfield. I can wholeheartedly assure you that it is far worse than any dragon lore suggests."

Aunt sank into the chair near the window. "Great heavens! How can that be?"

"I do not know what to make of it. All is well now. There is no need to worry. I am simply tired, and pleased to be home. Enough of such things, though. Tell me of these darlings." Elizabeth lifted Heather and Phoenix.

"Heather is quite the sweetest, most beautiful creature in the world." Mary's eyes glittered. "I understand now why you encourage April to accompany you nearly everywhere. The children are quite fond of her and Phoenix, too. They hardly want to be out of the dragons' sight."

"And you, Aunt?"

"I find that they have become far easier to hear with practice. Rustle is quite patient with me now. He even spends time in the nursery. Moreover, he and Phoenix are striking up what looks to be a promising friendship."

"I would never have imagined him accepting a fairy dragon as a friend. You must be very special." She nuzzled Phoenix. "And Longbourn?"

Mary smiled a broader smile than she had in months. "I have been to see him nearly every day as you told me. I prepared the oil according to your recipe. Oh Lizzy, your book is wonderful. Aunt and I have been studying and copying it nearly every day."

"Mary is quite right. I have even shown your uncle. He is impressed and has generated quite the list of questions to discuss with you."

"But it is just my random collection of musings and observations."

"You sell yourself short, my dear."

"It was ever so helpful to help me soothe Longbourn's itches and moods. He has not been happy about your absence, but he has accepted me as a tolerable substitute for the interim. I suspect it is only because I knew his favorite snacks and the way to drive away the mites attacking his tail." Mary stroked Heather's chin. "If only he had a disposition like hers."

"He can be such a crosspatch. I am glad he has not been too difficult."

"Speaking of difficult crosspatches," Aunt chuckled. "Your father wishes to talk to you. I was to bring you as soon as your mother finished with you this morning, but obviously that has not happened."

"You should rest, not talk," April scolded.

"Tell Papa that. He might listen to you."

"I am afraid he is most impatient to speak with you about what you have found. Are you feeling strong enough? I can ask him to come up and speak with you here if you wish."

"There is no need, I shall go to him." Elizabeth struggled up from bed. The room spun a bit, then settled back to right ways up. She smoothed her rumpled dress and tucked untidy hairs behind her ears. "I look a fright, but I can make it."

"At least permit me to help you down the stairs." Aunt caught her under the arm and supported her on the trek downstairs.

Had the staircase grown as long as the grand stair at Netherfield in her absence? They paused twice for breath on the way down.

Papa and Uncle awaited her in the study. Uncle encouraged her to sit near the fire and gave her some sort of soothing tea that felt very, very good on her raw throat. Papa offered her a lap rug and waited for her to settle in before beginning his interrogation.

Elizabeth relayed the details of Mr. Darcy's trip to Ware and their aborted attempts to recover the maps, at least as much as she could remember in the moment.

"Dragon venom, are you sure?" Papa asked.

April darted to him and hovered in front of his face. "Have you suddenly grown hard of hearing? It was venom, dried and deliberately placed as a ward against trespassers. It hangs in the air now. We cannot even enter the room. If you had asked, I could have told you that myself and spared her the trip downstairs."

"I thought perhaps you might know a counter to the poison, or be able to find one in all your dragon lore." Elizabeth said softly, but it was as loud as she could speak.

"Darcy had no ideas?" Uncle asked.

"He tried twice more to enter, masking his face in various ways, but the venom was too potent. He has written to the Blue Order for advice."

"It will take them weeks to come up with anything useful! I am sure I will have something here." Papa threw his hands in the air and rose. He shuffled to his book case. "I need the ladder."

Uncle brought the library steps around and climbed them to retrieve an armload of tomes at Papa's direction.

Papa sat at his desk and started opening the books. "You might also ask Longbourn whilst I study here."

"She needs to go up and rest. Do not send her for a tramp about the woods." April stood on the page he was reading and stomped.

Papa closed the book, sending April dodging out of his way. "You need to go to him immediately. He has been quite distraught in your absence."

"The ninny works himself up unnecessarily. He is spoilt by constantly getting his way. Her sister will do well enough for him. What needs of his are left unmet? She should be in bed."

"I understand your concerns, but he must be satisfied first, lest we find him in the cellars below the house. You know what happens when he does not get his way. I doubt anything could persuade Mrs. Bennet to ignore such a thing." Papa folded his arms before his chest.

"I know, Papa, Longbourn is hardly patient. I will be fine." She pushed up on the arms of the chair, but quickly fell back into the seat.

Why could not Longbourn be more reasonable?

"I will accompany her." Uncle rose and helped her up.

"Very good. Oh, and you should know, Lizzy, we have had a letter from Collins whilst you have been away. He should arrive tomorrow."

"So soon?"

Papa sighed. "Yes. The sooner he begins to learn the nature of the estate, the better. I do hope you will find yourself recovered tolerably well enough to keep society with him by then."

"Yes, Papa." She took Uncle's arm and left. April followed, chittering her displeasure.

Once they were away from the house, Uncle slowed their pace. "Are you sure you are strong enough for this?"

"I have no choice, it seems, but perhaps we might sit for a moment." She pointed to a garden bench.

The sunlight burned her eyes. The light, soft breeze scoured her face like rottenstone. Perhaps April was right.

He helped her sit. "I am worried indeed, Lizzy, this is not like you."

She leaned back and dragged in deep breaths, though they still seared all the way into her spine. "What is to be done? I hardly think a call to the apothecary is in order. What would we tell him? That I ate a bad piece of mutton? I have faith that this will run its course and with a little time and rest, it will all be well."

"I hope you are correct. There have not been many cases of dragon poisonings in recent memory. You will write everything in your book, will you not?" He sat beside her.

"Just as I write everything. I think I could hardly do otherwise. But do you really think it so significant?"

He took her hands in his. "Yes, my dear, I do. Your aunt has shown me what you have compiled. I am deeply impressed. You have your father's passion for lore, but with a far more practical bent. I am quite convinced that it should not be kept to yourself. With your permission, I should like to help you compile it. Then you might come to London and present it to the Order for publication among the Dragon Friends. Keepers and Mates both can benefit from your advice."

Her little commonplace book of dragons? Surely it could not be that significant.

"Does Papa know of your idea?"

"Not yet. I thought I should talk to you first. But I will approach him. He will agree with me. I am quite certain. What greater honor for him as Historian than to have you add to the body of dragon lore in a very significant way?"

She clasped her hands in her lap. "I think perhaps he might. He does so love dragon lore. But what of Mr. Collins? He is to arrive soon. I know Papa wants to begin his own transition to Elder Keeper as soon as may be possible. That means I could easily be married by Twelfth Night. We would have to consult Mr. Collins' opinion as well. And if he does not hear dragons—"

"Regarding that," he squeezed her hands hard. "You can have no doubts about how I feel in regards to this match. If you were to like him, genuinely like him, then I am in no way opposed. Even if he does not hear dragons, if he is an amiable man and you truly wish for the match, then I support you, entirely. But forcing you into a match with a man who we know nothing of—except that his own father was a hateful, abusive creature who did not speak a civil word to your father for the last three decades of his life—let us just say that does not make for an auspicious start."

"But it is the way of the Blue Order, is it not? We trade some of our personal freedoms and preferences for our connections to the dragons." She pressed her eyes with the back of her hands. "What choice do I have?"

"Whilst I was in London, I took the matter to the Secretary of the Order. Things are changing, Lizzy, and even the dragons know it. Though the major-dragons may live five hundred years or more, they are coming to understand we are far more ephemeral creatures. Our society and ways change far faster than theirs. The last Dragon Conclave discussed how to manage situations like yours."

"I suspect that Longbourn did not attend that Conclave."

"Little matter, the chief dragons were all there: Buckingham was there, as were York, Clarence, Cornwall, Norfolk and Lancaster. They all agreed that they would accept the changes necessary for Keepers to wed more freely. The details remain to be sorted out, but the precedent is there. Longbourn must concede to the Conclave."

"I doubt he will be willing. It is hard to tell who is more stubborn, he or Papa."

"It is not a matter of willingness, but a matter of dragon law—or it soon will be. The letters are being written now and will be delivered soon."

"All the more reason for Longbourn to rush us into marriage, before the changes have the weight of law." She pressed her temples

Her head throbbed so loud it was hard to hear.

"You have only to say the word, and your aunt and I shall intervene."

While very dear of him to offer, had he any idea of the chaos that would bring?

"You are very good to me. But I am determined to keep an open mind and a cheerful countenance, and hope for the best."

"As you should. There is no need to borrow trouble for today, is there?" He patted her arm.

They rose and continued into the woods, slowly.

His offer was kind and thoughtful, but he did not fully understand the bonds between a Keeper and a major-dragon. A small dragon, a fairy dragon, cockatrice or tatzelwurm might be argued with, even denied their way. But it was not that way with a major-dragon of any sort. What they wanted was what they would have, one way or another. They were stubborn on a whole different level to companion dragons and their displeasure was frightful, as was the threat of losing their friendship should they be displeased enough. Perhaps some were willing—and able—to suffer such a breach, but she was not among those strong enough for that sort of loss.

April flew ahead of them, probably to give Longbourn a stern talking to. She was such an opinionated little thing. Longbourn might banish her from his company for months.

What if April took a dislike to Mr. Collins ... heavens that could be a disaster! Collins could insist that she keep April contained to her cage. If he was of a sufficiently stubborn disposition, April might not be able to persuade him to change his mind.

Elizabeth gulped. The possibility of a strong-willed heir to Longbourn had not crossed her mind until now. If he neither heard, nor was susceptible to persuasion—that was a truly horrid thought.

No, she must not dwell on that. Not now.

Longbourn waited for them just outside his cavern, April perched on his top-most head ridge. He snorted and stomped and roared as he saw them.

Maria Grace

Another tantrum? He might require a visit, but that did not mean she would tolerate his petulant games. He would offer as much respect as she demanded.

She stopped and crossed her arms, her knees threatening to buckle. "Another fuss like that and I am going home."

"You see, I told you she is unwell. You unfeeling beast, dragging her out here like this." April pecked at his head, not that he was likely to feel it through his thick hide.

Longbourn paused and stared at Elizabeth, sniffing. His eyes bulged, and he trumpeted a sound she had never heard before. Something between a deep, brass horn and a crash of thunder.

Hopefully it would not scare the children back at the house.

"The flufflebit was right. It is venom." Longbourn leaned in close and smelt her head to toe.

His hot breath, acrid and moist, chafed against her exposed skin, not unlike the venom had.

"I think we have established what it is."

"I am not pleased."

"I gathered that as well."

"I am very displeased." Longbourn growled. The ground beneath him rumbled. "You should not have been exposed."

Her stomach knotted and cold prickles traversed her limbs. He never took that tone with her.

"What do you want me to do about it? It has already happened, I cannot change the facts."

"You must wash everywhere; your hair, your clothes. With very hot water. Twice, no thrice. You are covered in venom dust." Longbourn snorted hard, blowing hot dragon breath over her. He shuffled

~218~

around to the right and left, doing the same. "That will help, but you must bathe."

"I will persuade the housekeeper she is to prepare water for your baths." April launched toward Elizabeth.

"No." Longbourn blocked her with his wing. "You are so tiny it is not good for you to be exposed to her. Keep the babies away until she is washed as well. Bathe yourself as well, fluffletuft."

"No wonder you are still feeling so poorly." Uncle caught her elbow and steadied her.

Longbourn circled her again. "Your boots too, they must be taken outside and brushed very, very well. Anything you wore since you were exposed. I would rather you burn it."

"Is that really necessary?"

"I suppose if it is washed well, it is not. But I will not have you endangered again." Longbourn stomped, shaking the ground under her feet. "You are to stay away from Netherfield entirely."

"Then I am freed from the obligation to dance with Mr. Darcy at the Netherfield ball?"

"No, you are not. He insulted you—us—honor must be satisfied." Longbourn roared again, slimy spittle flying from his lips. "Do not play games with me. You will do as I say."

"I do not understand why—"

"You do not need to understand. Just obey me." He lashed his tail, sending rocks and branches flying.

He had never ordered her about so, knowing well she did not appreciate it any more than he did. "Mr. Darcy should be told about bathing."

"I shall go and take him word." April zipped away.

She had probably been looking for an excuse to do

that for quite some time. Too bad Elizabeth could not join her.

"Stay away from Netherfield and stop stalking about the hillside caverns. You must not visit the militia anymore."

"We expect another segment of the militia to arrive soon. We have great hope that the egg is with them. Papa will insist that we continue the search when they arrive."

"You shall not."

"Then who? You do not think Papa, who can barely make it here, is able to traverse the countryside—"

"Seeking the egg is too dangerous for you. I will not have it. Stay to your home and meet your future mate."

She edged back. "What do you know of him?"

"What does it matter? You are to stay here, with me. That is the way it will be accomplished. I have chosen my next Keeper."

Something about the tone he used …

"And if I do not agree?"

Longbourn rose to his full height and spread his wings, churning up dust. She choked and sputtered, stepping away. He leaned down and wrapped his wings around her, the way he would his prey. "Do not argue with me, Keeper."

His cold tone slithered down her spine, raising chills in its wake. Her heart raced and her chest burned as she gasped in the hot dragon breath. His fangs were so close, so sharp, glistening. She pushed and kicked, but his wings formed an impenetrable cage. Her knees buckled.

He caught her in his massive, taloned foot, lifting her toward his face.

She shoved at his grasp, but it would not give way.

A shriek as she had never screamed before tore from her throat.

The woods went black.

Heat. Darkness.

Bitter, fetid air.

Roaring—so loud. Ears ringing.

Terror. Deeper, more encompassing than anything before.

Chest tight, shaking. Pain—how it burned!

"Lizzy, Lizzy?"

She forced her eyes open. Uncle stood over her, face white as death.

"Longbourn?" The words scoured her throat.

Uncle helped her to sit. She braced her forehead in her hands, unable to hold up her throbbing head.

"What happened? I thought … I ... did he harm you?" He held her shoulders tight.

"He … he …" She began to shake so hard she could not speak. "Take me home, pray, take me home."

Uncle supported her as she walked and carried her when she failed. Papa met them at the doorway, demanding an explanation.

"April was right, she is very ill indeed." Uncle shouldered Papa aside and took her up to her room.

"Pray, tell him nothing more," she whispered into his shoulder.

"Longbourn may explain himself to your father. I have no desire to get involved in that conversation. Tell me again, he did not hurt you?"

"No, he did not. But I have never seen him in such a fury. I … I have never been afraid of him before." The words caught in her throat with a sob.

No she would not cry. That was foolish and weak. A Dragon Keeper was made of sterner stuff.

"Nor have I. I doubt your father has ever seen him thus. But you are well, and that is all that matters. I will tell him Longbourn forbids you from any further dealings with Pemberley's egg. He will have to step up and manage his part as he should have from the first."

"But how can he? He covers it well, but he is so limited—"

"Not nearly so limited as he would have you think. He is much like his dragon, preferring not to bother with things he is not interested in. I will assist your father in anything else that is necessary while you recuperate. Do not concern yourself with anything else. Hot water will be up shortly."

April, with a little help from Rumblkins, convinced Hill that she very much wanted to heat water for a bath and bring it directly up to Elizabeth. Mama wondered at the odd behavior, but was easily convinced that it was a most appropriate treatment for Elizabeth's 'cold.'

To his credit, a thorough scrubbing left her feeling much improved. That made up for Longbourn's beastly behavior. But only a little.

Never in all her days of knowing dragons had she been afraid of one. Even Bedford, the ancient firedrake, had proven to have a sweet disposition after she had discovered his broken tooth. Once she was able to pull it and relieve the pain in his mouth, they were fast friends.

Every time she met an ill-tempered dragon, it always had a good reason for its ire. Once she discovered the cause of its distress, all was well and they were delighted with her company. She had never believed one would actually hurt her.

Until today.

This must be the way the dragon-deaf saw dragons. No wonder there were dragon wars.

This was why they had to remain hidden.

And why she wanted to as well.

The following morning, while she bathed, April informed her that Mr. Darcy was following the same advice and was much better for it. He acted a bit peculiar when she flew in and joined him whilst he bathed, though. Walker was there, so clearly he did not object to dragon company during his toilette, so what was his problem?

Elizabeth snickered, but it would be pointless to try to explain. She poured a pitcher of water over her hair.

"Are the babies well? Did they suffer for being near me?" Elizabeth toweled her hair.

"They were a bit out of sorts over the evening, but they are well enough now. They were only with you a short time, so there was little harm done."

"And you? Why did you not tell me you were suffering?"

"I went directly to take a dust bath shortly after it happened and have been largely well since."

"And you did not think to suggest the same to me?"

"You have made it clear that you do not like dust baths. I did not think water could accomplish the same thing." April hung her head.

Did the poor dear feel guilty? Elizabeth raised her hand for April to perch. "I was only teasing, dearling. You take wonderful care of me and are not at all to blame for what happened at Netherfield."

"Longbourn does not agree. He has scolded me

quite soundly." April trembled a little.

Elizabeth pulled on her chemise and sat on the edge of her bed. "Something has him in a frightful temper. I do not know if we shall ever know what it is."

"Gardiner told me what happened."

"I am sorry—"

"He was correct to. You know it was wrong of him to act so. Just because Longbourn is a major-dragon does not mean he is permitted to act threateningly to you." April hopped to the bedpost and looked eye to eye with Elizabeth.

"While that may be true, I do not think Papa would permit me to file a complaint over his behavior with the conclave. And really, what purpose would it serve? They might reprimand him, but it would not change what has been done ... nor how I feel about it." She shrugged on her dress.

"No Keeper should feel threatened by their own dragon. I should very much like to tell him that." April pecked at the bedpost as though it were Longbourn's hide.

"I have—that is to say I will forgive him. I do not know how I shall ever be easy with him again, though. But what choice have we? We must muddle through as best we can. Now, see if you can help me with the top buttons and we shall go down to breakfast."

"It would be better for you to stay in bed and rest. You do have a—" April snorted, "—a cold, after all."

"You know I cannot lie-abed. I will not push myself too hard and you will, no doubt, convince Mama to excuse me from anything too arduous. Come."

Besides, Mr. Collins was expected sometime today. After Longbourn's outburst she dare not keep to herself. Somehow he would know and—she shuddered.

She would not have him angry with her again.

April perched on her shoulder as they made their way to the morning room.

Papa, Mama and her sisters were gathered around the table, engaged in quiet pursuits: reading, sewing, hat trimming. Exactly what Elizabeth might have hoped for, a calm, quiet morning.

"I hope, my dear," Papa set his paper aside and looked from Mama to Elizabeth, "that you have ordered a good dinner today, because I have reason to expect an addition to our family party."

"Who do you mean, my dear? I know of nobody that is coming, unless Charlotte Lucas should happen to call in. I hope my dinners are good enough for her." Mama sniffed, her lip curling slightly. She had no good opinion of Lady Lucas' table.

"The person of whom I speak is a gentleman and a stranger." Papa fixed his eyes on Elizabeth.

She squeezed her eyes shut as the room threatened to spin.

"A gentleman and a stranger! It is Mr. Bingley, I am sure. Why Jane, you never dropt a word of this. You sly thing! Well, I am sure I shall be extremely glad to see Mr. Bingley. Lydia, my love, ring the bell. I must speak to Hill this moment."

"It is not Mr. Bingley. It is a person whom I never saw in the whole course of my life." Papa leaned back, a satisfied expression creeping across his face.

He so enjoyed this sort of game. Mama, Jane, Kitty and Lydia all obliged him.

Elizabeth sat next to Mary, who grasped her hand under the table. From the look on her face, she knew something of Longbourn's recent temper, too.

"Who is it, Papa?" Lydia bounced in her seat. "I

know! It is one of the officers."

Kitty turned to her, hands clasped, "Perhaps one of the new ones? Have they arrived already, Papa?"

"Officers? What a delightful idea. You are so good to us, Mr. Bennet."

Papa shook his head. "It is not Mr. Bingley nor any militia officer. I received this letter from my cousin, Mr. Collins, who, when I am dead, may turn you all out of this house as soon as he pleases."

"Oh, my dear," Mama gasped and drew out her handkerchief. "Pray, do not talk of that odious man. I do think it is the hardest thing in the world that your estate should be entailed away from your own children. I am sure if I had been you, I should have tried long ago to do something or other about it."

Elizabeth bit her tongue. Mama simply could not comprehend there was no way around the entail. The entire affair was iron clad and even the dragon con-clave would be forced to see someone—or several someones— eaten in order to make any material change in their fate. Still mama railed bitterly against the cruelty of settling an estate away from a family of five daughters, in favor of a man who had nothing to do with them.

"Granted, nothing can clear Mr. Collins from the guilt of inheriting Longbourn. But if you will listen to his letter, you may perhaps be a little softened by his manner of expressing himself." Papa removed a letter from his pocket, and extended it toward Elizabeth.

"Pray sir, I cannot read this morning. My eyes are still weak, and my head aches." She handed it back to him.

He glowered.

"Stop it, she is unwell, can you not see?" April

hissed.

His eyes bulged.

Mama waved her handkerchief before her face. "You may as well read it yourself. I am sure that I shall not improve my opinion of him, though. I think it was very impertinent of him to write to you at all, and very hypocritical. I hate such false friends."

"It seems he has some filial scruples, as you will hear." Papa unfolded the letter, grumbling under his breath. "Dear Sir, the disagreement subsisting between yourself and my late honored father always gave me much uneasiness. Since I have had the misfortune to lose him, I have frequently wished to heal the breach. For some time I was kept back by my own doubts, fearing it might seem disrespectful to his memory for me to be on good terms with any one with whom it had always pleased him to be at variance.

"My mind, however, is now made up on the subject. I received ordination at Easter and have been so fortunate as to be distinguished by the patronage of the Right Honorable Lady Catherine de Bourgh, widow of Sir Lewis de Bourgh, whose bounty and beneficence has preferred me to the valuable rectory of this parish, where it shall be my earnest endeavor to be ever ready to perform those rites and ceremonies which are instituted by the Church of England."

"Dear heavens, his sentences are quite as long as your mother's. Could two such people ever exist together in the same room without coming to fisticuffs over who would speak?" April whispered in her ear.

Papa snorted and continued. "As a clergyman, moreover, I feel it my duty to promote and establish the blessing of peace in all families within the reach of my influence. On these grounds I flatter myself that my present overtures of goodwill are highly commendable and will lead you to accept the offered olive branch. You see, Mrs. Bennet, he offers an olive branch to us."

"I cannot image what he could possibly offer that would make any kind of difference." Mama sniffled.

"Listen to what he writes. I cannot be otherwise than concerned at being the means of injuring your amiable daughters, and beg leave to apologize for it, as well as to assure you of my readiness to make them every possible amends. I remain, dear sir, with respectful compliments to your lady and daughters, your well-wisher and friend, William Collins." Papa folded up the letter. "We may expect this peacemaking gentleman at four o'clock this afternoon."

"There is some sense in what he says about the girls, I suppose. If he is disposed to make them any amends, I shall not be the person to discourage him." Mama tucked her handkerchief into her sleeve.

"Though it is difficult to guess in what way he can mean to make us the atonement he thinks our due, the wish is certainly to his credit," Jane said.

Could she really not imagine? Jane was hardly that dull.

"He must be an oddity, I think," Mary said slowly, hesitantly. "I cannot make him out. There is something very pompous in his style. And what can he mean by sounding so apologetic for being next in the entail? We cannot suppose he would help it, if he could. Can he be a sensible man, sir?"

Elizabeth cringed a little as Papa glared at her. "I suppose we shall know more at four o'clock, then."

Her stomach roiled. It would be a very long wait.

Mr. Collins was punctual to his time, and was

received with great politeness by the whole family. His letter had done away with much of Mama's ill-will. She saw him with a degree of composure—an astonishing, if unsettling, transformation.

Papa said little, instead standing back to watch as Mama and her youngest sisters took the dragon's share of the conversation. Interesting that Aunt and Uncle were not among them for the great introduction. Was it by coincidence or contrivance?

Knowing Papa, probably the latter.

Mr. Collins was a tall, heavy-looking young man of five and twenty who seemed ready to launch into a great deal of conversation with his hostesses. His air was grave and stately, and his manners were very formal—too formal to be appropriate to a family setting—as Mama ushered him into the parlor.

"I must say, Mrs. Bennet, you have a very fine family of daughters. I have heard much of their beauty, but in this instance, fame has indeed fallen short of the truth. They are beyond lovely, every one of them. I am quite certain you shall enjoy the blessing of seeing them all, in due time, well disposed of in marriage."

Disposed of? What a ghastly turn of phrase. Did he consider females some sort of refuse to be cast away as conveniently as possible?

No, that was short-tempered and ungracious. It was not appropriate to judge him so very quickly. But April huffed unhappily from her perch in the curtains. Not a good first impression, it would seem, and her first impressions were very hard to disabuse.

Mama fluttered her fan in front of her face. "You are very kind, sir, I am sure. I wish with all my heart it may prove so, for else they will be destitute otherwise. Things are settled so oddly."

"You allude, perhaps, to the entail of this estate."

"Ah sir, I do indeed. It is a grievous affair to my poor girls, you must confess. Not that I mean to find fault with you for such things."

Elizabeth clutched her forehead. How entirely impolitic—and entirely typical—of her.

"I am very sensible, madam, of the hardship to my fair cousins. But I can assure the young ladies that I come prepared to admire them. At present I will not say more, but perhaps when we are better acquainted—"

"What is he looking for? A harem?" April shook her head forcefully enough to rustle the curtains.

Hill bustled in. "Dinner is ready, madam."

Mr. Collins offered his arm and escorted Mama to the dining room. Jane and Elizabeth followed closely enough to hear Mr. Collins' excessive admiration; the hall, the dining-room, and all its furniture were examined and praised. Was that just his way of making himself welcome, or was it inspired by a consideration of it all as his own future property? Only further acquaintance would tell.

Uncle and Aunt Gardiner joined them in the dining room and were in due course introduced to Mr. Collins. Aunt was everything sweet and gracious. Uncle, though, said little, his brow drawn in uncharacteristic, taciturn knots as Mr. Collins took the opportunity to fully introduce himself to the family.

More than merely offering an introduction, Mr. Collins proved beyond anyone's doubt, he was not a sensible man. The deficiencies afforded him by nature had been but little assisted by education or society. Though he belonged to one of the universities, he had attended classes while quite possibly learning nothing useful.

A fortunate chance had recommended him to Lady Catherine de Bourgh when the living of Hunsford was vacant. The respect and veneration which he felt for her high rank and patronage, mingling with a very good opinion of himself, his authority as a clergyman, and his rights as a rector, made him altogether a mixture of pride and obsequiousness, self-importance and insipid humility.

Having now a good house and very sufficient income, he intended to marry. In seeking reconciliation with the Longbourn family, he meant to choose one of the daughters, if he found them as handsome and amiable as they were represented by common report. Thus he would make amends for inheriting their father's estate. He thought it an excellent plan, full of eligibility and suitableness, and excessive generosity and unselfseeking on his own part.

Unselfseeking—provided they were attractive and pleasant enough for him. How endearing.

Over their heads, April kept up a running commentary of her diminishing opinion of Mr. Collins. Every time he spoke, it seemed, she found another trait to dislike. She did have a good humor about it, making it difficult for any at the table who heard her not to laugh aloud.

When Mr. Collins paused his conversation as the second course was brought in, April poked her beak above the curtains, looked directly at him and whispered, "You are a condescending, ingratiating, self-important mammal, with the arrogance of a cockatrice and the appeal of the Snake King."

Elizabeth tried not to stare, but it was difficult to decide who not to stare at. Papa was struggling not to choke. Uncle Gardiner's jaws were clenched so tight he might break a tooth. Aunt held her napkin to her face as she turned red while Mary hid her face in her hands. Mr. Collins' brows furrowed as he looked not at his struggling family members, but into the very curtain where April hid.

Could he hear her? Elizabeth's face grew cold and prickly and she held her breath.

Mr. Collins blinked several times, and he looked away.

Elizabeth chanced a brief look toward April.

"I am not sure. He does not hear clearly, that is certain, but he might be hard of hearing, perhaps with enough ability to be trained to hear passably. But I am not sure."

How odd for her not to be certain. She always knew.

The looks on Papa's and Uncle's faces suggested they thought the same thing.

"You seem very fortunate in your patroness. Lady Catherine de Bourgh's attention to your wishes, and consideration for your comfort, appear very remarkable." Papa sipped his wine and sat back a little in his chair.

Mr. Collins' face brightened to almost blinding. "I have never in my life witnessed such behavior in a person of rank—"

Just how many people of rank had he been in the presence of?

"—such affability and condescension, I have myself experienced from Lady Catherine. She has graciously approved of both the discourses which I have already had the honor of preaching before her. She has also asked me twice to dine at Rosings, and has sent for me to make up her pool of evening quadrille. Some, I fear, reckon her proud, but I have never seen anything but affability in her. She has always spoken to me as she would to any other gentleman and not had the smallest objection to my joining in the society of the neighborhood. Why, she has even approved of my leaving the parish occasionally for a week or two, to visit my relations."

"That is all very proper and civil, I am sure," said Mama, "and I dare say she is a very agreeable woman. I think you said she was a widow, sir? Has she any family?"

"She has only one daughter, the heiress of Rosings, and of very extensive property. She is a most charming young lady indeed. Lady Catherine herself says that in point of true beauty, Miss De Bourgh is far superior to the handsomest of her sex; because there is that in her features which marks the young woman of distinguished birth."

"That means plain features and a big nose, which only fortune and substantial property can make beautiful," April whispered.

"She is unfortunately of a sickly constitution, which has prevented her making that progress in many accomplishments which she could not otherwise have failed of."

"So not only is she dreadfully plain, she has no real accomplishments to speak of. I wonder if she can even read." April stared directly at Mr. Collins.

He did not look up. "Her indifferent state of health unhappily prevents her being in town; and by that means, as I told Lady Catherine one day, has deprived the British court of its brightest ornament. Her ladyship seemed pleased with the idea. You may imagine that I am happy on every occasion to offer those little delicate compliments which are always acceptable to ladies. These are the kind of small things which please her ladyship, and it is a sort of attention which I conceive myself peculiarly bound to pay."

"It is happy for you that you possess the talent of flattering with delicacy. May I ask whether these pleasing attentions proceed from the impulse of the moment, or are the result of previous study?" Papa asked.

"They arise chiefly from what is passing at the time. Though I sometimes amuse myself with suggesting and arranging such little elegant compliments as may be adapted to ordinary occasions, I always wish to give them as unstudied an air as possible."

At least it was now clear, Papa thought him ridiculous as well.

This was the man to whom she would be tied for the rest of her life? A dragon-deaf windbag, who cared little whom he married so long as she pleased his eyes, eased his conscience and looked good to his patroness?

A man who preferred such an easy life probably had no scruples about complaining when he did not find things so easy. His temper was probably ferocious. Not unlike Longbourn's.

This was the man Papa and Longbourn expected her to marry? She would be hemmed in on all sides by those demanding she provide them with ease and comfort with no consideration to her own desires.

Managing one would be difficult enough, but both? And then if there were children? How could she care for them—especially if they could hear while their father could not—and the man, the dragon and the demands of the Blue Order?

No, that was more than anyone could manage.

She wrapped her arms around her waist, tight, but it did nothing to alleviate the emptiness within.

She cast a pleading look at Papa, but he closed his eyes and turned aside.

What had her life just become?

10
Chapter

Morning sun streamed into the dressing room as Darcy lingered in the tub of hot water, having scrubbed every inch of his skin nearly raw. His clothing had been sent out to the laundress and his boots brushed and polished until they shone. He ducked down and scrubbed his hair once more. The bath last night had left him feeling so much improved, he did not want to miss any possible advantage this one might impart.

He needed to remember to thank April for bringing the news herself. That was an unexpected courtesy that his attitude toward her had done nothing to warrant. It seemed something was bothering the little blue flutter-tuft, though.

Perhaps it had something to do with the dragon-thunder he heard in the distance. Longbourn must be in a very ill humor to be so loud. What could have upset him so? It was difficult to tell with dragons. Sometimes they seemed so capricious.

Walker certainly could be so when the mood struck

him. Though he had only been gone a few days, the cockatrice's absence was difficult to ignore. How much longer until he might return?

Darcy clambered out of the copper tub. Stiff joints and uncertain knees reminded him of his first—and hopefully last—encounter with dragon venom. But at least drawing breath no longer had him bracing for the pain. That alone was reason to celebrate. His stomach grumbled a bit—had his appetite returned as well? Perhaps one more soak and scrub would leave him set to rights.

He dressed and opened the window. The crisp smells of the morning always helped him begin the day.

In a great flapping of wings, a cockatrice landed on the window sill. Walker?

No, Rustle, dusty and droop-winged.

He squared his jaw against the disappointment.

"Have you eaten recently? Shall I call for a tray?" Darcy asked.

Rustle hopped to the edge of the tub. "Food would be welcome. Might I?" He dipped his wing in the bath water.

Darcy bowed and retreated. It was not wise to stand too near a bathing cockatrice. They enjoyed their baths a great deal.

A tray arrived at his door in short order. Darcy took it from the maid, denying her entrance. Through the door, Rustle suggested that she did not think it unusual and that she had a great deal to do. She curtsied and hurried away.

Darcy offered Rustle kippers and ham, which he wolfed down with aplomb. Darcy contented himself with toast and jam and a bit of cheese.

Belly slightly distended, Rustle settled on the back

of the chair opposite Darcy's. "We encountered the militia company just a day out from here. Walker insisted he delay the remainder of his journey until we could search the company thoroughly. The good news: he is certain that the egg is with that company."

Darcy exploded from his seat, barely containing a shout.

"That is the only good news to be had, though." Rustle squawked as if to make his point.

"No doubt, nothing will be simple." Darcy returned to his seat, heat creeping up his jaw.

"Far from it. We could not determine precisely where the egg was hidden in the accoutrements of the militia. It was as if the scent had been deliberately spread throughout. Moreover, the supplies and rations are closely guarded. So closely, we could not approach without being shooed off like crows." A shudder began at Rustle's beak and rippled all the way down his body.

"It cannot be that bad, with only a limited amount to be searched—"

"The company arrived in Meryton yesterday evening. I stayed near, hoping I might be able to detect its presence as the supplies were moved. But I could not. And now there has been sufficient time for the egg to have been secreted away in some place where we might not even be able to smell it."

"Oh, bloody hell." Darcy raked his wet hair.

"Walker says, and I agree, it is too much for you to search alone. Bennet's assistance is essential."

"Bennet's assistance? How precisely am I to obtain that? I do not think he will admit me to his house."

"There is Miss Elizabeth ... no, did you offend her again?"

"No ... yes ... I do not know. Truly I do not know.

I had not thought so at the time, but in retrospect, I am not sure. I never am." He kneaded his temples.

"You offended her, I am certain. You could try to go to Gardiner. He has not Bennet's resentments."

"Why do I not go to Longbourn directly and ask his assistance?" Darcy threw his hands in the air.

Rustle shrugged and bobbed his head. "That is a thought ... perhaps a very good one."

"You must be joking."

"Not at all. Who better to assist you? Come, I shall make the petition for you." Rustle pointed toward the window with his wing.

"He will not see me."

"He may surprise you. If it does not work, then you can see Gardiner. You can ill afford to turn aside any possibility of help."

Rustle was right, though Darcy loathed admitting it. He hurried out, and followed Rustle into the woods.

What was that sound? He paused and closed his eyes.

Thunder perhaps? He peeked one eye open. No, there were no dark clouds. He shut his eyes again and concentrated.

Those were dragon voices! The words though were unfamiliar ... were they speaking their own tongue? That was not possible though, who could Longbourn be talking to at that volume? Only another major-dragon could be that loud. And from the sound there was an argument brewing,

Darcy tensed. Should he run to it, or away?

Silence.

Birds began chirping as though nothing had ever been different.

Rustle circled back to him. "Why are you standing

about so stupidly?"

"Did you not hear?"

Rustle cawed and flew into the woods.

Darcy followed.

Rustle approached Longbourn's cavern while Darcy waited behind the shrubbery. The ground was no more disturbed than it had been the last time he was here. Two arguing dragons could not possibly have occupied this space.

Lovely. Now he was hearing dragon voices where there were none. If he did not find the egg soon, he would be a candidate for Bedlam.

"Laird Longbourn," Rustle called, bowing toward the dark opening in the hillside.

Grumbles and growls came from within. The ground thumped and a toothy, scaly head appeared. "Leave me. I have no wish for company."

The deep, rumbling voice resounded in Darcy's chest. Was it possible to feel a voice more than hear it?

Rustle bowed, touching his forehead to the ground, wings extended. "Pray excuse the intrusion, but the matter is urgent. Most urgent."

Longbourn leaned down and snorted, ruffling Rustle's feather-scales and stirring a cloud of dust. "What do you dare consider urgent in my presence?"

Who was this creature with all the power and pride of true draconic presence? Was this the same dragon that wagged his tail and all but purred with Miss Elizabeth's ministrations to him?

"The missing dragon egg—"

Longbourn reared up and roared. "That egg has caused me nothing but grief! I wish to hear no more of it."

Darcy rushed out of the bushes. "Then pray, Laird

Longbourn, assist us in finding it, and we shall have it gone from your territory."

Longbourn's eyes bulged. He huffed and grunted—was he preparing a poison breath? He stomped toward Darcy and leaned down close to his face.

"This is your fault. Everything is your fault. You failed your Keep. You endangered my Keeper. You bring trespassers to my territory." Longbourn's tail whipped across the ground, sending small stones and branches flying.

A drop of ocher venom dripped from his fang and landed, burning, on Darcy's cheek. He squeezed his eyes shut, eyes watering from the fumes. Lifting his shoulder, he rubbed the cheek against his coat. It would probably be ruined, eaten through by the noxious acid.

A smart man would run. A major-dragon in high dudgeon was nothing to be trifled with.

Darcy swallowed hard. "The fault is not all mine. I was betrayed by one who I trusted as a brother. Not once, but twice. He…"

A low roar began deep in Longbourn's throat. The wyvern's patience was short—dangerously so.

Why tell the dragon such things?

But what else could he say?

"He tried first to steal my sister—elope with her. I stopped that and banished him from Pemberley grounds, sending him into the militia. I was assured by the head of the Order it would be enough to protect my sister, and Pemberley Keep. It never occurred to me that he—he was not bound by the laws of the Order—he could not actually hear. He was a trickster, a charlatan. When he could not take my sister's fortune, he went after something of greater value. He knew the grounds of Pemberley well enough to sneak in and steal the egg."

"Why do I care for any of this?"

"Because, the man is here now, with the egg. Help me find it, and I shall take it from your territory."

Longbourn's eyes narrowed. "I do not trust you. You permitted my Keeper to be injured."

"The Order commanded us to do everything in our power to retrieve the egg. If there is anyone to blame, it should be them."

"You should have protected her." Longbourn's breaths came faster. Deeper, pungent, potent.

"Had there been any reason to suspect—"

"Any idiot would have anticipated maps that valuable would be protected." His tail thumped the side of the cavern opening. A small shower of dirt tumbled down.

"Valuable? To whom? Only to smugglers and thieves. They would hardly have access to dragon venom." Darcy's eyes bulged and his jaw dropped. "You knew they were warded against intruders?"

"You permitted her to be hurt. Now she is weak and angry. It is your fault we quarreled."

"You quarreled with your Keeper?"

With Miss Elizabeth, whom all dragons adored?

Oh, this was bad.

Very, very bad.

"She has not returned to me. She used to come to me every day, but today the sister came. The sister said my Keeper will not see me."

The anger in Longbourn's voice was clear, but there was something else … was it sadness, loneliness, fear?

Did dragons even feel those things?

Whatever it was, it was dangerous, perhaps even

deadly.

Longbourn stomped. "It is her duty to tend me."

"It is a Keeper's duty to see to their dragon's needs. But it is also her duty to obey the Order, for the good of all human and dragonkind. That is why she was helping us find the egg."

"I have forbidden her. She is not to be endangered again." His tail swung hard enough to break bones.

"Then, pray, assist me. You are surely better able to search the caverns than I. Meanwhile, I can contrive to search the encampment again, something you are unable to do. Together—"

"And what will you do with the egg once you find it?" Longbourn rounded on him, roaring.

Darcy stood his ground, though his ribs rattled and knees turned to jelly. "Take it home—"

"Then why do you have a sword, a Dragon Slayer blade?" Longbourn reared up and extended his wings, flapping. Leaves and dirt swirled around them.

A wyvern might only be the least of major-dragons, but his fury was awesome.

Darcy held his breath and considered his words. He might have only one chance to explain. A wrong word and there would be nothing left of him to find.

"What happens when an egg hatches without human presence?" Darcy asked very softly.

"It happens all the time in the woods. Fairy dragons, tatzelwurms, cockatrices, there is even a tiny basilisk that shares my woods. Wyrms that pass for snakes, in the small lake the legend of the giant, one eyed—"

"Those are minor dragons. When they do not imprint on humans, they want nothing to do with men—and think nothing of attacking them. Since they are small, though, they do little harm. But a major-dragon?

Humans are easy prey."

Longbourn folded his wings across his back. "It is a crime for a Dragon Friend to kill a dragon."

Good, he was listening.

"When it is a dragon who has imprinted on humans, it is a crime of the worst shade. But not so in defense against a wild dragon."

"You would kill the dragon of your Keep?"

"Not if there were any other choice."

"You would be anathema to all dragon kind. Reviled, stalked … even paying with your life."

"I know the consequences." Darcy clenched his fists. "I suffer them each night in my sleep. But if that is the price to be paid to keep the Pendragon Treaty, then I will pay it. It is the cost of hearing dragons."

Longbourn huffed over him, spittle dripping from his lips.

"I want more than anything to return that Dragon Slayer to the Order, untouched by dragon blood, and to restore Pemberley to its rightful Keep." Darcy counted ten long breaths.

Longbourn stepped back.

Cool, fresh air blew against Darcy's face, chilling the sweat on his neck.

"I will assist you. Then you will be gone. I want the Dragon Slayer, the egg, and you away from my territory."

Darcy bowed. "It will be as you say, then, Laird. I am most grateful for your assistance."

"I will begin now. Rustle, assist me. You know the smell of the egg." Longbourn turned sharply.

Darcy jumped away from his pounding tail. It would be difficult to search without a dragon companion—nearly impossible. But to argue about that now would be beyond foolish.

"The cockatrice will bring you news." Longbourn disappeared into his cavern.

"Tell Gardiner I am in the service of Longbourn and the nature of our task." Rustle called over his shoulder as he disappeared after the wyvern.

Darcy sank down on a convenient stone, and scrubbed his face with his hands. His cheek burned and bled where the venom had landed. The shoulder of his coat was now frayed away, the lining showing through. And he had no companion dragon to convince his valet it was nothing to be concerned over.

When would Walker return?

At least Longbourn had agreed to help. That was the material thing.

He pushed up to his feet, knees arguing all the way. His vision wavered. Another bath was in order immediately. Afterwards he could worry about the Dragon Slayer in the barn, Miss Elizabeth's condition, and how he was going to search for the egg amongst a camp full of soldiers.

After another bath, which would cost him in considerable vails to the staff, Darcy headed downstairs. He needed something far more substantial than the bread and cheese he had begun his day upon before he could face any more dragons—or men. Thankfully a cold luncheon had been laid out in the small dining room, and the room was empty. What more could he possibly ask for? Such good fortune could not last long though, so he sat down to sate himself before Miss Bingley appeared.

Bingley sauntered in. "Finally taken to lying abed and enjoying a bit of a respite, I see? Never thought I would see the day. I am heading into town in a bit. Care to join me? Colonel Forster invited me to dine with himself and his new wife. He included you in the offer."

Darcy nodded vigorously, struggling to choke down his bite. "Yes, yes, I should be happy to join you."

"Do not choke yourself, man, have a care. I have never seen you excited about a social engagement. Are you feeling well? What happened to your face?"

Darcy touched his cheek. "Dull razor. My man nearly scraped my cheek clean off."

"Ah good, thought your bird might have finally taken a dislike to you." Bingley laughed and sat down.

"I suppose that is some sort of canny remark about—"

"About your general deportment in society. Yes, you are starting to develop a reputation as a curmudgeon, and you are far too young for that. Save it for your dotage. Really, Darcy, I insist you come down off that high horse and actually enjoy yourself. The ball is the perfect place for that. You must attend."

"If it makes you feel any better, I have already requested a set of dances from Miss Elizabeth Bennet."

"You have? Excellent, I am proud of you." He clapped Darcy's shoulder. "I had not thought it likely, but you are showing some real promise of being tolerable in company. Are you finished eating? Shall I call for the horses?"

How rapidly Bingley's mind leapt from one idea to the next.

"Yes, do." Darcy wiped his mouth and set his napkin aside. "I shall meet you in a quarter of an hour."

The ride to Meryton was blissfully uneventful. Just

the opportunity Darcy needed to regain his composure and consider how he might obtain unimpeded access to the encampment, without dragon persuasion. Several families from Pemberley and Lambton had men in that regiment. Perhaps if he offered to bring letters home for them, or to write to those families himself and report on the excellences he found. Either might suit. Perhaps even offering to write a letter to Clarington, praising Forster's efforts in the full Colonel's absence. That had potential as well.

Meryton's main street was cobbled and quaint. It had not the traffic of a larger town, but it was sufficient to be called bustling. Neat country shops lined the street, with proud window displays to catch the eye. More refined than Lambton, but not up to the standards of Derby.

Bingley pointed toward the windows of a millinery shop. "I believe, yes, I am sure of it. Those are the Bennet sisters. Come, we must pay our respects."

Before Darcy could suggest otherwise, Bingley's horse was already moving in that direction.

What else was there to do but follow?

Darcy could only make out four Bennet sisters. The middle one was missing. Had she gone to tend Longbourn? Would he tell her Darcy had been to see him? Could he expect an angry summons from Bennet in the offing? A message to Gardiner was definitely the first order of business when he returned to Netherfield.

Miss Elizabeth stood slightly away from her sisters, near a tall man who looked vaguely familiar. They had never been introduced, but his face ... yes! Richard had pointed him out in London just a few months ago. Aunt Catherine's new vicar. He was heir to some sort of estate and she, as always, was looking to extend hers and Rosings' influence among the Blue Order.

Dragon fire! Was he heir to the Bennet's estate? He hardly needed one more Bennet to complicate matters.

Bingley called out a salutation and Miss Bennet answered, bringing the entire group close enough to converse.

April launched off Miss Elizabeth's shoulder and started toward Darcy.

"My dear cousin, do you not think it wise to leave your pet behind when you walk? A cage would be a far more fitting place for it. Really I think it unseemly—" the man said.

"I do not like him at all. I am not a pet." April cheeped, circled once around Darcy and returned to Miss Elizabeth's shoulder. "Has Rustle returned?"

Darcy nodded, looking toward Bingley and Miss Bennet.

"Has the egg been recovered?"

He shook his head.

"Is there hope?"

Miss Elizabeth glanced at him from the side of her eye.

He nodded.

"Gardiner will call on you later." April tucked herself into Miss Elizabeth's generous hood.

So the heir of Longbourn estate could not hear dragons. No wonder Longbourn was in such a temper. Bennet could not be any happier than the dragon about this either. That certainly explained his generally ill temper.

A flash of red just beyond the little group caught his eye. Two officers …

"Denny! You are back!" Miss Lydia shrieked and beckoned the two red-coated men toward them.

Bloody hell! Wickham!

His innards knotted and his pulse pounded in his temples. How often had he considered what he would say to Wickham should they meet again? None of that was possible in this company.

"I have indeed returned from my errand, and with my friend, and our much-missed supplies in tow. May I present to you, Mr. Wickham." Denny bowed with a flourish.

Wickham stepped forward and bowed. "I am enchanted to meet such a lovely party of ladies."

Miss Lydia and Miss Kitty tittered.

Wickham entertained them with his typical inanities, the ones which young females found so enchanting—that Georgiana had found so enchanting.

A fresh course of loathing raced through him.

His horse shied.

"I thought you a better horseman, Darcy," Wickham called.

Miss Elizabeth stared wide-eyed from Wickham to Darcy and back.

"Imagine meeting you here. Who would have thought you would deign to visit a town where the militia might encamp?" Wickham laughed, encouraging the young women to join him.

Darcy gritted his teeth, feeling eyes staring at him.

"How is your sister, is she well?" Wickham winked and grinned.

"She is doing very well. Richard and I are very pleased with her new companion." One who might never permit Wickham access to Georgiana again.

"When you write to her next, offer her my greetings, will you not?"

Darcy grunted.

"Always so formal, so proper, you would not even consider it, eh? You are so attentive to everything in your Keep ... keeping, are you not? How is Pemberley? It has been so long since I have seen—"

Enough! This was not to be borne!

Darcy dug his heels into his horse's side and rode away at a smart clip.

Wickham had always been far too brash, too bold. Why should that have changed now? But to gloat about his sins in front of company, some things were beyond the pale.

But now he knew that Darcy was about. What would that drive him to?

It would have been better to keep the secret a little longer, but there was little to be done for it. Best dine with the colonel and get as close to the militia as he could.

Later that evening, Papa's coach conveyed all five sisters and Mr. Collins to Aunt Phillips'. Mama gave up her seat in the coach to him, clearly deeming it far more necessary for him to spend time with his cousins than for her to mingle with the officers. While it was pleasing not to have to fend off Mama's advice on how to be most appealing to the officers, Mr. Collins' comparisons between Papa's equipage and Lady Catherine's were almost as tiring.

His single-minded adherence to the topic continued when they reached Aunt Phillips' house. He was immediately so struck with the size of the rooms and the furniture that he declared he might almost have supposed himself in the small summer breakfast parlor at

Rosings. At first blush, Aunt Phillips found the comparison less than gratifying and did little to conceal her offense. When he went on to explain what Rosings was, who was its proprietor, the splendor of its drawing-rooms, and that the chimney-piece alone had cost eight hundred pounds, her ire dissipated.

Given the look on her face following his explanations, she would hardly have resented a comparison with the housekeeper's room. Considering how much she was like Mama, Aunt Phillips was probably already planning who among her neighbors she should share the story with on the morrow.

In the midst of Mr. Collins' next monologue, Mr. Wickham walked into the room, bringing with him a breath of fresh air and the greatest hope for pleasant conversation Elizabeth held in some time. Compared to the other officers, he was far beyond them all in person, countenance, air, and walk, as they were superior to Mr. Collins.

She was hardly the only one to notice. Though nearly every female eye in the room was turned on him, he sat beside her. She blushed at the implied compliment.

Good sense cautioned her not to become fond of him. It would only end with heartbreak. But with Longbourn's recent treatment of her, and the discovery that Mr. Collins was all the things she dreaded, some solace was required.

What harm could a single conversation occasion?

"How far is Netherfield from Meryton?" he asked, glancing over his shoulder at the lively game of lottery tickets behind them.

Lydia and Kitty laughed raucously at something one of the officers said.

Maria Grace

"On the order of two miles, quite an easy distance."

"Would you know how long Mr. Darcy has been staying there?"

"Slightly more than a month. Do you wish to call upon him? He is a man of very large property in Derbyshire, I understand." She raised an eyebrow and cocked her head.

Would he take the hint or was she trespassing too much upon his privacy?

"His estate there is a noble one. A clear ten thousand per annum." The corner of his lips drew up in a handsome expression. "If you are interested in his affairs, you could not have met with a person more capable of giving you certain information on that head than myself. I have been connected with his family from my infancy."

From infancy? Was he somehow related to Mr. Darcy? There was some resemblance about the jawline and the brow. "Indeed? I would never have guessed."

"You may well be surprised, Miss Bennet, at such an assertion, after seeing the very cold manner of our meeting today. Are you much acquainted with Mr. Darcy?"

She lowered her voice and leaned a little closer. "As much as I ever wish to be. I have spent four days in the same house with him, and I think him very disagreeable."

He seemed very pleased with her answer.

"I have no right to give my opinion, as to his being agreeable or otherwise. I have known him too long and too well to be a fair judge. It is impossible for me to be impartial. But I believe your opinion of him would astonish those who know him. He has very fine connections, you know." He hunched his shoulders and ducked his head, leaning a little closer to her.

"Perhaps he does, but he is not at all liked in Hertfordshire. Everybody is disgusted with his pride. You will not find him favorably spoken of by anyone. Even on my slight acquaintance I count him to be an ill-tempered man."

Wickham only shook his head and glanced at the ceiling, tapping his lips with his fingers. "Do you think him likely to be in this country much longer?"

"I do not know how much longer it will take him to conclude his business here. I hope your plans will not be affected by his being in the neighborhood."

"Hardly. I plan to enjoy all that Meryton has to offer. It is not for me to be driven away by Mr. Darcy. If he wishes to avoid seeing me, he must go. We are not on friendly terms, and it always gives me pain to meet him, but I have no reason for avoiding him." He crossed his arms in front of his chest.

"That you would say so suggests there is some serious tension between you."

"His father, the late Mr. Darcy, was one of the best men that ever breathed, and the truest friend I ever had. I can never be in company with his son without being grieved by a thousand tender recollections. This Mr. Darcy's behavior to myself has been scandalous, though. I believe I could forgive him anything and everything if that might prevent his disappointing the hopes and disgracing the memory of his father."

Elizabeth bit her tongue. As much as she would like to press further, delicacy required she hold her peace.

He glanced about the room, pausing to observe each group of his fellow officers, and sighed a bit wistfully. "A military life is not what I was intended for, you must understand. Circumstances have now made it an eligible option as I have been a disappointed man. My spirits will not bear solitude. I must have employment and society, and I might find both in the regiment."

"Might I ask where your earlier hopes lay?"

"The church ought to have been my profession. I was brought up for the church. I should at this time have been in possession of a most valuable living, had it pleased Mr. Darcy. His father bequeathed me the advowson of the best living in his estate. He was my godfather, and excessively attached to me. He meant to provide for me amply, and thought he had done it; but when the living fell vacant, it was given elsewhere."

Godfather? The preferment he directed toward Mr. Wickham suggested it might be more. A natural son perhaps?

"Good heavens! How could his will be disregarded? Why did not you seek legal redress?"

He shrugged and shook his head. "There was so much informality in the terms of the bequest as to give me no hope from law. A man of honor could not have doubted the intention, but Mr. Darcy chose to treat it as a merely conditional recommendation. He asserted that I had forfeited all claim to it by extravagance, imprudence, any behavior of my own he might not have liked. No doubt you are well aware of how easily his disapproval may be earned."

"I can believe he would be so judgmental. His opinions seem entirely fixed as to what constitutes acceptable deportment." She glanced at Lydia and Kitty.

Oh, the things Mr. Darcy would say of them!

"We are very different sorts of men. I have a warm, unguarded temper. I may perhaps have sometimes spoken my opinion of him, and to him, too freely. I can recall nothing worse. What is certain is that the living became vacant two years ago, exactly as I was of an age to hold it, and that it was given to another man."

"Shocking! He deserves to be publicly disgraced."

"Some time or other he will be—but it shall not be by me. Till I can forget his father, I can never defy or expose him." He smiled, though the sadness of the expression threatened to bring tears to her eyes.

"What can have induced him to behave so cruelly?"

"A thorough, determined dislike of me—a dislike which I attribute in some measure to jealousy. Had the late Mr. Darcy liked me less, his son might have borne with me better. But his father's uncommon attachment to me irritated him very early in life. He had not a temper to bear the sort of competition in which we stood—the sort of preference which was often given me."

"I had not thought Mr. Darcy so bad as this. Though I have never liked him, I had not thought so very ill of him—descending to such malicious revenge! Then again, I do remember his boasting at Netherfield, of the implacability of his resentments, of his having an unforgiving temper. His disposition must be dreadful. You grew up together, did you not? Has it been so all his life?"

"The greatest part of our youth was passed together; inmates of the same house, sharing the same amusements, objects of the same parental care. My father began life as a solicitor, as your uncle, Mr. Phillips, but he gave up everything to be of use to the late Mr. Darcy as his steward. He devoted all his time to the care of the Pemberley property. Mr. Darcy often credited my father with much of Pemberley's greatness. I believe the elder Mr. Darcy's promise to provide for me came as much from a debt of gratitude to my father, as from affection to myself."

Elizabeth chewed her lip. Delightful as he was to listen to, it would be pleasing if he would actually answer her question.

"The current Mr. Darcy has always been a prideful man, but out of that pride, I think, if you will excuse the speculation—good has come. He has a reputation of being liberal and generous, giving his money freely, displaying hospitality, assisting his tenants, and relieving the poor. Not to appear to disgrace his family or lose the influence of the Pemberley House, are powerful motives for his Christian charities. He has also brotherly pride, which with some brotherly affection, makes him a very kind and careful guardian of his sister. You will hear him generally cried up as the most attentive and best of brothers."

"What sort of a girl is Miss Darcy?"

He winced. "I wish I could call her amiable. But she is too much like her brother, very, very proud. As a child, she was affectionate and extremely fond of me. I have devoted hours and hours to her amusement. But I never see her now. She is a handsome girl, about fifteen or sixteen, and, I understand, highly accomplished. Since her father's death, her home has been London, where a companion lives with her, and sees to her continued education."

"How can Mr. Bingley, who seems the embodiment of good humor itself, and is, I really believe, truly amiable, be in friendship with such a man? How can they suit each other? He cannot know what Mr. Darcy is."

"Probably not. Mr. Darcy can please where he

chooses. He does not want in those abilities of disguise. Among those who are his equals in consequence, he is a very different man: liberal-minded, just, sincere, rational, honorable, and perhaps even agreeable."

The whist game broke up and the players dispersed to another card table. Mr. Collins used the break to return to his favorite topic, Lady Catherine, in tones so loud the whole room took note.

Mr. Wickham leaned a little closer. "Is your cousin very intimately acquainted with the family of de Bourgh?"

"Lady Catherine de Bourgh," she replied, "has very lately given him a living. I hardly know how Mr. Collins was first introduced to her notice, but he certainly has not known her long."

"You know, of course, that Lady Catherine de Bourgh and Lady Anne Darcy were sisters. She is aunt to the present Mr. Darcy."

Elizabeth grimaced. One more addition to the list of Mr. Collins' many appeals. "No, indeed, I did not. I knew nothing at all of Lady Catherine's connections. I never heard of her existence till the day before yesterday."

"Her daughter, Miss de Bourgh, will have a very large fortune, and it is believed that she and her cousin will unite the two estates."

"Mr. Collins speaks highly both of Lady Catherine and her daughter. But from some particulars that he has related of her ladyship, I suspect his gratitude misleads him, and that in spite of her being his patroness, she is an arrogant, conceited woman."

"I believe her to be both in a great degree." He chuckled behind his hand. "I have not seen her for many years, but I very well remember that I never liked her. Her manners were dictatorial and insolent despite her reputation of being remarkably sensible and clever."

Aunt Phillips called them all to supper, putting an end to their conversation.

Elizabeth went away with her head full of Mr. Wickham, though in the carriage on the way home she could hardly think. Neither Lydia nor Mr. Collins were once silent for even a moment. Lydia talked incessantly of lottery tickets, of the fish she had lost and the fish she had won. Mr. Collins described the civility of Mr. and Mrs. Phillips, protesting that he did not in the least regard his losses at whist, enumerating all the dishes at supper, and repeatedly fearing that he crowded his cousins. He had more to say than he could well manage before the carriage stopped at Longbourn House.

Jane followed Elizabeth upstairs and to her room, under the guise of helping Elizabeth with her hair. As she removed pins, brushed and plaited, she waxed on about the superiority of Mr. Bingley to all the officers and all other men in general.

At last Jane paused, and Elizabeth related what had passed between Mr. Wickham and herself.

"I do not know how to believe that Mr. Darcy could be so unworthy of Mr. Bingley's regard. Yet, how might I question the veracity of a young man of such amiable appearance as Wickham? Mr. Bingley and Mr. Wickham, they have both been deceived, I dare say, in some way or other. It seems to me, interested people have perhaps misrepresented each to the other. It is, in short, impossible for us to conjecture the causes or circumstances which may have alienated them, without actual blame on either side." Jane set aside the hairbrush.

"Very true, indeed. Now, my dear Jane, what have you got to say in behalf of the interested people who have probably been concerned in the business? Do we clear them too, or we shall be obliged to think ill of somebody."

"Laugh as much as you choose, but you will not laugh me out of my opinion. My dearest Lizzy, do but consider in what a disgraceful light it places Mr. Darcy, to be treating one whom his father had promised to provide for in such a manner. It is impossible. No man of common humanity, no man who had any value for his character, could be capable of it. Can his most intimate friends be so excessively deceived in him? I am sure not."

"I can much more easily believe in Mr. Bingley being imposed on, than that Mr. Wickham should invent such a history of himself as he gave me. Names, facts, everything mentioned without ceremony. If it be not so, let Mr. Darcy contradict it. Besides, there was truth in his looks."

"It is difficult indeed. Perhaps I should consult Mr. Bingley's experiences. One does not know what to think."

"I beg your pardon. One knows exactly what to think." Especially if one were to add consideration of a stolen dragon's egg to their understanding.

11
Chapter

After three days spent in the company of the militia, Darcy was certain of two things. He detested Colonel Forster's society only second to Mrs. Forster's society, and the egg was not hidden amongst the encampment.

He had seen Wickham not less than half a dozen times. The man must have sought him out for the opportunity to gloat. Each time he looked more smug than the last, knowing where the egg was hidden and knowing that Darcy did not. There was little that seemed to please Wickham better than getting the best of Darcy.

But he would not win this time. He could not.

Surely Longbourn would send word soon. How long could it take a highly motivated dragon to find an egg in the hillsides when accompanied by a cockatrice who could actually smell it?

Darcy called for a breakfast tray and paced his room. Joining the company in the breakfast parlor was out of the question. With the ball to be held the next night, the household's frenzy was more than his fragile composure could tolerate. Perhaps he could escape the house entirely for the day and fortify himself for the dread event with a generous dose of solitude.

A squawk at the window!

He jumped.

Walker, at last!

"Come in, come in. I had begun to despair that something untoward had happened to you." He swept the curtains out of Walker's way.

"I should have anticipated a se'nnight delay at least. The Order is not known for moving quickly, even when urgent matters are at hand." Walker hopped from the window sill to the back of the nearest chair, flipping his wings neatly to his back.

"I am sure you have seen the militia with their supply trains as you came. Unfortunately, Wickham discovered my presence here before I could search the encampment without his knowledge. Nonetheless, I have spent the last three days determining that it is not among them."

"And the hillsides?" Walker picked at one of the buckles holding a small satchel to his chest.

Darcy released the straps. "Longbourn and Rustle are combing them."

"Longbourn? Something has moved that dusty, crusty creature to activity?"

Darcy snorted. "He was tremendously disturbed at Miss Elizabeth's injury. He forbade her from any more searching for the egg and volunteered to take her place."

"I can understand his being upset."

"Why so?"

"According to the description I gave the Order, it

was wyvern venom you encountered in the map room."

"Wyvern?" Darcy set the satchel aside.

"Yes. But how it got there no one can say. Wyverns do not give up their venom easily, only to their Keepers—and victims—if at all. There has been no other wyvern in this region in a century."

"There was black trade in venom at one time. It is possible it was a family heirloom, passed down to some Netherfield resident."

"That has been suggested. But it is mere conjecture and not at all useful. Unless Bennet has come up with something, no one in the Order has the means by which the venom, once airborne, can be neutralized. Once it settles again, the room may be entered, with certain precautions taken. But it will take months for that to happen."

Darcy pinched the bridge of his nose. "So those maps can be of no use to us. Have you any welcome news?"

"I brought some papers from the Order. You will be pleased, but your aunt will not."

Darcy opened the satchel and pulled out a bundle of blue taped papers, sealed with the Order's blue wax. "They have tackled the marriage issues?"

Walker bobbed his head. "It seems that the unthinkable has happened. Dragons have changed their minds. I have been charged to help spread the word."

Darcy sank into the nearest chair. "Pray, tell me you are not joking. This is not the kind of jest I can tolerate."

"As it means I may well not have to endure the company of Anne de Bourgh for all of her natural life, I do not consider it a matter of jest, either."

"There is recourse to the marriage the old Pemberley and Rosings arranged?" Darcy held his breath.

"I am not sure I would go that far, but the signs are very favorable that that will soon be the case. You have only to defer the unhappy event for perhaps another year, maybe just a few months. I believe the Conclave will have a final mandate drafted by then. Given their current attitudes, it seems likely the Conclave will no longer insist that dragon-dictated marriages must be honored."

"Second to finding Pemberley's egg, this is the most heartening news I can imagine. I had no idea the Conclave would consider such an issue important enough to discuss."

"Do you think we regard our relationships to our Dragon Friends so lightly as to be insensible to their feelings?" Walker had that offended look in his eye and his hackles rose.

"Hardly. It is just that dragons do not mate as we do, and there has been little basis of understanding on that matter since the penning of the Pendragon Treaty."

The feather-scales on the back of his neck smoothed. "Buckingham is quite future-sighted. He has been studying the writings of your philosophers and examining the unrest that has been plaguing the continent. It is his conclusion that a significant social shift is happening, one that could threaten the Pendragon Treaty. I think this is the first of many changes, changes that will help the Accords to remain strong. It would not do to have them break down after eight hundred years."

Darcy scrubbed his face with his palms. "When our life-spans are so much shorter than dragonkind's, it is sometimes difficult to remember the full scope of considerations that must be dealt with."

A knock at the door drew him away. He took the breakfast tray and dismissed the maid.

"Kippers?" Walker sniffed the air. "You hate them."

"But you do not. I requested them just in case you might arrive in time to partake." Darcy placed the tray near Walker.

He grabbed a kipper in his beak, flipped it into the air and caught it, swallowing it whole.

"You could stop to chew, you know."

"Later. The last se'nnight has been such that it is best to swallow and bring it up later when there is time to savor it."

Darcy swallowed and smacked his lips. Some dragon manners he would never become comfortable with. He buttered a piece of toast and looked aside as Walker downed the remainder of the kippers.

A loud squawk and another cockatrice flapped at the windowsill.

Walker reared up defensively, but quickly settled.

Rustle.

"You may enter." Walker extended his wing toward the window.

Rustle hopped to Walker and bowed his head. Walker touched his beak to the back of Rustle's neck.

They did so enjoy their shows of dominance.

"I come on behalf of Longbourn. He requires your presence." Rustle's feather-scales were covered in dust and his wings drooped.

Darcy leapt to his feet. "He has found it? The egg? It is recovered?"

"I am to say nothing in that regard. You are to

come." Rustle's voice was weary, far deeper weariness than mere physical exertion.

Had the urgency of the situation affected the dragons as well? They so rarely evidenced anything resembling anxiety.

"We will leave immediately." Walker tossed a piece of ham toward Rustle, who wolfed it gratefully.

Darcy shoved a plate of cold ham toward Rustle. "Please, consider yourself my guest."

Rustle jumped to the table's edge and gobbled the meat so fast Darcy was hardly certain it was ever there.

"My deepest thanks, to both of you. I will inform Longbourn you are coming." Rustle bobbed one more bow and dove through the window.

A quarter of an hour later, Darcy approached Longbourn's cavern, Walker flying just ahead of him. Though it was still early, shadows enveloped the little copse. Rustle stood at the opening in the hillside talking to the darkness just within. They spoke dragon tongue. Perhaps Walker would offer some insight into their conversation later.

"Laird Longbourn," Darcy called, still in the bushes. "You summoned us to an audience."

"Approach." Longbourn stomped out of the shadows.

His hide was dull and grimy, face creased in an expression of draconic displeasure. That did not likely bode well for any of them. Neither did his lashing tail that swept the ground and bounced off the cavern mouth with painful thuds.

Walker landed. He and Darcy approached, bowing deeply.

"Where have you been?" Longbourn bent low and

glared at Walker.

"To see the Order for information on wyvern venom—"

Longbourn roared hard enough to set Darcy's ribs trembling.

Walker flapped for balance. "I offer my services, now I have returned. Merely tell me how I may be useful."

Longbourn huffed and snorted, clawing at the exposed rock. "The only use I have for you now is to leave my territory, and take all your troublesome companions with you."

"Pray, Laird Longbourn, does that mean you have—" Darcy steeled himself for another roar.

"The egg has been recovered."

Darcy's knees failed and the world wavered around him. He sank to one knee, his breath coming in labored pants.

It was found! It was found. The Dragon Slayer could be returned to the Order, and the egg to its Keep. All would be well.

"We are deeply in your debt, Laird Longbourn." Walker said, nudging Darcy with his wing.

"Indeed we are. Since you want us gone, I will make arrangements. We will depart this very afternoon."

"No, you will not."

What? No, he could not have heard that correctly.

Darcy pushed to his feet and dusted off his knees. "Pray excuse me. I do not take your meaning."

"You shall not have the egg … not yet." Longbourn pulled himself to his full height.

"The egg is too near hatching, you cannot risk keeping it. Preparations for hatching must be made. Rosings is ready to receive the egg and provide all that is necessary for the hatching and time of great hunger afterwards," Walker said.

"You owe me for what I have done. I mean to see the debt repaid before you depart." Longbourn's tail whipped back and forth.

"We are grateful for your help, but how are we to repay such a debt?"

Did it not matter to Longbourn that the unhatched egg remained a real threat to his own territory and all of dragonkind?

"My Keeper still refuses to see me." Longbourn ducked his head into his shoulder. "She sends the other one to me, but it is not the same. I want my Keeper."

"I do not take your meaning."

Longbourn sat back on his haunches, his tail dragging patterns in the dirt. "She has not been the same since you offended her. We never quarreled before that happened. It must be the source of her distress. You must make things right. Make reparations to her, and see that she comes back to me. Then you shall have the egg."

"You want me to go to her father's house and bring her here, then you shall return the egg to me?"

"Make reparations—you promised to dance with her. Then she will see that I have upheld her honor, and she will come back to me."

Darcy dragged his hand down his face. Dragon logic could be tenuous at times. Probably best not to try and explain that now.

"You wish me to attend the ball and dance with her?"

"You have already asked her. Just do as you said you would."

"I cannot promise that will have any influence on—

"

Walker spread his wings and flapped, slapping Darcy's legs with his wings. "It will be done, Laird Longbourn, just as you say. Tomorrow he will dance with her and bring her to you. You shall have your Keeper returned to you, and you will return the egg."

Darcy bit his tongue. Walker would not act so if he did not have good reason for it.

"Bring her to me tomorrow after the ball, and you will have the egg."

And if he could not, then what? That was definitely not the question to ask right now, though the answer did seem rather essential.

Longbourn snorted and lumbered back into his cave.

Rustle launched and waved for them to follow to a clearing a quarter of a mile away.

He landed on a skeletal tree. It must have been struck by lightning, with one side charred and dead and the other supporting wispy tendrils of new life. "He is in a foul temper. Elizabeth's absence torments him."

"Is she unwell still? Is that what keeps her away?" Darcy asked.

"I do not know. She has never done such a thing before. He is inconsolable."

"She is nearly as stubborn as Longbourn. What if I am not able to convince her to return to him?"

Walker landed on a branch slightly above Rustle. "You will not have to convince her of anything. She is as dedicated to the Blue Order as you. Tell her the truth of the situation, and she will willingly go."

"You have that much faith in her?" Darcy raked his hair.

"I do not think there has been a woman who has so

loved dragonkind in centuries. She will do what must be done."

Perhaps she would, but putting something so critical in the hands of another? Gah! Nigh on intolerable.

Still, it was only until tomorrow. At last there was an end in sight to this nightmare.

On the morning of the Netherfield ball, Elizabeth lay in bed just a little longer than usual. A sunbeam peeked through light clouds to tease at the foot of her bed. The morning was crisp, but not unpleasantly cold. Perhaps the rains would hold back today, after all. A clear evening was everything she might ask for.

Tonight she would have the pleasure of dancing a great deal with Mr. Wickham. She would have to dance with Mr. Darcy as well—she dare not fail to fulfill her promise to Longbourn. There was already enough snorting and stomping going on from that corner. No need to add to that.

Not that she had any intention of seeing Longbourn anytime soon.

She wrapped her arms over her shoulders and rubbed them briskly, shuddering.

After that thought, there would be no more sleep. An appearance in the morning room would be appropriate. She dressed and braced herself for the ball-related effusions which were sure to greet her downstairs.

"Captain Carter has already asked me to dance a set with him tonight." Lydia skipped past her and into the morning room.

Her parents, Mr. Collins, and her sisters were

already assembled in a domestic scene fraught with the kind of energy only a ball could occasion. Perhaps she should have joined April with the Gardiners in the nursery. The fairy dragons liked to keep company there for good reason.

"He has asked me too, so you need not think so much of yourself." Kitty snorted and looked back down at her stitchery.

What was she doing to those shoe roses? They had only just come from the haberdasher. She was as likely to ruin them as to improve them.

"Well, Denny and Chamberlayne have asked me as well. Can you say the same?" Lydia reached across the table for a pot of jam.

"They would have, had I been permitted to go out with you instead of staying here and—"

Mama silenced Kitty with a glower. "That is enough, dear. You will not want for partners today, none of you will. So, Mr. Collins, I know you have great concern for your reputation. Have you determined if you will attend tonight?"

Elizabeth held her breath. Was it foolish to hope?

"I am by no means of the opinion that a ball of this kind, given by a young man of character, to respectable people, can have any evil tendency. I am so far from objecting to dancing myself that I hope to be honored with the hands of all my fair cousins in the course of the evening."

Apparently it was. She forced herself to smile, only because it would be less noticeable than if she frowned. Kitty and Lydia were not so circumspect, but, in what appeared to be his characteristic fashion, he did not seem to take notice.

He rose and bowed toward Elizabeth. "I take this

opportunity of soliciting your hand, Miss Elizabeth, for the two first dances especially—a preference which I trust my cousin Jane will attribute to the right cause, and not to any disrespect for her."

Elizabeth's stomach churned—to be so ambushed first thing in the day!

Papa leveled one of his looks at her, the kind that she could hardly ignore.

"Thank you for the honor, sir. I accept." What else could she say? She swallowed hard. No doubt this was a prelude of what was to be the rest of her life. Bowing to the unwelcome wishes of one master or another.

Papa was unmoved, supporting Longbourn's right to insist she uphold her responsibilities to her role as Keeper. Including her responsibility to marry as the dragon directed.

But Uncle Gardiner said things were changing. Did Papa not realize, or was it simply too inconvenient to deal with? He had little use for things bothersome or inconvenient.

Papa rose and beckoned her to follow. Would that Mama should object and insist she remain where she was. Keeping company, even with Mr. Collins, was preferable to an interview with Papa right now.

He shut the door behind her and shuffled to his desk, leaning against it rather than taking a chair.

She pressed her lips hard. If he was too anxious to sit, he was truly vexed indeed.

"I do not know what to make of you, Elizabeth. You have hardly been yourself since returning from Netherfield." He tried to make eye contact, but she avoided him.

"Yes, Papa."

"Longbourn is beside himself, you know. He says

that you refuse to come to him, that he has sent Rustle and April for you, but you deny him. Even Mary cannot entreat you to come."

"That is true, Papa."

He rubbed his hands together. "He is frantic, disappearing from his caverns, then suddenly appearing in the cellars below the house. You realize how dangerous that is? If Hill were to see him, the shock could easily kill her."

"You are exaggerating. Rumblkins has become excessively fond of her. He will protect her from any such shocks."

Was that why the tatzelwurm had recently taken to following Hill around constantly?

"That is beside the point. Your duty is to tend the dragon, and you are shirking. I demand to know why." He folded his arms over his chest and tapped his foot.

Elizabeth edged back half a step and wrapped her arms around her waist. "Mary is full well capable of ministering to Longbourn's needs. He wants for nothing. His hide is oiled, his lair is swept. He has all the food he can stuff himself with. If Longbourn is not happy about that, then perhaps he is being petulant."

"That is not for you to decide, not that it matters in any case. If a major-dragon wishes to be petulant, then petulant he shall be."

"Then he may be that way without me." She ducked her head and slipped back another step.

"He is a dragon, Elizabeth, a dragon. Perhaps you are too accustomed to getting your way with him. Have you forgotten? He does not have to bend to your wishes." He threw his hands in the air.

"Perhaps it is time that changed."

"What are you saying? Have you been listening to

that stuff and nonsense Gardiner has been spouting about changes from the Conclave?"

"If there are changes, then it behooves us to follow them."

He leaned close to her face. "Longbourn will not tolerate it. Dragons do not change."

"If the Conclave demands it, he has no choice."

"Have you tried telling a dragon that?"

"He has tried telling me." She turned her back to him.

"You fought with him over Collins?"

She shook her head.

"Good, and you will not either. It is not good for a dragon to be challenged. It disrupts the entire Keep. You will go to him then."

"No, sir. I will not."

"You will explain to me why."

"No, sir, I will not. You may ask Longbourn, he fully understands why. He may explain it to you."

"Lizzy…"

She turned and met his gaze.

"Stop this impertinence immediately. I have it half in mind to forbid you from attending the ball tonight."

"Perhaps that is a very good idea. Then, I will not have to dance with Mr. Collins or Mr. Darcy. You will have to explain to Longbourn why I am not going, though. He seems to think it is essential for me to go."

"Lizzy, please. You have known all your life that this was the way things would be. I am sorry you do not like Collins. I understand, truly I do. I will find some way to make it bearable for you—heaven alone knows how—but I will not rest until I do. I promise you that. Just do not take it out on Longbourn."

Her chin dropped to her chest. "I am grateful for

your promise. I am sure I will come to rely upon it before all is said and done. As for Longbourn, this is a matter between us. It must be settled between us. If I am to be his declared Keeper soon, then we must establish what that relationship will look like going forward. I will not permit him to be master and I, slave. There are certain … courtesies that I require, even if I am only a lowly human. He must understand that."

Papa removed his glasses and peered at her. "Pray tell me, what did he do?"

"He must learn to control his temper."

"My dear girl. I had no idea." He wrapped her in his arms and held her tightly.

A sob welled up in her throat, but she forced it back, though she could not fully contain the trembling in her shoulders.

"A dragon can be a fearful force, to be sure. A force that is beyond our control. I am sorry he showed that to you. It is a burden Keepers must bear at times."

Perhaps Papa was right, it was merely part and parcel of the Dragon Friend's lot. But what kind of Friend would leave her in fear of her own life?

Perhaps that was not a Friend she truly wanted to have.

Far from insisting that she stay at home from the ball, Papa determined that it was essential she attend. Her spirits needed lifting and an evening of music and dance was the surest balm for her soul. Moreover, he decided he too would attend. Perhaps she had really unsettled him, confessing the truth about Longbourn.

But it had unsettled her as well. Dragons had always been trustworthy companions, ones she trusted better than people. Not long ago, she knew, beyond any doubt, that she had nothing to fear from them. Now, though—she shuddered. Would anything ever be the same? After being caught helpless in a dragon's paw, held up to a gaping, venomous maw, powerless in the face of it, how could she ever trust a major-dragon again?

She spent the better part of the evening assisting Jane and Mary with their gowns and hair and accepting their assistance in return. There was something wholly entertaining—and fully distracting—about preparing for a ball.

Mr. Collins rode on horseback with Papa whilst the ladies took the carriage. It looked as though Papa wanted to speak with Mr. Collins on the way, but it was unlikely he would have any useful conversation. Mr. Collins had words enough for them all.

So did Kitty, Lydia and Mama. Usually irritating, to-night that was a blessing. Her responses were not required, and she could be alone in her thoughts.

The driver handed them out into the chill night air. Mama and her sisters swept inside with the force of a whirlwind—they were there for a purpose and nothing would stand in their way.

Elizabeth lingered behind. A few more breaths of the bracing night air and she would be better able to take on the crush within. Besides, she had the real pleasure of Mr. Wickham's company to look forward to. That was real motivation to go inside.

A loud squawk echoed from the side of the house, sending a shiver down her spine. Rustle or Walker? She could not be sure, but it was definitely a cockatrice. She pulled her cloak a little tighter around her and crept toward the sound.

The torches planted along the drive in front of the

house cast an eerie glow, far more sinister than should be present at a ball, leaving her shadow long and obvious. She pressed closer to the house, taking cover in its shadows. The shrubberies planted near the house reached for her, plucking at her cloak and her hair. If she was not careful, all Jane's hard work would be ruined before she danced even the first set.

"If it was not you, then who?" That was Wickham's voice.

"I am sure I cannot tell you." And Mr. Darcy?

"I do not believe you. Were that true, you would not be so calm."

"So I am the guilty party because I remain calm in the face of calamity? That is a weak argument for my guilt," Mr. Darcy said.

"You enjoy winning, do you not? Once again, you have taken from me, reveling in what you have reduced me to."

"I am not reveling nor have I reduced you in any way. Look to your own actions for responsibility, not to me."

"You may think you have won, Darcy, but I assure you—"

Squawk!

She jumped and turned.

Walker landed beside her and tugged at her cloak. "You do not need to hear this. It is not—"

"I think it is very much what it appears to be. But you are quite correct, I do not need to be here listening in the shadows."

"Do not be so quick to judge!"

"I thank you for your advice, but I find perhaps that I have not been quick enough in the past to recognize—others—for what they are. I shall endeavor not to make that mistake again." She flipped her cloak around her and stormed toward the front doors.

Shortly after her entrance, Mr. Darcy appeared, but not Mr. Wickham.

So it seemed her favorite partner would not attend the ball now, and Mr. Darcy was answerable for that.

Mr. Darcy greeted her in the front hall with great politeness and reminded her of their promised dance, taxing her civility in providing a response. She muttered under her breath as a servant directed her to the ladies' changing room where she removed her cloak and donned her dancing slippers.

She ducked out and into the main rooms. Heat from the multitude of candles and fires and the bodies milling about mixed with the fragrances of perfumes, vases overflowing with flowers, and sweat. Oh, the noise! How much noise so many people made, even when they were all being quite polite. She paused a moment to adjust to the assault on her senses.

"Eliza?" Charlotte approached through the crush, hands outstretched. "You look quite well tonight."

"As do you. Did Maria do something new with your hair?"

Charlotte patted the elegant twist. "Indeed she did. I hesitated to let her try, then thought I may as well as not. Did your cousin come with you tonight? I have heard tell—"

"That he is quite interesting?"

"That was one word I heard bandied about."

"I am not sure that is the word I would choose, but we may settle on that as it is easiest. You see, he is there, standing with Jane and Mr. Bingley." Elizabeth pointed with her chin.

"He is tall, but beyond that, he seems ordinary

enough. I wonder that you would call him interesting."

"You have no idea!" Elizabeth rolled her eyes.

"He is not agreeable?"

"Not in the conventional sense of the word—"

Charlotte twitched her head. "He is coming this way."

"Cousin Elizabeth!"

"Mr. Collins, may I present my friend Miss Charlotte Lucas."

Bows and curtsies were exchanged.

"I am pleased to be introduced to any friend of my dear cousin."

"I do not think Charlotte is engaged for the whole of the evening yet. Perhaps you might consider a dance with her?" Leaving one less possibility that she might have to dance two with him.

"How very agreeable. After I have danced with all of my fair cousins, might I have your hand for, that would be, the sixth dance of the evening?"

"Thank you, I would be delighted." Charlotte smiled.

Would she still be smiling after dancing with him, though? At least they would have a jolly conversation then, probably at Mr. Collins' expense.

"But now, dear cousin, the musicians are calling us to the dance floor." He extended his hand and led her to a place in the line of dancers that crowded the floor.

The floor was chalked with ships and celestial designs. Draco was included among the constellations. How grand the dragon looked, though clearly the artist had never seen one in the flesh. The proportions were all wrong.

Who had Miss Bingley got to do the work? It was not the style of any of the local artists. It was a little sad that the designs would all be brushed away by the end of the evening.

Miss Bingley announced the first dance. How kind of her. Courtesy dictated it should be something even the less skilled dancers might manage. Pride, of course, demanded that it be the most fashionable, complicated steps possible. There was little question which would win out.

The music began and in three steps she lost hope of surviving the encounter unscathed. Mr. Collins offered his right hand instead of his left, turned her once instead of once and a half, leaving her on the wrong side of the line, and tried to correct the dancers beside them who were already in their correct places.

During the next phrase of music, he trod on her toes twice, her dress once, and on the feet of the man next to him, though how he managed that was beyond imagination. Though he apologized for his mistakes, it was at the expense of him attending to the music. The cycle of shame and misery continued for far longer than anyone should have had to endure. The moment of her release from him was ecstasy.

She danced next with an officer, and had the refreshment of talking of Wickham, and of hearing that he was universally liked. The intelligence came as no surprise, but it was gratifying to hear, nonetheless. When those dances were over she returned to Charlotte.

"If only Mr. Wickham might have stayed," Elizabeth said.

"He was here?"

"Yes, I saw him before coming in, but he quarreled with Mr. Darcy, and left."

"If he could be driven away by a mere quarrel,

perhaps he is not made of stern enough stuff to be an officer, much less dance at a ball. If I may be so bold as to suggest you not be a simpleton and allow your fancy for Wickham make you ignore a man of ten times his consequence. I dare say you will find Mr. Darcy very agreeable."

Elizabeth pressed her hands to her cheeks. "Heaven forbid! That would be the greatest misfortune of all! To find a man agreeable whom one is determined to hate! Do not wish me such an evil."

"You are a peculiar creature indeed. Pray excuse me a moment." Charlotte tipped her head, pointing at Maria, who waved frantically.

Miss Bingley came towards her in a storm of silk, taffeta and feathers. She wore an expression of civil disdain that only she could possibly affect.

"So, Miss Eliza, I hear you are quite delighted with George Wickham! Your youngest sister has been talking to me about him, and asking me a thousand questions. I find that the young man forgot to tell you, among his other communications, that he was the son of old Wickham, the late Mr. Darcy's steward."

"He showed no reservation in sharing that confidence with me."

Miss Bingley's eyebrows rose, almost touching the ringlets framing her forehead. "I am indeed surprised. Let me recommend you, however, as a friend, not to give implicit confidence to all his assertions as to Mr. Darcy's using him ill."

"Why ever would you think he said such a thing?"

"As I understand, this would not be the first place he came into as a stranger and initiated calumny against Mr. Darcy."

"I wonder why?" Elizabeth turned her eyes toward

the ceiling, a painted and plaster-worked masterpiece.

"As well you should. It is perfectly false. Mr. Darcy has been always remarkably kind to him, though George Wickham has treated Mr. Darcy in a most infamous manner. I do not know the particulars, but I know very well that Mr. Darcy is not in the least to blame. He cannot bear to hear George Wickham mentioned. Though my brother thought he could not well avoid including him in his invitation to the officers, he was excessively glad to find that Mr. Wickham had, at the last moment, taken himself out of the way. His coming into the county at all is a most insolent thing indeed. I wonder how he could presume to do it."

"How indeed. It does seem quite outlandish that he should have the audacity to appear in the county to which his regiment is assigned."

"I pity you, Miss Eliza, for this discovery of your favorite's guilt. But really, considering his descent one could not expect much better."

"His guilt and his descent appear by your account to be the same. I have heard you accuse him of nothing worse than of being the son of Mr. Darcy's steward."

Miss Bingley straightened her spine. "I beg your pardon. Excuse my interference. It was kindly meant."

"As kindly meant as your remarks about my family in the labyrinth outside?"

Miss Bingley's face lost all color, and her jaw dropped.

"But then I do not know all the particulars of your conversation, do I?" She raised her brows and walked away.

Insufferable, insolent, arrogant, prideful …

Jane intercepted her. "Miss Bingley looks quite ill. She is so pale. Was she unwell when she spoke to you?"

"I think perhaps the conversation did not agree with her. But do tell me, what you have learnt about Mr. Wickham? Or perhaps you have been too pleasantly engaged to think of any third person. In that case you may be sure of my pardon." She forced her voice to be light and her lips to smile.

Jane looped her arm in Elizabeth's and leaned down closer to her ear. "I have not forgotten him. But I have nothing satisfactory to tell you. Mr. Bingley does not know the whole of his history and is quite ignorant of the circumstances so offensive to Mr. Darcy. He will vouch for the good conduct and honor of his friend. He is perfectly convinced that Mr. Wickham has deserved much less attention from Mr. Darcy than he has received. I am sorry to say that by his account as well as his sister's, Mr. Wickham is by no means a respectable young man. I am afraid he has been very imprudent, and has deserved to lose Mr. Darcy's regard."

"Mr. Bingley does not know Mr. Wickham himself?" Elizabeth avoided Jane's gaze.

"No, he never saw him till the other morning at Meryton."

"What does Mr. Bingley say of the living?"

"He does not exactly recollect the circumstances, though he has heard them from Mr. Darcy more than once, but he believes that it was left to Mr. Wickham only conditionally."

Elizabeth squeezed Jane's arm. "I have not a doubt of Mr. Bingley's sincerity, but you must excuse my not being convinced by assurances only."

"It is not like you to be so resentful, Lizzy. You say you have been worried about my rapid attachment to Mr. Bingley, but I am equally fearful of your quick attachment to Mr. Wickham. Mayhap you should take the same advice you have given me. Take the time to truly know his character."

"Thank you, the advice is of course sound. Excuse me." Elizabeth hurried off.

Now Jane was against her too?

The one person to whom she could always go for support had overturned her for Mr. Darcy.

Gah!

The musicians began again, and Darcy approached to claim her hand. They took their place in the set. Farther down the line, Lydia stood with Mr. Collins and did not bear the trial gladly. She giggled and tittered and poked fun at their cousin as he stood solemnly, not answering her high spirits at all. Either his forbearance was the stuff of legend, or, more likely, he simply could not think fast enough to answer her. It was difficult to determine for whom to feel sorry.

Mr. Darcy observed as well, hands clasped behind his back. His face revealed nothing, but it was a cover for disapproval, no doubt. He could hardly observe such a model of impropriety without feeling so. He glanced at Elizabeth.

Her face heated, and she turned aside. But that would not do. To stand like this, in silence, virtually avoiding one another was not the way to spend a dance. "We ought to have some conversation, you know. It is decidedly awkward to stand here with one another without it. Perhaps, by and by, I may observe that private balls are much pleasanter than public ones. You ought to make some kind of remark on the size of the room, or the number of couples."

"Do you talk by rule then, while you are dancing?" He screwed his lips thoughtfully.

"It is a done thing."

"As you wish, then. Do you and your sisters very often walk to Meryton?"

"It is one of our chiefest amusements, to be sure. When you met us there the other day, we had just been forming a new acquaintance."

A stain the color of port wine crept up Mr. Darcy's jaw. "Mr. Wickham is blessed with such happy manners as may ensure his making friends—whether he may be equally capable of retaining them, is less certain."

"He has been so unlucky as to lose your friendship, and in a manner which he is likely to suffer from all his life."

Mr. Darcy drew a breath, but released it with no further comment.

Clearly he could find no way to defend himself.

Mr. Darcy glanced over his shoulder, his expression very serious. He shook his head and blinked, turning back to her. "Pray forgive me, what we were talking of?"

"We were speaking of friends and acquaintances and how our treatment of them might impact the future."

"Ah, yes. I have been speaking with an acquaintance of yours, a great tall one as a matter of fact. One who is devastated by your neglect and pines for your companionship."

He had been talking to Longbourn?

"I pray sir, that you would weigh carefully what you have been told. A biased report is not always favorable to both parties."

"And yet there was sincerity in all his looks."

"Do not suppose to lecture me on my duties, sir.

There is a great deal you do not understand."

"I am sure that is the case. Yet, is there not truth in both sides of an argument? Is not the only way to re-solve—"

Ear splitting thunder shook the room.

12
Chapter

Dragon-thunder!

Darcy cast about the room. The musicians paused. Women shrieked and clung to their partners who laughed at the silliness of their being frightened by a little thunder, even though their eyes betrayed less bravado than their words.

Another clap of dragon-thunder shook the room.

Miss Elizabeth caught his eye, her face ghastly pale.

"Your ankle, it is hurt," he said, offering her his arm.

She stared at him, blinking. Her eyes widened, and she reached for her ankle. "Yes, thank you. I cannot imagine what I have done to it, but I am quite unable—"

He held her arm in his and helped her off the dance floor to an unoccupied corner, near a window.

"I hear—I think it is Walker," she whispered, leaning against the wall.

He yanked the window open a hand span.

Wings rustled and scratchy taloned feet landed in

the windowsill. Walker contorted himself to shove his head into the opening. "The egg, it has hatched! An hour ago, it has hatched. The hatchling is loose in the woods. Longbourn is—"

"No! He would not! It is just a baby!" Miss Elizabeth grabbed her skirts and ran off.

Perhaps to find her father? He lost her in the crowd.

"Come now! We cannot wait!" Walker's voice rose to nearly a shriek.

Several ladies gasped and huddled closer to their partners.

"Meet me at the barn." Darcy shut the window hard against another roar of dragon-thunder.

The egg had hatched? Hatched!

No, it could not be.

But Walker could hardly be wrong about such a thing.

Darcy ducked out of the house and broke into a run. Cold, silver light from the full moon lit the path to the barn nearly as bright as day.

What choice did he have? What else could be done? A wild-hatched dragon would destroy the peace. That was a far greater harm than anything Darcy could suffer.

He burst into the barn, startling the horses and dashed to the straw nearest his own horse. He and Walker tore through the hay and freed the Dragon Slayer blade. Long, heavy, and wickedly sharp, tailored specifically for one task and one dreadful task alone.

One unthinkable task.

One necessary task.

The belt holding the scabbard was wide and heavy, weighing as heavily on his hips as it did his mind.

His horse shied.

"Do not think so hard about this. Saddle your fool beast and be off." Walker flapped as he scolded.

"Stop frightening the horse." Darcy fought to cinch the saddle.

He led the horse out of the barn and mounted. "Which way?"

Walker raised his head and breathed deeply, then closed his eyes, concentrating. He raised a wing and pointed. "That way, toward Longbourn's lair."

Darcy urged his horse toward the woods. Walker took to the air.

"How could he have missed the signs of an egg hatching? Why was he not there with it?" Walker muttered. "That wyvern will have much to answer for from the Conclave before all is said and done."

"Indeed." Darcy gritted his teeth and urged the horse faster.

Walker was right. Do not think. Focus on duty. Accomplish that.

There would be time enough for the other when the treaty and all it protected were safe.

They entered the woods and the horse slowed. The beast tensed beneath him, recoiling at his every command. Was it the darkness that hampered his speed, or something else?

Each step slower than the last. It might be faster for him to take to his own feet and run. Ridiculous beast.

He had to move faster.

A shrill cry exploded from the dark woods ahead.

Piteous.

Terrified and terrifying.

The hair on the back of his neck stood on end.

That must be the hatchling.

The horse balked and refused to walk on.

Enough of this nonsense. He moved to dismount.

A dark shadow, a shape unlike any he had ever seen, rose up before them and roared. Walker swooped on it, shrieking.

The horse reared and screamed. When its feet landed, it took off at a blind run.

Darcy clung to its back, gasping for breath. He lay close over its neck lest the low branches sweep him out of the saddle entirely.

A dark blur swooped down from the trees in front of the horse's face. It reared again, throwing Darcy from its back.

He bounced hard on the ground, losing his bearings for a moment. Walker landed beside him, fanning cool air in his face with his wings. Head pounding, Darcy clambered to his feet and clutched a tree for support until the dizziness passed.

Ahead, the horse screamed. A sick thud followed.

Walker took off. Darcy staggered after. Several hundred yards ahead, the horse lay frantic on the ground.

"Damn creature broke its leg." Darcy hissed under his breath.

"I told you this one was worthless. Shall I?" Walker landed near the horse's head.

"Quickly." Darcy turned aside, steeling himself.

Walker severed its spine in a stomach churning crunch, and the horse stopped struggling.

The woods stilled as the smell of blood wafted on the breeze. Beads of sweat dried cold on the back of his neck.

Dragon screams before and behind him. Were those merely echoes or separate voices? How many dragons were in these woods tonight, and why were they all screeching? He shut his eyes and concentrated.

The sounds ahead were shrill, like a baby's cries.

"Come back for the horse later. We must get to the hatchling!" Darcy plunged through the undergrowth toward the piercing shrieks.

Elizabeth dashed out of the nearest door into the chill night. Was that dragon-thunder Longbourn?

Who else could it be?

A tiny, shrill cry, plaintive and fearful, drifted from the woods. Those were the sounds of a baby.

One alone and afraid.

No Keeper could ignore such a sound.

Gathering up her skirts, she pelted toward it.

All of dragon lore said a hatching must take place in human presence for imprinting to occur. No alternative would do.

Elizabeth had attended no less than six dragon hatchings. While they were only small, companion dragons, they could not be so different from a fire-drake, could they? In every one of those, the baby did not really seem to alert to their company until after they had their first taste of meat—or was it blood? There was something in that first feeding, what it was and where it came from that made a difference. The tatzelwurm that did not eat from the Dragon Friend's hand was the one that chose to leave after hatching. Those hand-fed, stayed.

Perhaps if the baby had not eaten yet, there was a chance proper imprinting could still happen!

If she was wrong, it would kill her, consumed with hatching hunger.

But how could she not take the chance, even die

trying if necessary?

There would be no dragon death tonight.

She increased her pace. Her dancing slippers offered little protection against the rough ground, turning to tatters before she made it into the woods.

"I have seen it! I have seen it!" Rustle circled above her.

Bless his keen sight!

She trailed after him, deeper into the woods. Dragon roars pounded against her from several directions. How many voices were echoing off the rocky hillside?

A baby shrieked.

Longbourn's roar answered.

No! He would not harm the baby!

She sprinted through a dense patch of undergrowth and broke into a small clearing.

Moonlight shone onto the open ground, glinting silver off the still wet hatchling.

Waist high to Elizabeth, it was long and gangly as a newborn foal; neck, legs and tail far too long for its body. Glistening red scales covered its clearly feminine face, fading to a darker red across the back.

A girl!

Sharp, baby teeth filled her mouth, matched by razor talons, like a kitten's claws, only deadly. It might be a baby, but it was far from helpless.

Her wings were still trapped in the eggshell. Scrapings in the dirt testified to frantic efforts to free herself.

Longbourn reared up behind her, engulfing the baby with his shadow.

The baby howled and tried to hobble away, overbalanced by the eggshell.

"No! Do not hurt her!" Elizabeth hurtled toward

the hatchling.

"Get away! It will kill you! It is wild." Longbourn roared. "I will not have you injured again."

Elizabeth flung herself between Longbourn and the baby. "No!"

The baby cried and pushed her back, shredding her skirt and slicing her arm with a forepaw.

Longbourn lunged for the hatchling, but Elizabeth covered it with her body. "I can save her, I can. Give me a chance."

The hatchling paused and stared into her face, nearly nose to nose with her. Stunning green eyes blinked, almost as though it understood her.

"Yes, that is right. Let me help you. I will free you from the eggshell." She slowly reached toward the baby's wings.

The hatchling backed up, tripping over its own feet.

"Your name is Pemberley, did you know? May I call you that?" Elizabeth inched closer.

Pemberley cocked its head and blinked at her.

"You see, you know your name." Elizabeth stroked Pemberley's glistening cheek. "Now let me help you." She grasped the edge of the eggshell with both hands and tore it. "Stretch your wings now, it should rip free."

Bits of eggshell flew, spraying cold egg slime across Elizabeth and Longbourn. Two oversized wings flapped free, knocking Elizabeth to the ground. A sharp claw on the edge of one wing cut her cheek.

She cried out and pressed her hand to her face.

Pemberley edged closer and sniffed at her cheek and arm, her little forked tongue peeking through her lips.

No, she could not taste human blood!

Elizabeth ripped off her petticoat. "Let me clean

you up. You will feel much better." Pushing to her feet, she held up the muslin for Pemberley to sniff.

Pemberley poked her head through the fragile muslin. Elizabeth scrubbed her face and neck with the tatters.

The undergrowth rattled and something broke through. Rustle dove for it.

Longbourn bellowed.

"Get away from it! It will kill you!" Mr. Darcy drew a huge sword.

A Dragon Slayer.

He lunged for the baby, Walker close behind.

She wrapped her arms around the hatchling. "No! She is imprinting now, give her a chance."

"She?"

Walker landed on the ground nearby.

"Look at her face closely. Look at Pemberley. Give me your cravat. She needs your scent." She held out one hand, the other stroking Pemberley's face.

Darcy fumbled with the knots, nearly strangling himself as he handed it to her.

Elizabeth rubbed Pemberley's face with the cravat. "Here is your Keeper. Smell him. You must know him. You have surely heard his voice. Talk to her, Mr. Darcy, quickly."

Darcy stepped closer. "Ah … she is right. I am your Keeper. I will take you back to your home and nothing shall ever threaten you again."

Pemberley's eyes widened. She recognized his voice!

At least he had done something right and talked to the egg before it was stolen.

The hatchling reached out her head and touched his shoulder.

"Clean her face with your cravat," Elizabeth said.

Darcy carefully brushed away the last remnants of the egg slime. "You are remarkable, Pemberley."

Pemberley squawked and turned toward Elizabeth, reaching her forked tongue toward the blood trails down Elizabeth's arm.

Elizabeth jumped back. "She must not taste human blood. Not now! We must have meat for her! Longbourn—"

"No! Rustle come!" Walker launched, Rustle in his shadow.

Darcy embraced Pemberley's head, pulling it toward him. "Be patient just a moment, little one. You will have plenty to fill your belly."

"That is right, keep talking to her, call her by name. Tell her yours." Elizabeth backed away.

Pemberley wrenched around in Darcy's grasp and staggered toward Elizabeth. "No leave me!"

Elizabeth's eyes burned and her vision fuzzed as she threw her arms around the scaly neck. "No one is going to ever leave you. Your Keeper is here to take care of you."

"Keeper?" Pemberley nosed the side of Elizabeth's neck.

She guided Pemberley toward Darcy. "Keeper."

Darcy embraced the hatchling and stroked her head. "Keeper."

The cockatrices burst through the trees and dropped bloody chunks of meat at their feet.

"Pray, Laird Longbourn, help us retrieve the carcass," Walker called.

Longbourn grumbled and stomped off behind Walker.

"What is it?" Elizabeth pulled one piece closer.

"Horse? How?"

"Yes. I will explain later. How do I feed her?"

"Cut it up in small pieces. Hatchlings are greedy in their hunger. She will choke herself if you do not restrain her."

Darcy unsheathed the Dragon Slayer. "At last! A good purpose for this!"

He hacked the meat into hatchling-sized bites.

Pemberley lunged for the meat, drool dripping from her fangs. Elizabeth restrained the hatchling. "She needs to have the first bite from your hands."

Darcy hesitated, but she could hardly blame him. Any sensible person would fear for the safety of their limbs near dragon teeth.

"She will not recognize you as Keeper if you do not feed her."

He scooped up bloody gobs of meat and held them out for Pemberley. She gobbled as fast as he could offer them.

Pemberley stopped for breath and looked longingly at Elizabeth. She picked up a sliver of meat and placed it in Pemberley's mouth.

She swallowed it whole and peered at Elizabeth, leaning close to her injured cheek. "Hurt?"

"It is nothing to worry about, dearling." Tears flowed down her face.

"Heavens, she is right!" Darcy leaned closer. "What might I do for you?"

"Do not worry, this is a good thing. You must see what this means! She has imprinted. She understands human blood is a reason for concern! She is safe!" Elizabeth wrapped her arms around Pemberley's neck and sobbed into her shoulder.

Darcy leaned back on his heels, panting. "You are

certain?"

"She knows my blood is an injury, not food. What more certainty is there?" Elizabeth dried her eyes on her sleeve.

"I had no idea this was possible." He dragged the back of his hand across his mouth.

"Nor did I."

"Then why—"

"I just knew—I cannot explain. If you knew there was the smallest chance you did not have to put that blade to use, would you not have taken it?"

"I am ashamed I did not know to even try. Why did the Order not even mention the possibility?"

"It is not in the lore. Just something I suspected from the hatchings I have seen. It could have turned out very different."

"Hungry." Pemberley looked from Elizabeth to Darcy and back.

Dragon-thunder boomed through the trees. Why was Longbourn bellowing about now? There was a small basilisk that lived in the Longbourn woods. Did he need to be that loud to scare it off?

"We must get you to a safer place, then there will be more to eat." Elizabeth said. "We should get her to Longbourn's cavern. Pick up the egg shell too. That should not be left where it can be found."

"Will Longbourn permit her there?"

"He is only a Laird. She is a Vikontes, if I recall my genealogies correctly. He should be honored to host her, and even if he is not, it is his duty. He will fulfill his duty. Help me now." She urged Pemberley to her feet.

He wrapped his arm around the drakling's shoulders. "Come along now, you need a nice safe place to eat. Follow Miss Elizabeth. She knows where to go."

Elizabeth glanced over her shoulder. Something in the tone of his voice and in the look in his eyes was very sincere and kind. Perhaps he would make a decent Dragon Keeper, after all.

Pemberley grew tired well before they reached Longbourn's cavern. Darcy picked her up and carried her the rest of the way. She wrapped her neck over his shoulders and rested peacefully in his arms, gentle and trusting as a lamb. Miss Elizabeth walked just behind him, stroking Pemberley's head and cooing encouragements to her when she became restless from hunger pangs.

How close had he come to following the Blue Order's protocols and destroying this creature that now clung to him like a child? Could he ever repay the debt he owed Miss Elizabeth? She had faced down a major-dragon to save Pemberley. Was there any other who would have—could have—done such a thing?

But how had such a thing happened? The egg was supposed to be safe in Longbourn's keeping. How could he have permitted it to hatch without warning any of them that it was imminent? Would he have intentionally endangered Pemberley? As capricious as the wyvern could be, that seemed extreme, even for him. But if not that, what had happened?

Maybe Miss Elizabeth would know. But it would be difficult to ask without sounding ungrateful, and that would not do. Better not to have an answer at all than to risk insulting her.

"There is the cavern. Give her to me now and make

up a bed for her of soft leaves and sand." She reached for the hatchling, wincing.

Fresh blood dotted the cut on her arm. The wound was more serious than she had let on. It would require some kind of treatment tonight. But how?

Pemberley shifted easily into Miss Elizabeth's arms, though the drakling must weigh at least half as much as she.

Moonlight streamed into the cold cavern, past the initial overhang, a good ten feet inside. Darcy grabbed a fallen branch, still covered with leaves and used it as a broom to pile soft sand against one wall. Several arm loads of leaves and Miss Elizabeth pronounced it sufficient. He took Pemberley from her and arranged the hatchling in the nest.

She whined. Piteous cries of hunger reverberated against the stony walls.

"Stop that racket." Longbourn lumbered up behind them, dragging the horse carcass.

Walker and Rustle landed beside it and began shredding it with beaks and talons.

"I did not invite—"

Elizabeth marched toe to toe with the wyvern, fury wrapped around her like a cloak. "A Vikontes does not require an invitation to stay with a Laird. You will do your duty toward her. I will not hear another word about it."

"You will stay with the baby?" Longbourn pulled back slightly and looked her in the eyes.

"Of course I will. A baby so young cannot be left on her own."

Longbourn snorted softly. "You do not expect me to leave, do you?"

"No, you are a host and must provide for our guest.

That horse will not last very long. She will need more meat, until the time of great hunger has passed. Deer will do very nicely for her." She crossed her injured arm over the other and squared her shoulders.

No creature with any sense about it would deny her anything when she wore that expression.

Longbourn scratched the dirt and bared his fangs.

Darcy gathered handfuls of the gory meal and presented the pieces to Pemberley. How fast could she manage to swallow the gobbets and just how many could she consume?

"You expect me to hunt for the drakling, too, I suppose." Longbourn's mouth turned down in a draconic version of a frown.

"If you do not, I shall bring her mutton myself."

"She cannot have my sheep." He stomped and the ground trembled.

"Then provide her deer."

"But you will stay?"

Miss Elizabeth edged back slightly. "I will stay."

"Scratch my ears." Longbourn presented his head near her hand.

She hesitated, hand trembling.

Why?

Longbourn whined almost as insistently as Pemberley.

Miss Elizabeth capitulated and scratched behind his ear. He leaned into her. She squealed and edged back, clutching her injured arm to her ribs.

"You are hurt!" Longbourn reared up. "The drakling—"

"Baby clumsiness, that is all."

Longbourn sniffed at her arm and face. "It smells bad. Like death."

How could it? Firedrakes had no poison.

Miss Elizabeth closed her eyes. "It must be turning septic. Dragon wounds often do. Rustle, fetch Rumblkins from the house, quickly, please."

"I will bring him straight away." Rustle flew into the darkness.

"What do you need the furry rat catcher for?" Longbourn asked.

"Have you ever seen a tatzelwurm's wounds get infected? Rats bite them all the time and yet they do not suffer infection. I am convinced that there is something about the way they lick their wounds that keeps them safe from it."

"I have never heard such a thing." Darcy offered Pemberley the last piece of meat. She sniffed at it, eyes half closed. She turned her head aside and fell asleep.

"You should have your fill while you can, Walker. These will be busy days for all of us." Miss Elizabeth wavered slightly.

Walker tore into the carcass with all the fury of a hungry dragon. It was not a pretty sight.

Elizabeth wavered and Darcy caught her elbow. She limped as he helped her to sit. She was a sight, covered in dirt, blood and egg slime, her ball gown in tatters and her dancing slippers long since gone from her feet.

"She needs water, Laird Longbourn, and warmth."

"I will bring water. Start a fire if you can." Longbourn turned into the depths of the cavern.

Darcy pulled his fire starters out of his jacket pockets and stripped off his coat. "Pray take this. You are chilled."

She allowed him to wrap it over her shoulders. "Do you always carry flint and steel in your pockets? It seems an odd thing to bring to a ball."

"I suppose so, but having been once stranded by a lame horse in the winter, I am never without." He chuckled.

"Pemberley will need the warmth, too. The fire should be near her. She will sleep several hours—no more. When she awakes, she will be famished."

Darcy helped Miss Elizabeth move to Pemberley's side, then went out to gather tinder and kindling.

By the time he had a fire going, Longbourn returned with a bucket of water. Where had the wyvern got a bucket and ladle?

Darcy ladled out some water and offered it to Miss Elizabeth. Her face was flushed and eyes fever bright. She took it, but without her usual energy.

Walker hopped to her and touched her forehead with his wing. "She is hot. This is not good."

Longbourn shoved his nose between Walker and Miss Elizabeth. "She must be made well!"

Elizabeth touched his nose. "No tempers now, I have not the strength for it."

"I will bring Gardiner." Walker flew off.

"Perhaps you should wash your wounds," Darcy said.

"You cannot stand to be idle, can you?" She propped herself on one elbow.

He wrung his handkerchief out in the water and handed it to her. "It is not my long suit."

She dabbed at the slash down her arm, now swollen and violently red. "I am afraid this color does not look well with my gown, or what is left of it." Her laugh ended in a grimace.

Rustle swooped in, with Rumblkins just a hairsbreadth behind. The tatzelwurm slithered up to her, purring loudly.

Pemberley stirred and lifted her head.

"Pemberley, dear, may I present my friend, Rumblkins of Longbourn's Keep." Elizabeth beckoned the tatzelwurm into her lap.

He climbed up and touched noses with Pemberley. He rubbed against her jaw with the top of his head. She flicked him with her long forked tongue.

"Hungry," Pemberley cried.

"Come here, and I shall feed you." Darcy moved toward the carcass.

"No. Stay her. She needs." Pemberley wrapped her neck across Miss Elizabeth's shoulders.

"Rumblkins is helping me. Go with your Keeper. I will be here when your belly is full." Miss Elizabeth stroked Pemberley's head and whispered something in her ear.

Pemberley carefully crawled off her nest and leaned against Darcy's leg. She looked up, mouth open, so much like a baby bird. One that guzzled down raw horse meat, pounds at a time. He dropped another chunk in her mouth and scratched her chin. She rumbled happily and rubbed the top of her head against his leg.

Rumblkins climbed higher in Miss Elizabeth's lap and sniffed her cheek. "This is not good. But I can clean it."

"I would be grateful." She clenched her fists, steeling herself.

Rumblkins' forked tongue was raspy as a cat's and opened her wounds anew. They bled and he lapped up the blood. A thoroughly disturbing image. But the cuts looked better when he was finished. Her cheeks glistened with wet trails, though she never voiced her discomfort. Ever thoughtful, she was probably trying not to upset Pemberley. Rumblkins curled up in her lap, purring loudly.

She ran her hand over his head, paying special attention to the spots behind his tufted ears. "Thank you my friend."

Belly distended, Pemberley's eyelids drooped. She crawled back toward the sandy-leafy nest and nudged her head under Elizabeth's arm. Rumblkins scooted to make room for her on Elizabeth's lap. A moment later, all three were asleep. Longbourn lay down beside them, head on his paws, and closed his eyes as well.

Darcy sat back on his heels and stared. What a peculiar tableau. Though beyond disheveled, Miss Elizabeth had never been more attractive, surrounded by the creatures that adored her.

It was easy to see why they did. She understood them, knew them in ways that no dragon lore had ever revealed. She laid down everything she had for them.

Remarkable.

Stunning.

She was a Keeper suited to a dragon of royal stock, like Pemberley. Why did her family and her connections have to be so shocking?

The fire flickered. It was getting low.

He forced himself to his feet. Best tend it now.

Dragon bones, he was tired. Weary to his very marrow. Weary, but relieved. Maybe that was it. The tension that had held him together all these weeks was finally relieved, and now all that had held him together was unraveling.

Thankfully Longbourn's tantrums had knocked down enough deadfall that firewood was easy to find. He fed the fire, cut some more meat against Pemberley's next feeding, and collapsed near the fire.

Bennet and Gardiner arrived just as Pemberley's hunger cries began anew. They immediately made themselves useful, hacking up more horse meat, insisting Longbourn go to procure a deer for Pemberley's next meal, stoking the fire and boiling water for herbal concoctions for Pemberley's hide.

Bennet might be insufferable in many respects, but the man knew dragons and was quick to share his knowledge. He deserved his appointment as Historian of the Order. How little Father had prepared him for the task of keeping an infant dragon. Did he know even half of what Bennet was pressing him to learn now?

Bennet set Darcy to reading and copying from books of dragon lore he had brought from his library. Pages and pages of instructions, lists, extracts from dragon law and etiquette—who knew a dragonet had to be presented to the Conclave by a sponsoring dragon? At least Rosings had already offered to mentor Pemberley—perhaps that was what she had meant by it.

Though he would not trade his place as Dragon Keeper to Pemberley, it would have been pleasing to have some understanding of the depth of what he was getting himself into. A dragonet was not like keeping livestock, it was more like having a child. A very large, very hungry, very carnivorous child.

Between feeding and tending Pemberley's needs, Bennet grilled both Darcy and Elizabeth on the details of the hatching. Over and over, he demanded every detail from their perspectives, Walker's, Rustle's, even Longbourn's. Apparently only Miss Elizabeth, and none of the dragons, had any faith that Pemberley could still imprint properly after hatching in isolation. It was a testament to their faith in her that they obeyed her commands and did not kill the hatchling outright.

Such a thing had never been recorded before. It was impulsive and dangerous, a very foolish thing to do— a point he did not fail to impress upon his daughter. Perhaps a little too firmly. Bennet was clearly an adherent to the old ways of men and dragons.

Longbourn avoided answering questions about why Pemberley was left alone to hatch. The capricious creature denied any accountability for the near disaster. Oddly, Miss Elizabeth did not attempt to cajole any details out of him. If anything, she was aloof and only engaged him at the dragon's insistence. Did she suspect some wrong-doing on the wyvern's part? Was she punishing him by withdrawing her attentions?

If so, it seemed an effective means of controlling the dragon. He was clearly unhappy about it and the attentions she lavished on Pemberley.

The drakling reveled in her kindnesses, never happier than when she was permitted to sleep in Miss Elizabeth's arms. Pemberley even willingly shared her nest with Rumblkins, Rustle, and the fairy dragons who visited often, all for the privilege of Miss Elizabeth's company.

Even though Miss Elizabeth insisted Darcy manage all the feedings, Pemberley still returned to cuddle with her after each one, utterly besotted with her. Bennet insisted that it was because Miss Elizabeth was the first to offer Pemberley human contact and comfort. Darcy dare not argue with the Order's Historian, but he was hard pressed to accept such an easy dismissal of Miss Elizabeth's uncanny understanding of the hatchling's moods and needs.

She made dragon-keeping look easy. Though he loathed admitting it, without her help even more than that of her father, the last few days would have done him in.

No wonder women sought the companionship and advice of other women when a baby was due. Infants were far more complicated creatures than their size would suggest.

Miss Elizabeth had also been right about the tatzelwurm's healing properties. Though Rumblkins' ministrations were clearly painful at best, her wounds were much healed in just a few days.

After five days, Pemberley's hunger ebbed. Her feedings shifted from hourly gorges to a daily deer across four feedings. Bennet assured him her hunger would continue to taper off as she grew and learned to hunt on her own—a skill another dragon would have to teach her. He also deemed her imprinting successful and promised to write a letter to the Order attesting to the fact, assuring Pemberley's welcome among dragon-kind.

At the end of the se'nnight Bennet deemed it safe to leave Pemberley in Longbourn's care whilst they returned to their respective houses for some much needed rest. Darcy would still have to attend her at least three times a day, but fresh clothes and a chance for a few hours in a proper bed would be very welcome at this point.

But how to explain his sudden removal from the ball and subsequent absence?

It should not have been surprising that Bennet had managed that as well.

Before leaving Longbourn, Bennet and Gardiner

had left a letter in the care of a fully complicit Mrs. Gardiner, explaining an emergency business trip calling Bennet, Gardiner and Miss Elizabeth away. With the help of all three fairy dragons, Rumblkins, and Rustle, the household had been kept in tolerable order.

Netherfield was a greater challenge. Walker and Rustle, with the occasional assistance from Longbourn lurking in the cellars, persuaded the Netherfield residents that they had all caught cold and were far too ill to leave their rooms. When Darcy returned, their 're-coveries' would begin and they would be encouraged to forget that Darcy had ever left the ball.

Once again, he was in Bennet's debt.

It helped that Bennet was an officer of the Order and charged to execute the duty. So it was a slightly less personal debt. Slightly. But to Miss Elizabeth he owed more than he could ever expect to repay. Pemberley lived only because of her courageous intervention. What could possibly repay that?

His return to Netherfield barely raised an eyebrow among the staff. Life slowly settled into a routine that revolved around thrice daily visits to Pemberley. More often than not, Miss Elizabeth was there as well, oiling and brushing both dragons, scratching their itches, and helping Longbourn to teach Pemberley the first tenets of the Pendragon Treaty. He had thought to leave Hertfordshire as soon as possible, but perhaps staying to learn from the Bennets made sense.

"I wrote down the receipt for the scale oil and the wash that will help with the scale mites. Your housekeeper should be able to make it up readily enough. The supplies are not difficult to come by. Given the quantities you will need as Pemberley grows, you may want to instruct her to plant beds of the herbs, though.

Your local apothecary might not be able to keep up with her demands for them." Miss Elizabeth handed him several sheets of paper.

He folded them and tucked them in his pocket. "Thank you, that is very kind."

"It is nothing. They can be quite cranky when their hides are itchy." She scratched Pemberley under the chin.

"You should go back to the house now. You are tired. You should rest before you attend the recital with Collins tonight." Longbourn nudged his head under her other hand. She attended the spot behind his ear.

"Why are you so concerned about whether I attend the concert tonight? I never knew you to be a great lover of music." She smiled tightly, shoulders stiffening.

"It is good for you to spend time with Collins. He is heir to this estate."

"I have not forgotten that." She withdrew her hand and stepped back.

Longbourn pressed closer to her. "You must—"

"Pray excuse me, Mr. Darcy. I am needed at home." She curtsied, gathered her skirts and hurried away.

Longbourn harrumphed and dropped himself on the ground, thumping hard.

"Why she go?" Pemberley whined, staring after her. "She not happy. She angry when you say Collins. What is a Collins?"

Longbourn snorted. "She is my Keeper."

"I like her. She is soft and she knows ... everything." Pemberley crept toward Darcy and leaned against his leg. "I sad when she goes."

Longbourn pushed up on his forepaws. "I must speak to your Keeper."

"You no leave, too." Pemberley shoved her head inside Darcy's coat.

Darcy dropped to one knee and took her face in his hands. "I will just step outside and be back very soon. I am not leaving you."

He led her back to her nest and scratched her back and between her wings until her eyelids drooped. Longbourn beckoned him outside.

A sunbeam penetrated the tree canopy and warmed a large circle just outside the cavern. Crisp breezes rattled the branches above and sent leaves scattering. Winter was not long off. How much shelter from the cold did a young dragon need? He would have to ask Bennet.

Longbourn paced along the cavern mouth, grumbling under his breath.

The wyvern's temper was bubbling—not something he wanted Pemberley to see—or learn from.

"Is there something wrong, Laird Longbourn?"

"Elizabeth is not happy."

"I noticed she seems troubled." Darcy bit his tongue. This was not the time to imply that Longbourn might have anything to do with it.

"She is tired. It is the baby—too much work for her. It is time for you to take her home." Longbourn's head swung around, and he looked Darcy straight in the eye.

"Take her home? She cannot travel now, she is far too young. Surely you can see that. Derbyshire is quite a distance for her."

"You were going to Rosings for the hatching. Send word that the Cowntess Rosings might make ready to receive you. Take Pemberley there. It is not too far. Rosings will teach her what she needs to know."

"I have not yet learned all I might from Bennet. I

had thought to stay—"

"No. I did what I said I would do and more. I found your egg. I have kept the drakling for you. Now it is time for you to leave."

The insufferable brute was throwing him and his dragon out? Darcy's presence had always been sought after! No one ever insisted on his departure. How dare he!

"It will take some time to make preparations. I have no idea how to transport Pemberley safely."

"Walker can fly to Rosings in less than a day. Their preparations can begin immediately. You can put the drakling on a wagon or in a cart if you will and be gone in a se'nnight. You should take Gardiner with you as well."

"I should welcome his assistance, to be sure, but I can hardly press the point."

"He upsets my Keeper with foolish ideas. She needs to be away from him. Take him with you." Longbourn punctuated the demand with a tail thump.

"His wife and children are here. He will return." Darcy dodged his lashing tail.

"All will be settled by the time he returns. I will see to it. She will marry Collins and stay here with me. It will be settled."

"Have you considered—"

Longbourn leaned very close into Darcy's face. A drop of venom hung off his fang. "It is Dragon Law, she will marry as I say and be my Keeper. You will not interfere."

"I only suggest that Miss Elizabeth is a strong woman. She will not respond well to being ordered about. It might be better—"

"I do not want your advice. Send Walker today. You

have a se'nnight to be out of my Keep." Longbourn huffed acrid, venomous breath in his face.

"As you say, Laird. Pray, tell Pemberley when she awakes that I will return soon."

Longbourn snorted and skulked back into the cavern.

No wonder Miss Elizabeth was at odds with Longbourn. He was a fool for trying to force her to do anything. Did he not realize the rare treasure he had in his Keeper? No doubt it was not going to go well for either of them.

Darcy scrubbed his face with his hands. How did one transport a drakling along fifty miles of good road?

A se'nnight later Elizabeth stood at the mouth of Longbourn's cavern, a thick journal under her arm. Pemberley whined beside her, trying to huddle under her generous green cloak. A chill breeze whipped around them, bearing a kiss of winter.

"No want to go. Stay with you. Please." Pemberley pressed her head against Elizabeth's chest.

Elizabeth wrapped her free arm around the baby's sinewy neck. "You must, my dear. It is time for you to learn from a proper firedrake. There are so many things she will teach you."

"I want you teach me." Pemberley licked Elizabeth's face. "You not like me?"

"Do not ever think that. I love you very dearly. I also want what is best for you, and wintering here with a cranky wyvern who is jealous over his own space is not the best thing. Rosings is waiting to welcome you."

"Then you come. She welcome you, too."

Pemberley spread a wing around Elizabeth, pulling her close.

In the cavern's shadows, Longbourn grumbled.

She glared at him over her shoulder. "Perhaps one day I shall visit. But I am Longbourn's Keeper. I must stay with him."

Uncle Gardiner approached. He wore a dark grey great coat with three capelets at the shoulder, well prepared for the coming weather. "We have the dog cart made into a dragon cart now. Nice and comfortable for you. Pray will you come and see if it is to your liking?"

"Go with him, you will enjoy traveling." Elizabeth ducked away from Pemberley's wing.

"You not come? Please come."

Elizabeth swallowed hard. "Perhaps, someday, I may visit you. I should like that very much."

"You must. You must."

Uncle laid a gentle hand on Pemberley's neck and guided her toward the refitted dog cart, complete with hound inside.

The four wheeled dog-cart had been rebuilt, raising the dog box up a good two feet. Inside, Pemberley would have enough space to sit comfortably as they drove. Darcy and Uncle would sit atop the box whilst Walker and Rustle had spots on the railing behind them. A smart new black and red coat of paint made it a very attractive little vehicle.

Mr. Darcy approached, somber as always. "Your father suggested adding a dog inside would assist with any necessary persuasions should someone peek within. The dog is deaf and nearly blind, far too old to be bothered by Pemberley. We introduced the hound to her a few days ago, and she took to him readily enough. The company should make the journey easier for her."

"How long do you think it will take?"

He clasped his hands behind his back. "I've arranged for fresh horses at all the posting stations. So we should be no more than eight hours on the road, I think, six if all goes very well."

"Pemberley has just had a good feed. That should keep her until then. But she will be hungry when she arrives." She turned aside, throat tightening.

"Walker says that they will be waiting with a meal ready for her when we arrive. Rosings seems quite keen on meeting Pemberley."

"I am pleased she will be properly welcomed. She is such a dear creature." Elizabeth blinked hard and dragged her sleeve across her eyes.

This was so beastly unfair. Why did he insist on taking Pemberley away now? Was he somehow afraid that she might contaminate his dragon with her low company?

She pushed the journal at him. "Here. I have copied as much of Papa's firedrake lore as I could for you. I have also included all the details of her hatching that I could recall, the signs of her moods, what to look for in case of severe scale mites, tail blisters, split talons and teething."

"Teething?"

"In about a month, her first molars will begin to come in. Expect her to be temperamental. I included several remedies that might soothe her."

Darcy leafed through the pages. "How long have you been at writing this?"

"It is no matter, so long as you will find it useful in caring for her." Her voice broke.

There was so much more he needed to know, so

much she wanted to tell him. But her words failed.

"This is more than I could have ever asked for. Thank you. I am in your debt."

"Take good care of her and your debt will be amply discharged." She stared as Uncle coaxed Pemberley into the dog cart.

The hound sniffed at her and woofed softly. Pemberley licked the hound's face and curled up around it. The dog turned three times and settled into the hollow made by Pemberley's tail.

Darcy cleared his throat. "May I ask one further favor of you?"

"Certainly."

What more could he possibly want from her? Was it not enough that he was tearing the baby from her side?

"My sister, she is but fifteen. She was so young when the old Pemberley died. I fear she knows little of firedrakes. She will no doubt have many questions about Pemberley and what she should do for her. May she write to you for advice?"

She would not have to lose contact with Pemberley entirely!

Elizabeth pressed the back of her hand to her mouth and sniffled. He might be an arrogant, insufferable man, but there was a real vein of kindness in him. "I will look forward to her letters. Tell her she may write to me as often as she likes."

"I will do that then."

Uncle approached them, brushing his hands together. "She is settled in and as comfortable as we can make her. Do you wish to say goodbye, Lizzy?"

"With your permission, Mr. Darcy."

"Of course."

Elizabeth blotted her eyes with the edge of her cloak and trudged to the cart. They had done an excellent job of fitting it for the drakling, including placing the lock on the inside. Walker perched on top of the cart.

He bowed as she approached. "Lady Elizabeth."

"You should not call me that, Walker."

"I will call you that, always. I do not know how to begin thanking you."

"Just promise me that if you or Pemberley ever need anything, you will not hesitate to find me. You know where to find me. Promise me that."

"You have my word." He ducked his head under her hand in a draconic expression of submission.

She scratched his neck and behind his ears.

He rumbled a happy sound. "May I visit you and Lairda April?"

"Of course you can, assuming Mr. Darcy—"

"I do not require his permission."

"Then I shall look forward to your company." She crouched beside the cart. "And you, my dear, be a good girl for your Keeper and Cowntess Rosings. Darcy's sister will write to me of you. You may ask her to write on your behalf as well, and I shall write to you. Mayhap you might even learn to read. Some dragons do, you know."

"I will learn." Pemberley propped her head on her forepaws, her green eyes large and sorrowful.

"I will always be here for you. Do not forget." Elizabeth stood.

Uncle patted her shoulder and climbed into the seat. "I will send Rustle with word when we arrive. I may be several days at Rosings, though."

Darcy climbed in beside him, and they drove off.

Once they were out of sight, Elizabeth sank to the ground, face in her hands.

Longbourn lumbered up and stretched out beside her. "This is best."

She shrugged, but did not look at him.

"You should go back to the house to be with Collins."

She scrubbed her face with her palms and rose. Longbourn reached his head for her, presenting his ear for a scratch.

It would be right to oblige, but her hands were too heavy to lift even that high. "I am tired. I shall return to the house."

Longbourn pressed closer. "You will return soon?"

"Mary has not been to see you since Pemberley hatched. She will come whilst I rest."

"Then you will come?" The tip of his tail lashed the ground.

"When I am rested." She plodded away.

Her feet were as heavy as her hands, her head, her heart. Everything was too much to bear.

Why was Mr. Darcy taking Pemberley away so soon? She could easily have stayed the winter.

But then, the pain would only be that much worse when she left. Maybe it was better like this. What chance was there she would see Pemberley again?

Longbourn was going to force her to marry Collins. Then Collins would hire a curate and begin taking over the estate under Papa's watchful eye. Elizabeth would become Longbourn's acknowledged Keeper, and he— and Collins—would run her life to his satisfaction and comfort.

The house came into view, but she turned aside to Mama's cutting garden and the little bench tucked in among the roses. There would be no roses now, but it was peaceful and that was what she longed for.

Dragon Keeping always carried a price. Until now, it had been easy to pay, a joy for the privilege of company that understood and esteemed her.

And it would be again. It had to be.

She drew a deep breath and squared her shoulders.

Her courage always rose when challenged. She was equal to even this.

Mary hurried to her. "April said she saw you from the window. Are you well?"

She forced a smile. "Well enough."

Mary grabbed her hands. "We are to walk to Meryton, Mr. Collins with us. Will you come?"

Heather peeked out from under Mary's hair. "We have missed you so."

"Allow me to get April, and I shall. It is time we put all this business of the missing egg behind us and get on with what is ahead."

Mary twined her arm in Elizabeth's and they returned to the house.

It was time indeed for life to return to some sense of normality.

As much normality as their dragons allowed.

For more dragon lore check out:
Dragon Myths of Britain
At RandomBitofFascination.com

Read the rest of the series:

Acknowledgments

So many people have helped me along the journey taking this from an idea to a reality.

Debbie, Anji, Julie, Ruth, and Raidon thank you so much for cold reading and being honest!,

And my dear friend Cathy, my biggest cheerleader, you have kept me from chickening out more than once!

And my sweet sister Gerri who believed in even those first attempts that now live in the file drawer!

Thank you!

Other Books by Maria Grace

Fine Eyes and Pert Opinions
Remember the Past
The Darcy Brothers

A Jane Austen Regency Life Series:
A Jane Austen Christmas: Regency Christmas Traditions
Courtship and Marriage in Jane Austen's World
How Jane Austen Kept her Cook: An A to Z History of Georgian Ice Cream

Jane Austen's Dragons Series:
A Proper Introduction to Dragons
Pemberley: Mr. Darcy's Dragon
Longbourn: Dragon Entail
Netherfield:Rogue Dragon
The Dragons of Kellynch
Kellynch:Dragon Persuasion

The Queen of Rosings Park Series:
Mistaking Her Character
The Trouble to Check Her
A Less Agreeable Man

Sweet Tea Stories:
A Spot of Sweet Tea: Hopes and Beginnings (short story anthology)
Snowbound at Hartfield
A Most Affectionate Mother
Inspiration

Darcy Family Christmas Series:
Darcy and Elizabeth: Christmas 1811
The Darcy's First Christmas
From Admiration to Love
Unexpected Gifts

Given Good Principles Series:
Darcy's Decision
The Future Mrs. Darcy
All the Appearance of Goodness
Twelfth Night at Longbourn

Behind the Scenes Anthologies (with Austen Variations):
Pride and Prejudice: Behind the Scenes
Persuasion: Behind the Scenes

Non-fiction Anthologies
Castles, Customs, and Kings Vol. 1
Castles, Customs, and Kings Vol. 2
Putting the Science in Fiction

Available in e-book, audio book and paperback

On Line Exclusives at:

www.http//RandomBitsofFascination.com

Bonus and deleted scenes
Regency Life Series

<u>Free e-books:</u>

- *Rising Waters: Hurricane Harvey Memoirs*
- *Lady Catherine's Cat*
- *A Gift from Rosings Park*
- *Bits of Bobbin Lace*
- *Half Agony, Half Hope: New Reflections on Persuasion*
- *Four Days in April*

✒ About the Author

Six time BRAG Medallion Honoree, #1 Best-selling Historical Fantasy author Maria Grace has her PhD in Educational Psychology and is a 16-year veteran of the university classroom where she taught courses in human growth and development, learning, test development and counseling. None of which have anything to do with her undergraduate studies in economics/sociology/managerial studies/behavior sciences.

She pretends to be a mild-mannered writer/cat-lady, but most of her vacations require helmets and waivers or historical costumes, usually not at the same time.

She writes gaslamp fantasy, historical romance and non-fiction to help justify her research addiction.

Contact Maria Grace:

author.MariaGrace@gmail.com

Facebook:
http://facebook.com/AuthorMariaGrace

On Amazon.com:
http://amazon.com/author/mariagrace

Random Bits of Fascination (http://RandomBitsof-Fascination.com)

Austen Variations (http://AustenVariations.com)

English Historical Fiction Authors
(http://EnglshHistoryAuthors.blogspot.com)

White Soup Press (http://whitesouppress.com/)

On Twitter @WriteMariaGrace

On Pinterest: http://pinterest.com/mariagrace423/